Stranded
in
Iceland

Victoria Walker

For Catrin

x

1

Felicity Thorne was walking around the supermarket hoping for inspiration to strike. She didn't mind cooking, it was having to think about what to cook that made her heart sink every day at about four in the afternoon. If she was a bit more organised, she would have a two-week rota of meals with all of the ingredients ordered weekly in a super-convenient, efficient online shop. But somehow, even at the age of forty-one, she couldn't manage to organise herself to that degree. Between juggling her day job as a receptionist in an independent school with her hobby-slash-side-hustle of writing psychological crime thrillers, two teenage children and their relationship with her ex-husband, there was never a single second of downtime.

It had been a long day. It was the middle of November and it had been raining for what seemed like months. Every morning, Fliss straightened her wayward hair which, being somewhere in between curly and straight, had to be forced to be one or the other. It had started out being presentable enough for work, but the damp air had made it grow to twice its usual size throughout the day. Catching sight of herself in a highly-polished metal shelf support, she made a vain attempt to smooth it down before she reached for a bag of salad that she didn't particularly want for dinner. It wasn't comforting winter food but it would help combat the ever-present motherly guilt and make her feel she was feeding her children something healthy. It was a balancing act between healthy food, which would lead to moaning from her daughter, and an easy life for herself by choosing something over-processed to win her over. While she was browsing the coleslaw options — would it be the delicious cheesy one or the reduced fat yogurt one? — her phone started ringing. It was a London number that she didn't recognise.

'Hello?' She tilted her head to one side to jam the phone between her ear and her shoulder so that she could continue with her shopping while she established what kind of scam was about to be attempted on her.

'Felicity? This is Eva Cushton from Blackwood Publishing. How are you?'

Fliss was so taken aback that not only was this not a scam call but that it was her publisher, that she dropped her phone into the chilled meat section that she was now perusing.

'Hello? Eva? Sorry, I think I lost you for a moment,' she said, rolling her eyes at herself.

Luckily Eva was still on the line. Fliss hadn't spoken to her since the first and only time they'd met when she'd been signed for a two book deal. Almost two years in and lacklustre sales of two books later, Fliss was under no illusion that she was not going to get another deal from Blackwood and had resigned herself to being quietly ghosted by them.

'I have some… interesting news regarding the international sales of your first book.'

International sales?

'Right. Lovely,' she said, trying to sound like an enthusiastic author and not at all bitter towards the publisher who she knew had written her off the minute it became apparent that the books weren't going to be award-winning bestsellers after all.

'We have had some moderate success in several of the Scandinavian countries over the last six months, particularly in Iceland. I suppose that shouldn't be surprising given that your books are set there,' Eva added as an afterthought.

It was still very surprising to Fliss to hear the word 'success' used in relation to her books. Given her last royalty statement, it was downright unbelievable.

'Are you sure it's my books?' The words were out before Fliss could stop herself. *For goodness sake, at least sound as if you believe in yourself!*

She heard Eva try stifling a snort of laughter before she said, 'Of course. It's not unusual for a book to take off somewhere other than the domestic market, although I have to admit we usually see some signs of that in the UK.' A polite way of saying they didn't see it coming because it hasn't done very well here.

'Well, that's great to hear.' Fliss began to wonder why Eva was calling. Was she about to offer her a new deal? Books three and four in the series were already written. It had started as a hobby and she wasn't going to give up writing just because she hadn't managed to find the right home for her books on the first attempt.

'Now that there's some traction, we feel it's worth putting some resource into the marketing. See where it could take us.'

'That sounds great, thank you.' Any kind of resource was pretty unbelievable. What did Eva have in mind? Posters at railway stations, on the Tube? Displays on tables in the doorways of Waterstones and WH Smiths?

'I'm calling to see if you're open to the idea of a book tour. We thought it would be a fabulous marketing opportunity to tie it in with *Jolabokaflod*.'

'Sorry?'

'*Jolabokaflod*.'

She still didn't know what Eva had said but clearly she was supposed to. She couldn't ask her to say it again.

'Yolo bokky flot?'

'Exactly.'

'Yolo bokky flot? Are you sure you heard that right, Mum? That literally doesn't mean anything.' Her daughter adopted the tone she always did when she thought Fliss had no clue about something, which was most of the time.

'I repeated it back to her and she said 'Exactly',' Fliss said, as she piled the odd selection of salad, pork pies, hummus and coleslaw onto three plates. 'Anyway, she mentioned doing a book tour, so it's something to do with that. Perhaps it's the name of a town and I misheard.'

'Why didn't you ask her to email you the details?' Her son, Josh, asked in a more reasonable tone than his sister.

'That's a good point, she did say she would email me, so we'll find out where it is sooner or later,' said Fliss, wondering how it was that her baby boy, now seventeen, had begun to have ideas that were very sensible.

'Did you get some crisps to have with the hummus?'

'Sorry, Emma, I got sidetracked by my *publisher* ringing me.'

'That's great, Mum,' Josh said, giving his sister a side-eye.

'Yeah, it's good. Even if you don't know what she's on about.'

'Well, a book tour, even if it's not to London or anywhere I've heard of will be fun. And she said that I've had some good sales in the last few months so hopefully that means we'll get a bigger royalty cheque than normal in the next few weeks.'

Emma's eyes lit up. 'Really? How much will you get?'

'I don't know. Let's not get our hopes up but maybe it'll be enough so that we can treat ourselves to a weekend away or something.'

'We could go to Alton Towers!'

'Or anywhere you'd like, Mum.'

Bless Josh.

'Will you two be alright if I have to be away for a couple of days?'

'Course. We can always ring Auntie Lily and Uncle Frank if we need to,' Josh said.

Later that evening, Fliss sat down in her favourite chair in the lounge and pulled her laptop out from underneath and onto her lap. Despite still believing on some level that the whole thing was a misunderstanding, there was evidence to the contrary in her inbox. It was an email with two attachments, one was named 'FL Thorne - Tour Itinerary' and the other 'FL Thorne - 2nd Quarter Royalty Statement'.

She hesitated, unsure which to open first. Eva had said that sales had been good. This royalty statement could surely only be an improvement on what she'd received before and how many sales were enough to have triggered the book tour? Curiosity about that won out over the tour itinerary.

'Oh my god!' she exclaimed, clapping her hand over her mouth and managing to grab hold of the laptop before it slid onto the floor as she flinched in shock. It was five figures and more money in three months than she could ever earn at work in the same time. She got up and jumped up and down a few times, trying to be quiet so as not to attract the attention of Josh or more importantly Emma, who might quickly burst her bubble of joy. She said the amount out loud to her reflection in the mirror over the mantlepiece and laughed at how excited she looked as she did a bit more jumping. This was the moment she'd longed for and had thought was impossible after the past couple of years. It was also one in the eye for anyone who had thought they'd been proved right in thinking that her writing career would inevitably end in failure. This was proof that she had done it.

Once she'd calmed down, made a cup of tea and opened the book tour schedule, the instinct to jump up and down had abated and instead, she looked in confusion at the document. Scanning down the list, she expected to see towns she might have heard of, obviously hoping in her heart of hearts to see London on there. It took her a moment or two to realise that the tour was apparently taking place in Iceland. When Eva had said the book had taken off there, she'd assumed that meant they were hoping it would pave the way for more sales in the UK, not that she'd be going to Iceland.

She'd been on a geography trip to Iceland when she was at school, not because she particularly liked geography but because it was better than going to Wales or the battlefields of Belgium, the only other choices, and more importantly, all her friends were going.

For a couple of minutes, she played the whole trip out in her mind, from sipping champagne in her business class seat on the plane, to the hotel room which would probably overlook the snow-capped mountains. She'd have to deal with queues of fans waiting, possibly through the night, for her to sign her books, giving each of them some one-on-one time so that they felt like the valued readers they were. There would probably be expensive, wine-fuelled dinners in the best restaurants, the bills picked up by her publisher who had finally recognised her for the shining star of their list that she had been all along.

Then reality hit.

She couldn't leave the children for - how long was this schedule? Five days? She'd never been away from them for more than a couple of days and that was only when they'd been away on guide or scout trips. Who would look after them? Lily and Frank loved the kids but not enough to take on that responsibility when they had a fair amount going on in their own lives. It was too much to ask. She trusted Josh to look after himself but it was spectacularly unfair to land him with the responsibility of trying to wrangle his sister for almost a week. Fliss would give it no more than twenty-four hours before she imagined Emma rebelling and doing exactly what she wanted, which at worst could include destructive house parties and at best might be staying out too late and making him worry. That wasn't his job.

But it was Duncan's job. He was their father, even though they weren't his only children anymore. It was the obvious solution. Fliss had made every effort to ask him for nothing since the day he'd left her for a woman he'd met on a team-building weekend three years ago. She'd kept from him the fact that her dream to be a published author had come true, mainly because for most of the two years she'd been published, there were only a few days right at the start when it had felt amazing. Given the fact that he hadn't mentioned it, she assumed he still didn't know. And with a fourteen-month-old baby he wasn't likely to have the energy to read anything these days.

Needing a second-opinion, Fliss rang her best friend, Abbie. She was a school-mum friend; they'd hit it off with when Josh had been in Reception with her son, Finn, and Emma and Ellie were friends too. She was almost the only person in the world that Fliss could talk to about her writing life who didn't think the whole thing was ridiculous.

'That's amazing, Fliss! You have to go!'

This was why she'd needed to ring Abbie.

'But I need to organise the kids for almost a week.'

'You know I'd have them but they'd be at each other's throats after a couple of days.'

'I know, thanks for sort of offering though. I think I'm going to have to ask Duncan.'

'You *should* ask Duncan. It's about time he pulled his

weight. This is a big deal for you, don't let anything get in the way. Think of me as a last resort option if that helps.'

Fliss laughed. 'The thought of you having to deal with Emma and Ellie and the ticking time-bomb of self-centred teenagerness does make me feel sorry enough for you to ask Duncan.'

Abbie was right. The time had come to ask him for a favour. He more than owed her, and at the same time perhaps she'd surprise him with news of her success. Make him see what she'd accomplished on her own when, at the end of their marriage he'd assumed that she wouldn't be able to cope without him. Hopefully, the joy it would bring her to prove him wrong would take the sting out of the fact that she needed to ask him for help after all this time. But she was determined that now, after two years of disappointment, she was going to grab the chance to have her five-day book tour and finally live the dream.

2

The next morning in a slow moment at work, Fliss sat with her phone in her hand, one finger poised over Duncan's number. They communicated almost exclusively by text; she couldn't remember the last time she'd actually spoken to him. But this, in a text exchange, would be a lot of typing.

She knew it was a good time to call. As a financial advisor, he always spent the mornings seeing clients and the afternoons doing paperwork so that when the kids were younger, they could take it in turns to pick them up from school. Before he'd met Shona, Fliss and Duncan had worked together. More than that, they'd started the company together and built it big enough to be taken over by a larger company. That was when it had all started to go wrong. When he'd met Shona. With all of his money tied up the business and the payout from the takeover contingent on performance over a number of years, Fliss was left with nothing but a reasonable downpayment on a house.

Last night, with the euphoria still running through her, this phone call had seemed like a small bump in the road to Iceland whereas now, it felt more like an insurmountable rock face. Her heart was beating so hard that her phone shook in her hand with every beat. This was ridiculous.

'Fliss.' He said her name with a hint of surprise.

'Duncan.' Might as well launch straight in. Small talk would be awkward. 'I need to go away for a few nights for work. Can you help with the children?'

He gave a low chuckle. 'They're hardly children anymore.'

'They can't fend for themselves for almost a week.'

This time he sighed. It was familiar, even if she normally read it between the lines of his messages rather than heard it. 'It's not the best time. What kind of work? A training course for school receptionists?'

Another chuckle.

Sometimes, despite what she'd been through, she did think Shona had done her a favour.

'It's for something else.'

There was silence while he waited for her to explain. Irritating, but she reminded herself that she did want to tell him, it was just more nerve-wracking now that the moment had come.

'My publisher has organised a book tour for me in Iceland.'

In her head, he'd have been drinking coffee when she said that because she was sure he'd have spit it all over himself. It was a satisfying thought.

'What? A book tour? Are you joking?'

'No. I'm not. So can you help out or not?'

'Christ, Fliss. You're a writer? That's what you always wanted.' He said it softly, making her heart ache briefly at the glimpse of the man she'd once known. The person who knew better than anyone else what her hopes and dreams were.

'So?' Time to press the point while he was still musing on the fact that she'd always wanted this. 'You can help?'

'I'll speak to Shona. We'll sort something out. When is it?'

'It starts on the seventeenth of December but I need to leave on the sixteenth. I'll be back on the twenty-second.' The timing couldn't have been better since the school she worked in would already have closed for the Christmas holidays by then.

'It's a bit close to Christmas.'

She sighed, loudly. 'It's not the best time but it was arranged before I knew that. It's to tie in with an Icelandic thing…'

'Jolobokaflod.'

'Yes.' How did he know about that? How did he know how to say it?

'Shona's family do that every year. Well, I guess the timing makes sense then.'

'So you'll let me know?'

'Sure. And congratulations, Fliss. It's amazing.'

Tears spring to her eyes. There was probably no one else who knew what this meant to her like he did and she was touched that for once, he sounded as if he respected her.

Later that afternoon, she had a text from him.

We can take the kids until 20th but then we're off to the in-laws for Christmas.

It grated that he used the term in-laws; it was verging on insensitive, but that was the Duncan she was used to now, and she had learned to try not to dwell on these things.

And he'd said yes. It wasn't the whole time, but she was sure Lily and Frank would be able to cover the last couple of days.

She was going to Iceland!

After spending an evening googling all the places she would be visiting in Iceland, Fliss realised that a good proportion of it was less of a book tour and more of a book wander around the bookshops of Reykjavik. There were a couple of days involving a bookshop to the south-east of Reykjavik and a library to the north, but a hotel in Reykjavik had been booked for her for all six nights, so neither of those places could be too far away from the capital.

The flight wasn't going to be business class and the hotel wasn't five star but Fliss was so looking forward to it. It was slightly nerve-wracking that the publisher didn't have the budget to send anyone with her but they'd organised someone from a company in Reykjavik to accompany her, even arranging for them to meet her at the airport.

Now that Duncan was on board, asking her sister to keep an eye on the children for a couple of days didn't seem so difficult, so the following day she invited Lily and Frank for dinner so that she could share her news.

'A book tour? I thought that only happened to people like Marian Keyes?' her ever-supportive sister said.

'Maybe Fliss is the Marian Keyes of Iceland?' Her brother-in-law, Frank, was so lovely, his comment backing up her assumption that she'd have a better chance of Lily agreeing to help with the kids if Frank was in the room as well, rather than asking over the phone.

'It's just...' Her sister struggled to find the words.

Helpfully Emma came to her rescue. 'It's so weird. I can't believe there are that many people in Iceland that have read your book. I mean, nobody here has ever heard of you.'

She made a good point and it was hard to be offended because Emma was at the age where she was never going to admit that anything her parents did was cool.

'It's surprised me too,' Fliss said. 'I'm sure even though it's sold well, it's probably not a bestseller. The publisher thinks the *Jolobokaflod* thing will help boost sales, that's all.'

'What is that?' Lily asked in an exasperated tone, as if she was asking for the hundredth time.

'It's an Icelandic tradition where people buy books for each other. They give them as gifts on Christmas Eve, and people spend the evening reading,' Fliss said, fresh from having looked it up. Although it sounded like the perfect way to spend Christmas Eve Fliss was reluctant to embrace it after hearing that Shona had already discovered it.

'It sounds so boring,' Emma said predictably.

'I wouldn't mind reading for a whole evening,' said Lily, 'but I wouldn't trust Frank to choose anything I'd actually want to read.'

'Ditto,' he said, with a laugh. 'You only ever buy me inspirational books written by male celebrities like Bear Grylls and Ben Fogle. It gives me a complex. I think it's fantastic, Fliss.'

'It is,' Lily relented. 'I'm proud of you. And Mum and Dad would be too.' They exchanged a look, a rare moment when they shared the closest bond they had, the shared love and loss of their parents.

'I'm proud too, Mum,' Emma said to the surprise of everyone. 'I suppose it is quite cool, if you're into books.'

Fliss smiled, because Emma was into books, just not the mainstream crimes, romances or best-sellers. She had recently developed a niche taste for American hockey high school romances that she now thought were superior to anything else in the literary world.

'Thanks, Em.'

'Where's Josh tonight?' Frank asked as they sat down to eat. Fliss had thrown together a quick meal of pasta with pesto sauce and plenty of garlic bread.

'He's helping out at the sixth form open evening,' Fliss said.

'He's such a nerd. He's always in the computer lab.'

'It's good that he has something he enjoys,' Frank said. 'He'll never work a day in his life if he gets a job with computers.'

Emma rolled her eyes. 'Whatever.'

Frank raised his eyebrows at Fliss and smiled. She knew he was politely highlighting that he thought Emma had backchatted him. Given what Fliss had invited them around for, it would have been nice if Emma could get through a conversation without comments laced with teenage derision.

'The garlic bread is delicious,' Lily said, sounding surprised and following up with a generous sip of her wine.

'Thanks. So are you two okay to keep an eye on the kids for a couple of days at the end of my book tour? Duncan can have them until the twentieth.'

'Of course,' Frank said, squeezing his wife's hand.

'Will Duncan drop them off with us?' Lily asked.

'I'm not sure yet but I'll sort out the details.'

'We don't need to stay with you, Auntie Lil. We could stay here and just ring if we need anything.'

Lily looked at Fliss. That basically meant that she was on Emma's side.

'Let me think about it.'

'Or we could come with you?'

Fliss shook her head, keen to squash that idea before anyone around the table could agree. 'I don't want to blow my first royalty cheque on a family holiday for you two while I'm working. And besides, you can't miss school. It's an important year for both of you.'

Another eye roll but at least it signalled that Emma accepted the decision.

'It's fine, Fliss. We've got a few weeks before we need to work out the logistics,' Frank said.

She gave him a grateful smile.

'You ought to treat yourself to something special with those royalties,' Lily said, passing the plate of garlic bread to Emma as she spoke.

'I don't need anything.' She'd already decided to save it. It was hard to make ends meet. Even with an affordable mortgage to pay, her salary only just covered everything. It would be nice to have a bit of a buffer for a change.

Lily put her fork down. 'You need some clothes that make you look like an author. No offence Fliss, but you've been wearing the same clothes for at least the past ten years. Treat yourself to a few new things to freshen up your look.'

It was hard to argue because it was true. Fliss was all too aware that she had let herself go over the past few years. Things had been busy. Tough. And she was at the bottom of her list of priorities. As long as she looked presentable for work, what else did she need to look good for? She didn't want to date, and on the odd nights out with friends, it was generally accepted that everyone wore jeans.

'Want to come shopping at the weekend?'

Lily looked surprised. 'I'd love that,' she said. 'You need someone with a critical eye, Fliss.'

Suddenly the shopping trip didn't seem like such a good idea.

3

The staff of Iceland Adventures were gathered for their weekly meeting in the company storage unit outside Reykjavik. As well as serving as a home for all of their equipment, it was a convenient meeting place since their office in the centre of Reykjavik was too small to fit all of them in. Whoever had arrived first had fired up the wood burner and it was already toasty warm, if you were sat close enough to the fire.

As the boss, Jonas Einarsson always led the weekly meeting with the first item of business being organising the rota for the week ahead. In the winter, especially this close to Christmas, they ran fewer excursions because of the limitations of the weather. But they still ran Northern Lights excursions every evening and a couple of Golden Circle trips every week as well as the usual airport transfers which sometimes incorporated stops at the Blue Lagoon.

'Also this week,' Jonas said,' we have a special booking from a publishing company in the UK. They're sending an author here for a book tour and need someone to collect her from the airport and then be her driver for the week. It should be an easy job. Anyone want to do it?'

'Is it someone famous?' Siggi asked.

'Someone called FL Thorne,' said Jonas.

'I can do it,' Brun said. He'd read the books and enjoyed them. It might be interesting to meet the author and get some extra insights.

'Are you sure? I've said we will be on call for whatever she needs. You are happy to do that? She arrives on the sixteenth and leaves on the twenty-second.'

'That's fine,' said Brun. What else would he be doing? Now that work was quieter, he was glad to have anything to fill the hours. He loved being busy and the winter lull, especially this year, was difficult.

'Great, thanks Brun. So that takes us up to Christmas, guys. We'll have our usual night out at the beginning of January, before we start to get busy again but I will email you all about that.

Rather than dispersing at the end of the meeting, most people, including Brun, stuck around for another cup of coffee and to finish off the pastries that Jonas's wife, Rachel, always insisted that he provide.

'Thanks for taking on this author job,' Jonas said to him as they sat down on the sofa nearest the fire. 'It's so close to Christmas, I thought I'd end up doing it myself. You know how everyone starts to wind down.'

'It's no problem. I've read the books. They're pretty good, actually. Not quite as dark and gruesome as our homegrown psychological thrillers.'

'Ah, I'm sure Rachel bought a copy take to England with her and she was keen for me to read it after her. I trust your recommendation more than hers,' he laughed. 'Don't tell her that.'

Brun grinned. He and Jonas had been friends for years, since before Jonas started the tour company and even though it hadn't been his dream to be a tour guide in Iceland, it was a job he enjoyed. Showing the beauty of his country to tourists was a pleasure that he never tired of. But a bit of variety was always a good thing.

'Where is the book tour? In Reykjavik?'

'No, there is Selfoss and Akranes as well. I'll send you the itinerary. Maybe you should take her to Skyrland?'

Brun laughed. 'Do you recommend it?' It was a relatively new attraction in Selfoss that Jonas had visited to see if it was somewhere they ought to be offering tours to.

'I recommend the food more than the history lesson on making yogurt but that is because I am not a twelve-year-old child.'

'I will keep that idea in my back pocket for an emergency.' He picked up another pastry, ignoring the voice in his head telling him that two was enough.

'Are you playing tonight?'

It was the regular open mic night at one of the bars down by the harbour. Since Ned Nokes, previously of boyband The Rush and currently resident in Reykjavik, had turned up looking for a low-key outlet for his new music, he and Brun had started to play together. After playing the odd open mic night, they'd more recently written a few songs together.

'Yes, we have a new song. It is not quite there but good enough to try out on you lot,' he said. 'You're coming?'

Jonas nodded. 'And Olafur and Gudrun. I guess you might not make it next week once Ms Thorne is here.'

'I will see how Ms Thorne and I get along. Maybe I will invite her.'

Jonas raised his eyebrows as if he thought it highly unlikely that a famous author would be interested in a local open mic night.

'You never know,' Brun said.

Later that day, he studied the itinerary that Jonas had sent him, determined to be able to offer Ms Thorne an Icelandic experience that didn't begin and end in a bookshop.

4

Fliss settled into her aisle seat. It was years since she'd flown anywhere, and the first time she'd ever flown by herself. She tried to adopt the persona of a self-assured solo business traveller because that was what she was. At least for the next six days. Despite Lily insisting that her brand new jeans, selection of blouses and sweaters and sheepskin-lined smart leather winter boots would make her feel like a new woman, inside she was the same, slightly harried single mother that she always was. The children had been collected by Duncan the day before. It was the first time they'd been to stay there since Dylan, the baby he'd had with Shona, had been born and she knew that Emma's bravado about the situation was hiding the fact that she was worried about the new dynamic with her dad, while Josh had been quiet, simply insisting that they'd both be fine and that he'd look after his sister. Being slightly older than Emma meant that he had been more aware of the tensions between his parents at the time Duncan left, whereas at only twelve, Emma had still been a little girl who thought the world of her daddy. She'd been more forgiving of Duncan than Josh had been able to be.

'Sorry, could I get to my seat?' A woman with a small carry-on case stood in the aisle waiting for Fliss to move.

'Oh, of course.' She smiled and slipped out into the aisle, grabbing the bag she'd left on the floor and pulling it out of the way.

'Thanks.'

The woman settled into the window seat leaving a seat between them and before long, it became clear that nobody else was going to sit there as the flight attendants closed the doors of the plane and began their safety briefing.

Fliss pulled her Kindle out of her bag, needing a distraction to keep her building nerves at bay. It wasn't that she didn't like flying, it was the thought of how far she was going from her children. A car journey away from them was one thing, a flight was quite another. She glanced over at the woman who had taken a paperback out of her own bag before she pushed it under the seat in front of her. Fliss almost gasped out loud when she saw that it was her own novel, the second one she'd written. Not only was this woman reading her book, right next to her on a plane, but Fliss assumed she'd enjoyed the first one enough to want to read the second. To hide her elation, she switched on her Kindle and began to read, although the words didn't sink in at all. Her mind was whirring.

The take-off distracted her; the views of London below as the plane banked away towards the north-west had her leaning across the centre seat for a better look and it wasn't long before the food and drink cart was on its way down the aisle.

Fliss ordered a gin and tonic and sensibly decided that she ought to eat something, opting for a sandwich and a packet of crisps. All of this came to an extortionate amount of money but she remembered that Eva had told her to keep all her receipts since Blackwood would cover the cost of all the essentials of her trip.

The woman ordered wine and then reached

down to her bag and took out a meal deal which she must have had the foresight to buy in the airport.

'That was a good idea,' said Fliss.

The woman grinned. 'I've taken too many flights without remembering to do this, but the hit to my bank balance finally drummed it into me.'

The gin and tonic had relaxed Fliss nicely and it seemed natural to carry on the conversation while they ate.

'Are you going on holiday?' she asked.

With a mouth full of food, the woman shook her head. 'I live in Reykjavik,' she said, once she'd finished. 'I've been back to see my family for a couple of days as we're staying in Iceland for Christmas this year. I'm Rachel, by the way.'

'Fliss. Nice to meet you. What do you do?'

'We have a tour company. Run excursions, that sort of thing. How about you? Are you on holiday?'

Fliss shook her head. She should have anticipated that the question would have come the other way. With her book on the seat between them, she couldn't possibly say that she was a writer because then the questions would almost certainly lead to Fliss having to admit to that being her book. She'd never told anyone that she was a writer in a conversation like this and despite longing to, all of a sudden it was too much.

'It's a work trip. I work in an independent school, it's a marketing thing.'

Rachel nodded thoughtfully. 'I've heard of a few Icelandic kids who go overseas for senior school. Are you going to a recruitment fair or something?'

'No, it's just a fact-finding exercise.' A vague enough answer to hopefully call an end to that line of questioning. 'So how long have you lived in Iceland?'

Rachel began to tell Fliss the story of how she'd worked in London and been seconded to Reykjavik to open a new branch of Snug, the homeware store. She'd fallen in love with

Jonas, a local tour guide who was now her husband and she'd stayed.

'He can't survive anywhere else,' she said with a grin. He comes to the UK with me sometimes but he's so outdoorsy, he hates been hemmed in in London. He might be okay in deepest Scotland or Wales but he needs the wilderness and that's not far from the middle of Reykjavik. My parents live in Oxfordshire which obviously to us is the countryside but to him isn't.'

They laughed.

'I live in Summertown in Oxford,' said Fliss. 'I grew up there, met my husband and we started a business so I've never lived anywhere else. You've had quite an adventure.'

'It has been amazing,' said Rachel. 'I never thought I'd leave London but I didn't know what I was missing. My friend, Anna lived in London too, well she still does, I suppose. She and her boyfriend split their time between the two places. You need to be careful you don't fall under its spell like we did.'

'I have two kids so there's not much chance of Iceland enticing me to that degree, although I did go on a school trip once and absolutely loved it.'

'A geography trip?' Rachel asked. 'Those are our bread and butter in the summer. The trips to the Golden Circle to see the geyser and the tectonic plates are so popular.'

'We saw all of that but not much of Reykjavik itself. I'm looking forward to exploring somewhere different this time.'

Rachel rummaged in her bag and handed Fliss a business card. 'If you need anything or want to see anything while you're here, give us a call. It's quiet for us at this time of year, the weather keeps tourists away, but we're still running Northern Lights excursions and trips to the Blue Lagoon.'

'Thanks. Hopefully I can fit something in,' said Fliss, taking the card.

They'd both finished eating and drinking. 'Sorry, I don't want to seem rude,' said Rachel, 'but I really want to finish the end of this book. I promised Jonas I'd pass it on to him when I get home and I still have a couple of chapters to go. Have you read it? It's amazing.'

Fliss took a deep breath, tried to dial down her smile to something that looked normal and polite rather than deranged, and said, 'No, of course. Enjoy.'

Stepping on this plane was like suddenly being in an alternate universe where she actually was a writer who wrote books that people read. She gestured to the flight attendant who was periodically speeding up and down the aisle with the trolley just in case anyone wanted a top-up and ordered another gin and tonic. This moment called for a celebration, even if it was by herself.

When they got off the plane, Rachel said goodbye to her in the luggage hall. With just a carry-on bag she didn't have to hang around.

'It was great to meet you. Hope your trip goes well.'

'Thanks. Have a lovely Christmas.'

Fliss waited for her case thinking how nice it had been to sit next to someone who was not only reading her book, but had been a pleasure to chat to. It had been a great start to the trip and if anything, Fliss was more excited than ever to find out what was so special about Reykjavik that it had made two English women want to leave all that London had to offer for what she imagined was somewhere with a slower, quieter pace; a city, yes, but in the midst of an unforgiving wilderness.

It didn't take long for her case to appear and as she made her way towards the arrivals hall, the butterflies were back. There were quite a few people waiting, the drivers holding signs were all gathered together and Fliss scanned the line until she saw her name FL THORNE. As she approached, the man holding it smiled. She couldn't quite see his smile, since it was hidden within a rather bushy beard but his eyes more than made up for it, lighting up as if he was genuinely pleased to see her.

'Ms Thorne? *Velkomin til Íslands.* Welcome to Iceland.' He held out his hand for her to shake, it was perhaps the biggest hand she had ever shaken, and his grip was firm, yet gentle. 'I am Brun,' he said.

'Nice to meet you, I'm Fliss.' She felt at ease with him straight away, as if they had known each other for much longer than the seconds they'd been standing there.

'Is it your first visit to Iceland?'

'Apart from a school trip years ago,' she said, relieved that he spoke flawless English.

'Ah, so you have already seen the geyser and probably the rift between the tectonic plates.' he said with a smile, then he took her case from her. 'Do you have a coat?'

'Yes,' she said, feeling silly for not having taken it out of her holdall already. The airport was constructed with enough glass for her to see that it was snowing outside. She bent down and extracted it, a long showerproof puffer coat which thankfully had a hood. It was another purchase fuelled by Lily insisting that her battered old floral Seasalt raincoat wasn't going to do, and now Fliss was thankful.

'We are ready,' Brun announced, once she'd zipped her coat up. Fliss picked up her holdall but before she could haul it up over her shoulder, Brun took it from her and pulled it onto his own. Against his large frame, it looked more like a handbag. She smiled and started following him towards the doors.

A blast of cold air hit her once they stepped outside and she pulled the drawstring on her hood tighter and put her hands as deep into her pockets as they would go, wishing she hadn't packed her gloves in her case. Brun appeared not to have noticed the drop in temperature, perhaps because he was used to it or perhaps because his fur-lined hat with earflaps was doing a better job of keeping him warm than her hood was.

'It is cold,' he said with a smile. 'But the car is not far.' Despite the gently falling snow, it was hardly settling and it seemed to be business as usual judging by the amount of people, cars, buses and general hubbub that was no different to any other airport.

The car was actually a four-by-four vehicle with huge tyres. Brun opened the passenger door, gesturing for her to climb in, and then closed it behind her before he stowed her luggage in the boot.

'Okay,' he said, as he sat down, pulling off his hat and tucking it into the door pocket while he ruffled his dark hair with his hand. He started the engine and manoeuvred out of the car park onto a road that looked highly unlikely to be the road to anywhere, particularly one between an international airport and the capital city. But obviously it was, otherwise Brun wouldn't be going that way.

Once they were properly on their way, he began to point out a couple of things along their route; a power station lit up in the dusk by colourful lights on its chimneys, and the road that led to the Blue Lagoon.

'It is the first time I have taken part in a book tour,' he said, glancing at her before he turned his eyes back to the road.

'Me too.'

'Really? Your first book tour is in Iceland?' He raised an enquiring eyebrow.

'Yes. My book hasn't sold very well so it was a surprise when I found out that it's been different here.

'Huh,' he said, in surprise. 'I guess Icelandic people have better taste.'

Fliss laughed. 'That's kind of you to say.'

'Not at all. Many of my friends have read your books.'

'Really?' She couldn't help herself. Did that mean he had read them?

'Yes. There are lots of dark, Icelandic stories but your book does not make Iceland seem like that. Your character, she is interesting. How she thinks about people, why they do what they do.' He paused and looked at her. 'Are you a psychologist?'

'No, I read a lot of books about criminals and their motivations, though. It comes from that, really.'

Brun nodded thoughtfully. 'And you capture the real heart of Iceland in your writing. That is why people love it.'

'Thank you. You've read them then?' Fliss had never felt braver, or more certain that if he had, he'd enjoyed them.

He looked at her, raised his eyebrows and nodded vigorously, his eyes smiling as they had before. 'Of course. It is great to meet the author of books that I have enjoyed.'

Fliss felt as if she must be glowing with pride. Today, for the first time since she'd started writing, she felt like a real-life author.

5

The following morning, Fliss was up early. She hadn't slept very well, worrying about the first day of the book tour. There was a lot to worry about. Would people speak English? Would anyone turn up? Would it be embarrassing to sit and sign books for people? What if she spelled someone's name wrong? What if she should have prepared something in advance and her publisher had forgotten to tell her?

Her hotel was on a main road, across from which was the sea. She hadn't managed to get a good look the night before since it had been dark by the time Brun dropped her off, but she'd noticed the choppy water glinting in the glow from the street lights. This morning wasn't all that much brighter. She'd been expecting short daylight hours but this strange light, somewhere between dusk and darkness was odd, as if it took much, much longer for the sun to rise or set. She suspected that's exactly what it was but hadn't paid much attention in physics lessons.

After breakfast, in the half-light, she crossed the road and strolled towards what looked like the centre of the city. It was quite windy next to the sea but with her hood up and plenty of layers on, she didn't feel too cold. The capsule wardrobe Lily had chosen had actually turned out to be very helpful since it removed all the indecision. This morning she had put her new jeans and boots on and then layered a long-sleeved t-shirt underneath a blouse and jumper. She also had another pair of identical jeans and two or three combinations of tops, including a slightly dressier one if she needed it. And as an afterthought, she'd packed a dress. Just in case.

The bracing walk helped to take her mind off things and her worries eased away in favour of thoughts of riding around the beautiful countryside with Brun. They were heading to Selfoss for the day, to visit the first bookshop. She hoped that by the end of the day, she'd feel as if the book tour was much more within her comfort zone than it had been at five in the morning.

Not wanting to venture too far, worried about getting sidetracked and being late for Brun, she walked as far as she could along the seafront without losing sight of her hotel, which was before the road turned a corner towards the harbour. At that point she turned around and headed back. Brun was outside waiting in the car. He greeted her with a smile and raised his hand.

'I'll be five minutes,' she mouthed, holding up her hand to indicate.

He gave her a thumbs up.

She went back up to her room to get her bag, and checked her minimal make-up just in case she had mascara down her cheeks. She ran a brush lightly through her straightened hair and added another smear of lipgloss.

'Good morning,' said Brun. He was standing by the passenger door when she went back down, and held it open for her while she climbed in.

'Morning, thanks.'

'It will take about an hour to drive to Selfoss. It would be a good idea to take your coat off,' he said.

She took her coat off as he suggested, and laid it on the

back seat next to his, which was already there. 'So I feel the benefit?'

He laughed. 'Yes. And we have heated seats in the car which is better than a coat.'

'What time does the sun come up?' she asked, as the road quickly led them out of the city.

'Around eleven. It will be almost light when we arrive in Selfoss.'

'Do you know Selfoss? Is it smaller than Reykjavik?'

Brun nodded. 'Yes, it is a small town but it is on Route One, the main road around Iceland, so it is visited a lot. As well as the bookshop, there are two museums. A new one, Skyrland and a turf house museum.'

'Skyrland like Skyr the yogurt?' Fliss asked, expecting Brun to laugh at her joke.

'Yes, exactly,' he said. 'I am your driver all week so if there is anything you would like to do, you tell me.'

'Thank you. I don't know how long the bookshop visit will take but I'd love to be able to see a bit more of the country while I'm here. It would be a shame not to if we have time.'

'It is good that you want to explore, Fliss.' He looked across at her with a look that she couldn't quite place. He was smiling but there was something else in his eyes too. And he pronounced her name 'fleece' which was very endearing.

'I don't really like Skyr but I'm sure the museum would be interesting.'

Brun burst out into a loud but deep laugh, taking Fliss by surprise, and she found herself laughing along with him. His laugh was infectious and entirely genuine. 'Ah,' he said, regaining his composure. 'British people are so polite, it is very funny. You will be glad to hear then, that Skyr is not all it has to offer.'

Fliss couldn't help but be intrigued. 'Okay, if we have time, let's go to Skyrland.'

The drive to Selfoss took them across miles and miles of barren, snow-covered landscape, the road clear of snow and ice on all but the edges, which were helpfully marked with yellow posts at regular intervals. It was familiar to Fliss from her geography trip years earlier in that she remembered the mountains that were rising up around them but they'd been in the summer when everything had been lush and green in comparison to the snowy landscape they drove through now.

They skirted a town on the way but other than that, there was nothing out of the ordinary until they arrived in Selfoss itself. It was situated next to a wide river that they crossed, over a bridge towards the centre of the town. Although the buildings were partly covered in snow, there wasn't enough fresh snow to disguise the coloured roofs. There were fairy lights twinkling on the buildings and trees, although the sun was starting to break through the long dawn, and the lights inside the shops made them look warm and inviting.

Brun pulled up outside a white, single storey building with large windows across its front and a sign that said *Bókakaffið* above the door. Fliss didn't need a translation to know that it meant books and coffee, the perfect combination.

'Here we are,' Brun announced. He pulled their coats from the back seat into the front and handed Fliss hers. He opened his door but before he could get out, Fliss put a hand on his arm, and he pulled it to.

'Brun, look,' she said, nodding towards the bookshop where someone had just gone inside, leaving the door half open for someone who was following behind them.

He leant forward and followed her gaze. 'I am not sure what you are showing me. This is the right place.'

'But look how many people are in there.'

Brun patted her knee. 'Fliss. Look at me.'

She tore her gaze away from the shop, panic rising in her chest. These people had misunderstood. She wasn't the person they were all here for.

'Fliss,' said Brun again.

She looked at him and saw a softness in his eyes.

'It is okay,' he said gently. 'You were not expecting this?'

'No, I wasn't. I'm not joking, Brun. No one has bought my book. At most I've had three conversations with my publisher over the past two years and aside from edits, about as many emails. This is too much.' She sat back in her seat and closed her eyes. 'I don't think I can go in.'

Fliss felt Brun's hand move from her knee and imagined the look of disappointment on his face that she'd wasted his time dragging out to Selfoss for nothing. Instead, she felt his hand wrap around hers, his fingers giving hers a gentle squeeze of reassurance. And for a moment she could think about nothing else other than how it felt to be touched by someone other than a friend or her children. How long it had been since anyone had held her hand.

'I will come with you, if you would like?'

She managed to stop herself replying on autopilot, saying that there was no need. Because now that he was here, holding her hand, she wanted him to stay with her.

'If you don't mind, that would be… I'd really appreciate it. Thank you.'

He gave her hand a final squeeze and got out of the car, pulling his coat on as he made his way around to her. He opened the door and took her coat off her lap, holding it open for her to shrug into once she'd stepped onto the pavement.

'There is nothing to worry about,' he said, his eyes locking onto hers as if he were trying to hypnotise her. 'You are FL Thorne. You write fantastic books and the people in there are only here because they love them and appreciate you for writing them. They are all on your side.' He nodded, raising his eyebrows as if he needed some sort of confirmation that she agreed with him.

She took a deep breath and shook her hands out in front of her. 'Okay. I can do this.' She nodded vigorously at Brun. 'Let's do it.'

He let out a loud burst of a laugh and said, 'Lead the way, Ms Thorne.'

Fliss pushed the door open, unsure of what to expect, but half expecting everyone to turn and stare at her, stopping their conversations mid-sentence so that a hush descended. But in fact, no one took any notice as she made her way, followed by Brun, over to the counter.

'Hi, I'm Fliss Thorne,' she said to the woman behind the counter, which was part sales counter, part coffee shop counter.

The woman's eyes widened and she grinned at Fliss. 'Oh my goodness,' she said in perfect English, 'Welcome to Book and Coffee Cafe! We're so happy that you could come.'

Fliss felt the eyes of a few surrounding people turn towards her but she kept her mind on what Brun had said.

'It's lovely to be here.'

'I'm Freyja. Can I get you both a coffee?'

'Yes please, a latte would be great.'

Brun nodded his agreement to that. '*Takk*,' he added.

Freyja began to make the coffee, chatting to them as she did so. 'We have a table ready for you and I hope we have enough books.'

The table was in a nook that was recessed back from the main area of the shop, still lined with floor-to-ceiling bookshelves but for now, cordoned off with a piece of rope slung across the entrance.

'I don't know what you prefer,' Freyja said, 'but we thought we would ask people to write their name on a piece of paper for you because of spellings?'

'That's a great idea,' Fliss said, beginning to feel more enthusiastic now that one of her biggest fears had been taken care of. 'Thank you.'

'Okay, so have your coffee and then we will get started.'

Fliss took her coat off and sat down, while Freyja stowed her coat and bag in a nearby cupboard. There was a pile of around fifty books on the table, copies of both her titles, more than she had ever seen together before. She pulled her phone out and took a photo.

'I will take some photos while you are signing the books.' Brun said.

'I don't know, do you think people will mind?' Fliss said, rummaging in her bag for the pen she'd bought specially for doing book signings, when she'd been in the first flush of excitement about the book tour.

'I think it is fine,' he said. 'You may get requests for selfies.'

When the first person came to the table, they stopped short of speaking to Fliss and instead said something to Brun in Icelandic. He smiled and nodded, holding his hand out to take their phone from them.

'Hello,' The first person sounded more nervous than Fliss had felt about twenty minutes earlier.

'Hi, thank you for coming.'

The young woman held out a piece of paper with her name written on it and picked up a copy of Fliss's second book, placing it on the table in front of her.

'I have already read the first one,' she said, with a shy smile.'I love Margot.'

'Thank you. I hope you enjoy this one.' Fliss carefully copied the name as it was written and then signed her own underneath. Then they both turned to Brun and the woman held the book in between them as they posed for a photo. He gave a thumbs up and handed the phone back to the woman who thanked him and gave Fliss a small wave before she made her way back to the main part of the shop.

Fliss exhaled and gave Brun a quick smile to show him she

was feeling better before she greeted her next... fan. Could she call them that? Yes, she probably could. The euphoria she'd felt that night at home a few weeks ago when she'd opened that royalty statement was back.

It was almost a couple of hours before Fliss finished signing books for everyone who had queued and then she'd had another coffee and chatted to some of the people who had stayed. She'd never imagined she would be able to spend two hours talking about her own books, her characters and for people to actually want to listen to what she said. She'd long ago stopped trying to sound friends and family out with storylines, endings and things like that. But these people wanted to talk about exactly that, and many of them were thrilled to know that there were at least two more books to come. Fliss didn't disappoint them by saying that they weren't part of her publishing deal, she'd have to sort that problem out when she got home. But these people had given her a reason to try and make that happen.

By the time she was ready to leave, it had started to get dark again and Fliss thought how nice it would be to stay at the cosy bookshop and curl up with another coffee and a good book but Brun had been patiently waiting while she chatted and it wasn't fair to keep him any longer.

'Thank you so much, Fliss,' Freyja said, pulling her into a hug as they said goodbye. 'We have never had such a successful event. You have been amazing.'

'Thank you. I can't tell you how nervous I was and I've enjoyed it so much. Your customers are fabulous.'

Brun held the door open for her and once they'd got into the car, they waved at Freyja and the others inside the bookshop until it was out of sight.

'I think you feel much happier now.' Brun said, smiling at her knowingly.

'I loved that so much. It was nothing like I'd imagined, not as bad, obviously, but I'd never dreamed it would be like that.' She felt as if she couldn't contain the joy.

'I think we need to celebrate,' he said.

6

Fliss wasn't sure that Skyrland and celebrating went together, but the glint in Brun's eyes made her want to go along with whatever he had planned.

Skyrland was in an old converted dairy. It was a cream-coloured building with a large arched window in one of the gabled ends which made it look more like a church than anything else, and she could see the pea-green corrugated roof peeking out from the gaps between the snow. There were fairy lights twinkling around the edge of the roof and a large tree just outside was festooned with tiny lights as well. The lying snow only added to the picture-postcard image.

'It's so Christmassy,' Fliss said, sighing happily.

'The lights are always there in the winter,' said Brun, smiling at Fliss's wide-eyed appreciation. 'They are not just for Christmas, they are winter lights. To bring some cheer when it is dark for so much of the day.'

'I love that idea,' Fliss said. 'I never realised. I'll have to make sure Margot has some fairy lights in the next book.'

They parked the car and made their way to the entrance. Fliss tried to pay but Brun insisted that her publisher wanted to foot the bill for any expenses, so she happily allowed him to. There was an exhibition telling the story of how Skyr was first made by a Viking a thousand years ago. Her children would have enjoyed the interactive exhibition a few years ago but she could imagine the eye rolls she'd get from Emma if she tried to take her somewhere like this nowadays.

Brun seemed keen to whip through the museum area so Fliss didn't linger for too long, after all he might need to get back to Reykjavik.

'Here we are,' he announced when they'd finished wandering through the exhibits. It was a food hall. 'Would you like to eat here?'

With a choice of several restaurants, a craft beer bar and a cocktail bar, it seemed like the ideal place and the atmosphere was relaxed but effortlessly cool and modern. It was almost like an indoor street food festival with a choice that included burgers, Thai food, pasta and pizza. They wandered around, checking out the menus for each place before they agreed on pasta.

'Are you happy if I have one small beer?' Brun asked Fliss.

'Of course, that's fine.' She was touched that he asked her and she knew that if she had objected he wouldn't have minded at all. Brun was no enigma. He was open and easy to be with, and given that she had only met him twenty-four hours ago, she felt as if he was already someone she knew. Someone she might count as a friend before too long.

'And you will have champagne? Or a cocktail?'

'Oh…' She had been about to say no, that she'd have a beer as well, but actually, she did feel like celebrating so she embraced Brun's gentle suggestion and had a look at a cocktail menu which was on the table next to them, settling on a sparkling wine-based cocktail which had something in it that made it shimmer. Perfect for a celebration.

They sat opposite each other with their drinks while they waited for the food.

'Tell me how today was for you,' Brun said.

Fliss didn't think she could remember the last time anyone had asked her anything like that. Josh would occasionally say, 'Had a good day, Mum?' But inevitably she always said she had even if it had been awful. Having someone sat opposite her, seemingly interested in hearing what her answer would be was a very welcome difference.

'You know I was nervous,' she said, waiting for him to acknowledge that which he did with a small nod. 'As soon as I sat down at that table and spoke to the first person in the queue, I didn't feel as if it was the first time I'd done it. I felt as if, somehow, it was natural. I didn't need to think about what to say or anything. It was the nicest day at work I've ever had.'

'*Skál*!'

'*Skál*!' Fliss said, then took a sip of her cocktail, looking at Brun over the top of her glass. He took a swig of his beer which left him with a little bit of froth on his moustache.

'You've got a bit of froth on you,' said Fliss, pointing to her own mouth to show him where.

'*Takk*.'

'So what do you usually do when you're not on a book tour with me?'

'The company I work for runs excursions, trips to see the Northern Lights, waterfalls, the geyser, things like that.'

Fliss rummaged in her bag for the card that Rachel from the plane had given her. 'I met someone on the plane who owns this company. That kind of thing?'

Brun laughed. 'Exactly this! It must have been Rachel. She is married to my friend, my boss, Jonas.'

'Small world.'

Brun shrugged. 'Not really in Reykjavik. Everyone knows everyone here.'

'You must have seen the Northern Lights lots of times?'

'Yes, many times. It is always a little different every time.

Sometimes they are hard to find, or they are there and you would only see them with a long exposure on your camera. Other times, they dance across the sky and put on a show for us. It is always a privilege to see them. It is my favourite excursion but you can go night after night with no lights and then it is disappointing to let our guests down. But the thrill of finding them is like an addiction.'

'When I came to Iceland before it was in the summer so it was light almost all the time. I'd love to have a chance to see them this time.'

'We may have a chance tonight, although I have not checked the forecast. We will drive slowly back to Reykjavik and we might be lucky.'

Fliss's phone began to buzz in her bag. She apologised and pulled it out. It was a FaceTime call from Emma. It was fairly quiet in the area where they'd sat, and Brun gestured that she should take the call and went to leave the table. She shook her head vigorously and he smiled and stayed where he was.

'Hi Mum! Where are you?'

'We're in an old dairy, we've just ordered dinner and I'm having a cocktail.' She held the cocktail up to show Emma.

'Cool. At least you can eat at a civilised time, we're getting forced to eat at five o'clock so that we can eat as a family. We could still eat as a family after Dylan goes to bed. The whole bloody house revolves around Dylan.'

'Emma,' Fliss said, in a tone that Emma would know meant she shouldn't have sworn. 'It's only for a couple more days and then you'll practically be at home again, just around the corner at Auntie Lily's.'

Emma exhaled loudly as if she was unlikely to survive another two days at her father's house.

'And how's Josh?'

'He's fine. He's out at that computer club thing.'

Which explained the FaceTime call. Emma was bored and

probably lonely.

'Why don't you take the opportunity to get some extra studying done while you're there, Em? Then you'll have a head start on your holiday homework and can have a few down days over Christmas.'

'It's hard to concentrate with Dylan crying all the time.'

Fliss suppressed a smirk of joy as she imagined how Duncan would be feeling about having a moody teenager in the house when he had to cope with a fairly unstable almost-toddler as well.

'I did my first book-signing today.' As soon as she said it Fliss knew she wasn't going to get the reaction she was hoping for.

'Nice one, Mum. Did anyone turn up?'

'Quite a few people. I'll send you some photos later. I must go, Em. Our food's here. I'll call you both tomorrow. Love you. Love to Josh.'

'Bye Mum, love you.'

Once they'd taken a first mouthful of pasta, a truffle and cheese affair that tasted divine, Brun asked, 'That was your daughter?'

'Yes. She's fifteen. It's a tricky age.'

Brun laughed. 'Would you like another drink?'

'Mmm, thank you.' It was turning into the perfect ending to a surprisingly enjoyable day and Fliss wanted to keep the good feeling alive. Another cocktail was exactly what she wanted.

Brun gestured to the barman for another cocktail and asked in Icelandic for what turned out to be a glass of water for himself.

When they'd finished eating, Fliss picked up her fresh cocktail and said,' I'll just finish this and we can get going.'

'Please, there is no rush.'

'You don't have anyone waiting for you at home?'

'No. Not at the moment.' He shrugged and looked down at his water with a half smile. 'I was in a relationship until about six months ago.' 'Oh. Had you been together long?' Fliss realised she had no idea how old Brun might be. It was hard to tell because of his beard. He had the rugged look of someone who worked outdoors a lot, but still, she had a feeling that he was a few years younger than her.

'We had been together for a couple of years. I have a big group of friends and everyone is in couples. I think it went on longer than it should have done because of that. We did not spend much time by ourselves, and it turned out we did not want to.' He smiled, letting Fliss know that this wasn't something he was still hurting about. 'How long have you been with your partner?'

Fliss realised that the conversation with Emma probably hadn't been enough to go on for Brun to be across the detail of their family set-up.

'We're not together anymore,' she said. 'The children are staying with him for a few days, just while I'm away. They have a half-brother who's just over a year old.'

'Ah,' said Brun. 'A toxic mix of teenager and toddler.'

'It seems to be. I can't help feeling as if it might be a bit of karma for their dad.'

Brun gave one of his loud guffawing laughs, which again, made Fliss helpless to do anything but join in. 'You have had one of your best days and he is perhaps having one of the worst. For you to think it is karma, Fliss, I know that it is no more than he deserves.'

They had both stopped laughing and were gazing at each other.

'Thank you, Brun,' said Fliss softly. 'It's been a long time since I've had a day quite as good as this.'

He acknowledged her with a small nod and a lift of his glass. 'I have enjoyed today. It has been good to see you find yourself.'

Although Brun hadn't used quite the right expression, she knew what he meant was that she had transformed from a quivering mess at the thought of having to walk into that busy bookshop and somehow manage to live up to anyone's expectations, to being a more self-assured version of herself. She felt that too, as if she had hit her stride in a race that had started many years ago, and she hoped more than anything that every day in Iceland was going to make her feel like this. Then maybe when she went home she wouldn't have to go back to being Fliss: ex-wife, mother-of-two, disappointing sister, with nothing on that list that was her. Perhaps over the course of the next five days, she'd morph into Fliss: mother-of-two, author, sister to be proud of, ex-wife who deserved respect. It was something to aim for, and after today, something that felt possible.

7

Disappointingly, although not unexpectedly according to Brun, they hadn't seen the Northern Lights on the drive back to Reykjavik the previous night.

'The skies are clear but the aurora forecast is not good for tonight,' he said, having checked on his phone before they left Selfoss.

Nevertheless, Fliss spent the whole journey staring at the skies, just in case. Brun had dropped her at her hotel, promising to pick her up at nine in the morning for the drive to Akranes, a town around forty miles from Reykjavik, to the north.

Her next event was being held at the library, so it wasn't going to be a carbon copy of the book-signing in Selfoss, but Fliss tried to tell herself that the first event would always be the worst one anxiety-wise, even if the library event did involve her being interviewed. It was way out of her comfort zone, but she had been looking forward to it, having enjoyed plenty of these events as an audience member. And now that the book-signing had gone well, who was to say the first interview wouldn't?

Brun had suggested she bring a swimsuit and towel with her since there might be the opportunity to visit some sort of outdoor swimming place. Fliss hoped it would be something like the Blue Lagoon — relaxing and indulgent, or at least that was how it looked in the photographs she'd seen. Luckily she'd had the foresight to pack a swimsuit, so before she went to bed, she put everything ready.

Brun was sat in reception waiting when she went down to meet him.

'Am I late?' she asked, feeling guilty about making him wait.

'I am early,' he said with a broad smile, standing up as she came towards him. 'Are you ready for another great day?'

'Yes,' she said, feeling less certain than she sounded, although the confidence Brun seemed to have in her was definitely helping.

Once they were in the car, he headed to Route One, the same as the day before but this time in the opposite direction.

'Is Route One the road to everywhere?'

'Yes,' he said. 'It is a ring road that goes right around Iceland, passing all the major towns. At this time of year it is not always possible to drive all of it because of the weather.'

They hugged the coast for a short while before the road took them through the snow-covered landscape where there was nothing of any note besides the occasional gathering of houses that could generously be described as small villages. Then they came back towards the coast and the road took them through a tunnel.

'This goes underneath the fjord,' said Brun. 'It saves maybe three hours for us today.'

The town of Akranes was situated right by the sea and there was a sturdy lighthouse on the rocky point. Fliss was pleased to see the place festooned in fairy lights, winter lights, just as Reykjavik and Selfoss were, and the colourful roofs were easier to see here since there was a little less lying snow.

Brun slowed right down as they drove into the very centre of the town so that Fliss could take a good look at everything, before he headed to the library.

It was a modern-looking, single-storey building with tall windows on each corner. Unlike the day before, there was no hint at how many people might be inside but there were quite a few cars in the car park which Fliss hoped was a good sign.

She turned and looked at Brun. 'It's not as bad as yesterday.' She was saying it as much to herself as to him but it came out almost as a question.

'No, Fliss, it is not. Because you know you will enjoy it.'

She nodded despite the anxiety which was threatening to overwhelm her, closing her eyes to try and keep it away.

'Fliss.' Brun laid his hand on top of hers. It was warm and as reassuring as it had been yesterday. Suddenly she was back in Selfoss in those moments before they'd gone inside the bookshop, and the feelings that were now willing her not to walk into the library were quickly replaced by the immensely fond memories she had of every moment of yesterday after that point. He squeezed his palm gently around her fingers and said her name again, the tone asking her to look at him. She did so and finally felt relaxed enough to smile.

'I think it'll be okay.'

'Yes. And we have an outing afterwards which we will enjoy either way.'

'Right. I'm Fliss Thorne, the author who had a very successful book signing yesterday.' Saying it out loud felt boastful but necessary, and it seemed to help.

Brun grinned and put his arm around her shoulders for a quick hug before he got out of the car and went around to open Fliss's door for her.

She introduced herself to the woman on the information desk near the entrance. The place had an informal feel.

Amongst the wooden bookshelves were chairs, beanbags, colourful rugs, leafy plants and even a hammock. It was so inviting, willing you to pick up a book and spend the day here reading it. What a heavenly thought!

On some level, Fliss was relieved that there weren't throngs of people packed into the place like there had been at the bookshop, but that was only because the library was bigger and everyone had already taken their seats.

Their host, Birta, took them through the maze of shelving to the middle of the building where a large space was filled with several rows of chairs laid out in a semi-circle facing a couple of more comfortable looking chairs with a standard lamp behind them and a small table in between. There were quite a few people seated already and others standing in groups, chatting.

Fliss turned to Brun and smiled. She could see 'I told you it would be okay,' in his eyes and loved that. He had got the measure of her so quickly and she was grateful to have him by her side, understanding how she felt and supporting her in what would otherwise be quite a lonely and anxiety-filled adventure.

'This looks great,' Fliss said.

'We hope it is okay,' Birta said, looking pleased at Fliss's reaction.

'Do you have set questions or will it be more of a chat?'

'I do have questions to begin with but we are hoping that the audience will have questions too.'

'Great.'

'We have a few minutes before we need to start. I will take you to the office where you can leave your things and we can make a drink if you would like?'

When Fliss was ready, she and Birta made their way to the two chairs, carrying their mugs of coffee. Brun took a chair on the end of the row at the back, pulling it away from the rest of the row to give himself some more legroom. Gradually, people noticed that Fliss and Birta were sat at the front and took their seats. It was so relaxed, with no need for anyone to bark instructions for people to sit down, and no overly-formal introduction.

Once people were settled, Birta produced a microphone from somewhere and began.

'*Velkommen*. We are very happy to welcome F L Thorne to the library today. As you know, her books are set in Iceland and have been at the top of the bestseller lists for a few months. And they are so popular here that they go in and out before we can put them back on the shelves.'

Fliss could feel a blush begin to radiate from her cheeks. Was that true? She was at the top of the Icelandic bestseller list? It did go some way to explaining the book tour, but it would have been nice to know that before she came. It was something to grill Eva about the next time they spoke.

'Thanks, Birta. It's lovely to be here in Akranes. And please, call me Fliss.'

Everyone clapped politely and Birta launched into her first questions which were mainly about how she came to write in the psychological crime genre, what made her decide to choose Iceland as a setting, what kind of research she did, and all the usual things she had heard other writers being asked at these kind of events.

'Are there any more books planned for this series?' Birta asked.

'I have actually written the next two books in the series,' said Fliss, without thinking because she felt as if she was having a chat with a group of friends.

Everyone clapped.

'When is the next one out?'

'Oh. I'm not sure.'

'A question for your publisher, Fliss? We are all looking

forward to it.'

Fliss smiled and wondered whether she could ask Eva about that. Was there more chance of another book deal now or was Iceland a drop in the publishing ocean that wouldn't make a difference to her fortunes by itself? The royalty statement she'd had was fantastic but since Brun had said that Iceland had a population of less than four hundred thousand, even if everyone bought her books, it wasn't going to turn her into Agatha Christie.

'Is Margot the star of the next books?' someone in the audience asked.

'Yes. As long as I'm writing about Iceland, Margot will be my star. She and Iceland are inseparable for me.'

'Will Margot find love?'

'I'm not sure I can say anything about that without spoiling what's to come,' said Fliss with a smile. The fact was, it hadn't crossed her mind at all to give Margot a husband or a boyfriend. Write what you know, that's what authors did and all Fliss knew was that being cheated on and then being single had overshadowed any memories she might have had of happy times in her marriage. She couldn't contemplate romance being in her life at all, not with the children, a full-time job and her writing. It was impossible. And so it had been impossible to immerse herself in those kind of emotions on Margot's behalf. But now she wondered if she was doing her character a disservice.

Once everyone in the audience had had a chance to ask their questions, Birta brought the proceedings to an end and everyone stood to applaud Fliss. She was torn between feeling mortified, not knowing how to graciously accept the adulation, and wanting to make sure this moment, however awkward she felt, was stamped in her memory for all time.

As soon as the clapping stopped, an orderly queue of people quickly formed in front of her.

'I forgot to ask,' Birta said, 'are you happy to sign some books?'

'Of course.' She had slipped the pen she'd used the day before into her pocket, just in case because surely that's what any author would do when meeting their readers. And Fliss was doing her best to keep reminding herself that that's exactly what she was here for.

It took quite some time to deal with the queue since many people had questions that they had been mulling over since the end of the talk. Birta made her and Brun more coffee, slipping it onto the table next to Fliss while she signed and talked.

By the time she and Brun were ready to leave, it was dark again and Fliss's heart sank, thinking that they'd taken too long to be able to go swimming after all.

'I'm sorry it took so long, I wasn't expecting that,' she said to Brun as she took her coat off and threw it onto the back seat before she climbed into the car.

'It is no problem. That is why you are here. I think it went very well again.'

Fliss grinned and nodded. 'I think it did.'

'And will Margot find love?'

'I already said, no spoilers,' she said, feeling playful and still on a high from the day.

'Ah, you can tell me.' He pulled away, heading further into the town rather than in the direction that they'd come from that morning.

'Do you think she needs a boyfriend?'

'I think she is sometimes lonely.' He looked across at her for a moment longer than a glance would take.

'I'm not sure she has time to be lonely.'

'Mmm. She is very busy but all of that is for other people, when she is working on cases, it is very consuming. But everyone needs time for themselves.'

'I'm not sure she would have time. It's difficult for her to think about finding a man when she is so committed to her work.'

'Her heart needs something, Fliss. Love of some sort, companionship.'

'Perhaps one day she'll have time for that,' Fliss said, staring determinedly out of the windscreen, wishing that she didn't think Brun was talking about her rather than Margot. 'Where are we going, anyway?'

'We are going swimming, if that is still what you would like to do?'

'But it's dark.'

'Yes, but the dark does not stop many things in this country. The place we are going is only open when it's dark, except at the weekend.'

'I've never been swimming in the dark before.'

'Then that is even better.'

8

Brun drove the short distance to the coast and parked in a car park overlooking the crashing Atlantic Ocean.

'We're not going for a swim in the sea, are we?' Fliss asked. Brun looked like he could easily survive a swim in the icy December seas but she hoped he realised she wasn't going to be joining in.

'Not at all,' he said. 'I am not trying to kill you, I want you to enjoy yourself, Fliss, leave Iceland with only good memories.'

Feeling bad for doubting him, she smiled and said, 'Let's go then.'

They made their way towards a small, curved building that was sat right on the edge of where the land dropped away towards the sea. Fliss was still not convinced there was anywhere to swim apart from the vast expanse of water to their right but she trusted Brun.

He paid for them both at the entrance to the building, handing her a pair of flip flops before arranging to meet on the other side of the changing rooms. She got changed, heeding the multiple signs asking her to shower without her swimsuit before she got into the pool. Luckily, she was the only person in the changing rooms which made that rule easier to go along with.

It was chilly, so she wrapped her towel around her before she went to find Brun. He was obviously more used to the cold than she was and was waiting in just his swimming shorts. It suddenly felt so odd, seeing him like this, and she couldn't help but assess him. He was entirely built of hard muscle. He was broad, yet toned, his body quite pale aside from his forearms and lower legs, and covered in a fair amount of dark hair. Overall, very positive, Fliss found herself thinking. It was a long time since she'd seen anyone to compare him to. Being an office worker and a gym shirker, Duncan, although slim, was not toned at all and if she was honest, it had been years since she'd felt physically attracted to him. She'd never minded about that; her own body, ravaged by carrying two children was probably equally unattractive to him.

But Brun had a very fine physique and Fliss tucked her towel more tightly around her chest.

'Come on,' he said, taking her hand as if it were the most natural thing in the world. It was so cold, Fliss couldn't imagine enjoying anything in these kind of temperatures. He led them down a set of stairs and out onto a terrace overlooking the sea. Not only overlooking, but right next to it; they could feel the spray from the waves which were crashing onto the beach the other side of the concrete wall that curved around the pool. It looked inviting, Fliss had to admit and Brun wasted no time in descending the steps into the pool. It was lit from underneath the water and although it looked warm, with the steam rising from the surface, when she stepped in, it wasn't as hot as she'd hoped.

'This is nice, yes?' Brun said. The look on his face was so hopeful, that Fliss didn't have the heart to say that it if was a bath she'd have needed to top it up with hot water.

'It's lovely,' she said. And if she didn't think about the

temperature, because it was hardly as cold as her local swimming baths, she was blown away by the fact that they were inches away from the Atlantic Ocean, in the dark of night and there was no one else here. As experiences went, it was pretty amazing. 'I've never been anywhere like this,' Fliss said.

'It is special. Come on.'

He stood up and made his way up the steps and out of the pool. Was this some strange Icelandic tradition that you only spent a few minutes in the geothermal waters? Is that why they had the place to themselves?

Fliss followed him, because what else was she going to do? It seemed like an awful lot of effort, with the naked showering, for such a short time but she trusted Brun and if this was the Icelandic way, she was going along with it. He looked behind to make sure she was following, and led the way back up the stairs. As Fliss headed to the changing rooms, Brun grabbed her hand.

'It's this way,' he said.

He led her outside to another pool, this time a circular infinity pool with a view across the darkness of the ocean beyond and the endless starlit skies above them. The steps into the water hugged the curve of the pool like a conch shell and this time, when Fliss descended the steps into the water, she sighed with happiness as it cocooned her in its warmth, right up to her chin. She closed her eyes, savouring the feeling for a couple of minutes.

'Why didn't we start out in this one?' she asked, once she'd gathered herself enough to join Brun on an underwater seat at the edge of the pool.

'This one is better because you went into the other one first,' he said with a smug grin.

She flicked some water at him, making him laugh.

'It is true, Fliss. Is it not?'

She nodded, reluctantly. 'It is true. Honestly, I was wondering what all the fuss was about geothermal water when we were in the pool downstairs.'

He laughed. 'It is good to have the contrast.'

'This is absolute heaven,' Fliss admitted.

'I am happy you think so.'

She turned to look at Brun. His head was tipped back, resting on the wall of the pool, a relaxed smile on his face. His hair, now that it was damp had formed curls around his forehead. Fliss was surprised by the sudden urge to twirl her fingers amongst them.

'Thank you. This is absolutely magical.'

'You deserve all the magical things in your life, Fliss.' He opened his eyes and looked at her intently. There was no hint of humour in his voice and she didn't know what to say. 'This trip is about you, and I am not sure that many things, when you are at home, are about you.'

How he knew that from the brief, however intense time they'd spent together, Fliss wasn't sure but he had an uncanny ability to know how she was feeling. And it was true. This was more than just a book tour. It was the first time she'd done anything for herself in years, perhaps even since she'd had the children. By the time she'd started to think that they were old enough to be able to be left with Lily and Frank for a night, and that she and Duncan might have the chance to grab a night away once in a while, he had left. And then, she'd been a single mother, too tired and desperate for a bit of peace to be able to properly take advantage of the odd times they stayed with Duncan.

'I feel as if I've been here for more than two days. So much has happened. I came here feeling like a total imposter, I was sure that quite quickly, someone would tell me that there had been a mistake and I would be on my way home, embarrassed and ashamed.'

'It is sad that you would think that. I hope you have seen how much people here love your books.'

'It's been truly amazing but I can't help thinking that at the next event, or the one after that, it will all unravel. I don't know, it just feels like too much of a leap to believe. If I'm honest, I don't think my publisher is interested in the rest of the series. Before they arranged this trip, I hadn't heard from them in over a year.'

'Really?' Brun shook his head. 'That is a terrible way to treat someone. So they do not tell you any information about how your book is doing in all that time?'

'No. I can look on Amazon at where it is in the charts but that's all I have to go on. The fact that it had done so well here was a huge shock, a lovely one,' she added, smiling at him, ' but I really thought my books were destined to be forgotten.'

'And now you know the opposite is true.'

'I think Iceland might be an anomaly. An exception.'

'But they have to want the rest of them after this.'

'They have first refusal on any further books in the series, but even if they don't want them, because the UK sales are so slow, I'm not sure Iceland by itself is enough to tempt a brand-new publisher anyway.'

Brun raised his eyebrows in surprise as he took in the reality of Fliss's situation.

'I think then, that it is even more important to make sure the days you spend in Iceland are special.'

'Thank you. You're doing a fantastic job, Brun. Without you, I'd never have found a place like this, or Skyrland.'

Brun laughed, 'Skyrland is the jewel in Iceland's crown.'

'Well, I had the best night out I'd had in ages.'

'That is not the best night out, Fliss. If you will allow me, I would like to invite you out in Reykjavik tomorrow night. You know Rachel, who you met on the plane? She will be there, and her husband Jonas and a few other people. We would love you to join us.'

How amazing to be invited to go on a night out in Reykjavik with locals. It was sure to be an experience she would never have had if she hadn't met Brun.

'I'd love that, thank you.'

'We are in Reykjavik tomorrow anyway.'

'I wasn't sure if you would need to come with me tomorrow as there's no need to drive anywhere.' She'd been nervous at the prospect of going anywhere without Brun, especially to one of the biggest bookshops in the country.

'Of course, I will be there.'

Fliss hoped that he wasn't putting himself out on her behalf if her publishers were only paying him to be a taxi service but she had to admit to feeling reassured that he was coming with her, and since he'd offered, decided not to question him.

As they sat in the pool, it began to snow gently. The cold of the flakes nipped at the exposed skin of her face but it was quite pleasant since the rest of her was so warm.

'I think we should go,' Brun said. 'If you are ready?'

'I don't think I am, it's so deliciously warm, I can't bear the thought of having to get out.'

Brun turned to her, his eyes dancing with pleasure at how much she was enjoying this place that he'd brought her to and Fliss's heart swelled. She reached her hand out to touch his, brushing her fingers against the top of his hand where it rested on the edge of the pool. His gaze was more intense, as he shifted slightly so that he was facing towards her. Her eyes were on his until he leaned towards her, and then they moved to look at his lips, knowing what was going to happen next. His kiss was gentle, his beard tickling her lips at first which only served to heighten the feelings that were already beginning to course through her.

He pulled away briefly, his eyes scanning her face for any signs that this wasn't what she wanted. She put her hand on his neck, threading her fingers into the damp curls and pulled him back to her, kissing him more deeply, to let him know that this was absolutely fine with her. More than fine, it seemed like a dream. To be in this place, with this man, someone who she had only known for a couple of days and yet who seemed to understand her more than anyone else. It was incredible.

9

Brun pulled up outside Fliss's hotel. Neither of them were ready to end the day they'd had together but Fliss didn't know what she wanted to happen next. The kiss had been lovely. More than lovely, but she wasn't ready for anything else. Before Brun, the last person she had kissed was Duncan, and before that, a couple of relative strangers when she'd been a student. This was huge. She'd put the possibility of kissing firmly out of her mind when Duncan left, imagining there would be no opportunity to pursue a relationship with someone new and then, it seemed too much trouble to launch herself into the world of dating after so long away from it.

They sat in silence, looking at each other. Brun had a lopsided smile on his face, he looked slightly bashful.

'Thanks for today. For everything,' she said, finally. He leaned over and gave her a final gentle kiss.

'Goodbye, Fliss. See you tomorrow.'

She turned and waved before she went inside, hearing him pull away once he'd seen her go in.

Her room was on the second floor and she was still feeling so relaxed from the hot pool, and from the warmth inside her after the kissing, that it seemed many more stairs to climb than it had before.

She dumped her bag on the chair in the corner of the room and collapsed onto the bed. It was so nice to lie down. She needed to go out and find dinner, unfortunately her hotel didn't do room service and the restaurant had already closed for the evening. But she'd allow herself a few minutes to relax before she ventured out again.

She closed her eyes and cast her mind back to the library talk. It had taken her by surprise that people might be rooting for Margot to have a love interest. Funnily enough, after not even considering it, now she wondered if it was something she should look to change. The kiss with Brun had ignited something inside her that had been dormant for years. She honestly didn't remember feeling like this over Duncan, unless she had just forgotten. But whatever happened next with Brun, even if nothing happened next, she knew she'd never forget how she'd felt in those moments before the kiss, when he'd turned towards her and she'd known exactly what was going to happen.

Her iPad starting ringing, startling her from her daydream which was just as well because she was about to fall asleep. It was Lily.

'Hi Lily!' It was nice to hear from her sister, no doubt it was to check arrangements for Duncan dropping off the children. Fliss almost blurted out that she'd kissed someone but luckily remembered that this was Lily, not Abbie. Lily might be very judgy about the fact she'd only known Brun for a couple of days.

'Duncan dropped Josh and Emma off with us today.' She was speaking in hushed tones.

Fliss wondered if she'd lost track of what day it was. 'I thought they were with him for another couple of days?'

'Yes, exactly. Those poor children. He gave them no warning, just asked them to pack and brought them over when he got in from work. Something to do with having to leave earlier than planned to go to his in-laws.'

Fliss closed her eyes and took a deep breath. It would be so easy to have a massive rant to her sister about what an arse Duncan was, but that wasn't productive and she didn't want to completely ruin her day by indulging in bitterness. 'I'm so sorry, Lily. I can get a flight back tomorrow. I'll have a look and let you know.'

'No, Fliss, stay where you are. Don't worry about the kids, I can go in late tomorrow and drop them off at school on my way.' Lily was a solicitor and worked crazy hours which was why Fliss didn't like to ask her to help out too much.

'Are you sure? I could change my flight. Or you could see if Abbie would help out?'

'I know. I'm only telling you what's happened so that you know, not because you need to do anything about it. They would have been coming to us the day after tomorrow anyway.'

'Well, thank you. What would I do without you.'

'I loved the pictures of you from the book-signing, I've never seen you look so happy, Fliss.'

It was lovely to hear that from her sister who was often a little dismissive of things but Fliss was distracted by something else she'd said. 'What do you mean, the pictures?'

'On your Instagram page.'

'Right…'

'Anyway, I think the children are planning to call you so I'll let you go. And please, don't worry about them, they're fine, whatever Emma says.'

'Thanks, Lil.'

'Keep enjoying yourself. I mean it.'

Fliss ended the call and went straight onto her Instagram account. Lily was right. There were photos of her at the book signing and the library visit, taken by Brun, judging from the angles. She knew he'd been taking pictures, he'd even told her that he would be, but she had no idea how they'd ended up on her feed. She was rubbish at posting, or anything to do with social media. Her publisher had asked her to set up social media profiles but aside from a few pictures she'd taken around her publication dates, she'd struggled to know what to post. These posts were written as if it were her who had posted. There were numerous hashtags and quite a few comments that it looked as though she'd replied to. As well as that, there were notifications that she'd been tagged in other people's posts and clicking on those, there were more photos that people had posted of themselves with her at the two events.

Realising that time was getting on, Fliss messaged Josh and Emma and said she was popping out for dinner and she'd call them when she got back. It was almost eight o'clock. Pulling on her coat and making sure her gloves were in the pockets, she headed back downstairs.

It was still snowing outside, it had been all the way back from Akranes, but Brun hadn't seemed worried about the road conditions or anything and here, in the centre of the city, the regular stream of traffic kept it from settling on the roads.

There was a keen breeze coming off the sea, so Fliss headed up the next side street in an attempt to find some shelter from it. The road she came out on was a shopping street, lined with trees, their bare branches wound with twinkling fairy lights, making Fliss feel festive. She had no idea where to head to for food, but wandered along the street enjoying her first real taste of Reykjavik. Most of the shops were closed but it was interesting to window shop and enjoy the atmosphere. She was surprised how many people were around, given that it was snowing but as she wandered along she found that there were plenty of bars and restaurants open. It was a capital city, after all.

Eventually, she came across a fish and chip restaurant

which had canteen style seating rather than small tables. It felt like a better option than sitting alone at a table for two. She ordered a beer and a small fish and chips and pulled out her phone to check her emails. She'd barely had time to look at them since last night and in fact, found an email from her publisher, Eva, letting her know that they were going to take over her social media posts while she was away. Apparently she'd sent them the logins when she'd set them up. It was so long ago, she wasn't surprised she'd forgotten. But it made her wonder why they'd never shown any interest in posting anything before now. It might have been helpful; they were supposed to market her books as part of the publishing deal. At least she knew now how it had happened and presumably as Brun had been booked by Blackwood, and was ultimately working for them, he must have been asked to send photos to them for exactly this purpose. Now that she knew what was going on, she couldn't help but be pleased that this was happening on her behalf because just thinking about having to tackle this sort of thing herself was exhausting.

Once her food came, she put her phone down and instead, people-watched discreetly while she ate. The fish was fresh and delicious and truly one of the nicest meals she'd had in ages. Well, since the meal in Selfoss with Brun. She smiled at the thought of him and resolved to ring Abbie later, after she'd caught up with the children. She needed someone else's perspective on what had happened, because what was she doing? Kissing Brun had been amazing and looking back, she didn't regret it even a bit. But she did wonder what it meant, because it couldn't mean anything. It couldn't be the start of something because she was leaving in three days. And it couldn't be a holiday romance, she wasn't that kind of person. Where did that leave her? And what was going to happen when she saw him tomorrow?

Unable to remember which street would lead her back to

her hotel, Fliss walked back along the seafront, not minding the bracing wind as much now that it had stopped snowing. When she got back to the hotel, she changed into her pyjamas and snuggled in bed to FaceTime the children.

'Hi Mum,' said Josh. He was in bed too.

'How are you, lovely?'

He shrugged. 'Okay. Bit pissed off with Dad.'

'I know. I'm not sure what went on there. I need to text him.'

'It doesn't matter. Shona was annoyed with him for saying we could stay. I was glad to get out of there.'

'Oh, Joshy, I'm so sorry.'

'It's not your fault, Mum,' said Josh, sounding indignant. 'He can't even help you out for a week when it's the only time you've ever asked him.'

Fliss bit her lip, a little uncomfortable at how grown-up her son sounded and how switched-on he was about what had happened. 'It's a difficult time for him.'

'No Mum, don't defend him. He shouldn't make you feel guilty about doing your book tour. It's important.'

'Thanks, Josh. And Auntie Lil wasn't too annoyed?'

'She was annoyed with him for dumping us but no, she's been ace. Uncle Frank even splashed for a Netflix subscription to cheer Em up.' Josh smiled, the frown disappearing from his forehead.

Fliss rolled her eyes dramatically, although she was smiling. 'She's going to want me to do that too now.' It had been on Fliss's list now that she had her royalties and it would be a relief to finally be able to give in to Emma for a good reason; she wanted to use this money for treats and was going to enjoy not having to say no to them, mainly Emma, so often.

'I saw your Insta posts.'

'Oh, god. I didn't do them, Josh, the publisher did. I didn't even know about it until Auntie Lil told me.'

'It's really cool, Mum.'

Fliss's heart swelled in her chest and she was a breath away from a sob. 'Thanks. I'll let you get to sleep. Love you, and give my love to Emma. I'll ring tomorrow.'

'Night, Mum. Love you.'

Fliss lay there for a second, gathering herself. Bless Josh. And her son being so lovely just made Duncan look more like a total arse. She typed an angry text to him, read it through and then deleted it. What was the point? He'd already dumped the kids without checking with her first. He didn't care what she thought, she should know that by now. She *did* know that. What would she gain by having a go at him, apart from making herself feel better, briefly? She couldn't force him to care about his first-born children, but she did feel the need to tell him not to hurt them. After three years, she still hadn't worked out how to do that, and every time he did something like this, messing them around to suit himself, it broke her heart.

Instead of ruminating on an appropriate response, she called Abbie.

'How's it going? Does it turn out you're famous in Iceland?'

Fliss laughed. 'Have you seen my Instagram?'

'What? No! I'm going to hang up and do that now.'

'No, wait. I kissed someone.'

'Sorry, I thought you said you kissed someone?'

'It's crazy isn't it?'

'Um, it's unexpected, Fliss. Who is it? A fan?'

'Very funny. No, it's the guy my publisher hired to look after me.'

'He's taking his job very seriously, then. Looking after you in every sense.'

'Abbie!'

'Sorry. But you haven't shown any interest in wanting to date. It's quite a turnaround in three days.'

'I'm as surprised as you. But it felt right. He understands me. He's nothing like the men I imagined having to date. I honestly didn't know someone like him could exist.' It sounded ridiculous to say it out loud, but she knew Abbie would try to understand what she meant.

'And what was the kiss like?'

'I don't know how to start to describe a kiss but I didn't need to decide whether it was a good idea or not. It had to happen and it's as if neither of us had any choice.'

'I've never heard you talk like this about anything, Fliss.'

'I know, it's ridiculous. I mean, where can it go?'

'It's not ridiculous, it sounds magical. Like it was meant to be,' Abbie said, sounding utterly certain.

Both of them were quiet for a moment.

'Lean into it, Fliss. Let whatever happens next happen. Who knows where it could lead?'

Abbie was right. She needed to see what happened. She didn't want to see Brun tomorrow and say it was a mistake, that they never should have kissed because it could never come to anything. They were both adults who knew the facts; that they had limited time together and each had lives that were firmly settled in different countries. As long as they both understood that, what was the harm in enjoying the next few days?

10

After he'd dropped Fliss at her hotel, Brun parked the car a couple of streets away, as close as he could get to his house. His friends Ned and Anna lived almost next door in the same small group of houses as him so rather than head home, he knocked on their door.

'Hey, Brun,' said Ned, looking pleased to see him. 'Come in. Anna's working in the kitchen but I can probably sneak in and get a couple of beers.'

Anna did PR for bands who were starting out and she ran an open mic night once a week in London where her bands were guaranteed a regular slot alongside other people who could just turn up and play. When she wasn't in London, she watched on a live feed and did social media posts to stir-up some interest. And it worked. She had two bands she was managing off the back of it and was doing PR for numerous others.

'I bet she is busy this time of the year?' Brun picked up one of the two guitars that were on stands in the corner of the room and settled himself on a chair.

'Hang on a sec,' Ned said and went into the kitchen to get the beer. Anna was sat at the table with headphones on. She smiled and waved at Brun and then gestured for Ned to close the door behind him. 'Shall we go through the song for tomorrow night?' He put the beers on the table and picked up the other guitar.

Brun and Ned had written lots of songs together over the past year but it was the first time they had planned to play one of their collaborations at the open mic night. They tended to play Ned's songs or cover versions. It was also the first song they'd written that had some of the lyrics in Icelandic.

'Sure, have you played it to Anna? What does she think?'

'She loves it,' Ned said. 'Reckons it's a surefire hit.'

'Ah. Do you need a hit?'

Ned laughed. He didn't need a hit at all. If he never earned another penny in his life, it wouldn't matter but he loved music and that was where his drive came from. Being friends with Ned had given Brun the confidence to take his love of music more seriously. He'd never have considered actually performing at an open mic night before but now, they played there together anytime that Ned was in Iceland.

'This one is more yours than mine.'

They ran through it once, then put the guitars down and sipped their beers.

'It sounds good,' Brun said.

'You look like you're thinking of someone when you're singing it. Is it Kristin?'

Brun smiled because Kristin was the last person he was thinking of. His head was full of Fliss. 'No, it's Fliss Thorne, the author who's here for the book tour.'

'FL Thorne? Even I've read one of her books. Anna made me, but it was really good.'

'I have been driving her to the places where she is doing signings and something has happened between us.'

'What kind of something?' Ned asked. 'Like you've had a moment or something?'

Brun shrugged. 'We've had a kiss.' He felt like a teenager

confessing to something as innocent as a kiss yet feeling like it was so much more than that.

'Really? Well good for you. Way to mix work with pleasure.'

Brun laughed. 'I guess I am. I have invited her to come tomorrow night.'

'Wow, you must really like her to invite her to watch you play.'

'I do. But it's strange, right? To feel like that so soon. We have only known each other a few days and already this has happened.'

'You can't put a timeline on these things,' Ned said. 'It is what it is. Isn't she English?'

'Yes and that is another reason to think it is not a good idea.'

'Stuff like this is never straightforward but if you like her, just go with it. See what happens.'

'She has kids.'

'Brun, you have picked a tricky situation to put yourself in. Even if you like her, that's potentially a lot to contend with. You think it's more than a holiday romance or whatever?'

He shrugged, 'I think it might be. She is amazing. She is funny and beautiful and she has no idea. I've watched her at these book events and she connects with her readers. They love her and it's as if it's a constant surprise to her that anyone even reads her books. It is wonderful to see.'

'That is definitely more than a holiday romance,' said Ned. 'That's the voice of someone who, dare I say it, might be falling in love.'

'No,' Brun said, shaking his head. 'Nobody falls in love so quickly.'

'Jonas and Rachel did, that story is folklore in our group and you were there, you saw it happening. What's different?'

'It's true, it was very quick but I think they took a chance on it being the right thing for them both and Rachel stayed in Iceland to find out if it was going to work. Fliss will leave in four days. It is too soon to declare that I might love her, even if that is what is happening.'

'Do you know what? Me and Anna had some ups and downs before we settled into what we have now.'

'I don't have the bank balance to live between countries, Ned, but thank you for believing it could work.'

'Come on, let's go through it again. You've got to kill it tomorrow night and then she'll be yours.'

Later that night, when he was lying in bed thinking about Fliss, Brun realised that whatever happened, he would have to let Fliss lead the way with what, if anything, the future could hold for them. It was no good dreaming of having a relationship when she had so much more at stake than he did. The only person he needed to consider was himself, in all his decisions. It wasn't like that for her and when he saw her tomorrow, he would make it clear that he had no expectations.

He smiled to himself. He couldn't wait to play that song to her at the open mic night tomorrow. She would have no idea what the lyrics meant but it was better that way. Better for her not to know the depth of his feelings for her because that would make everything more complicated. Even if he only had this week with her, it would be devastating when she left, but better to have had it than not.

11

The following day was Fliss's first venture to a Reykjavik bookshop. In the end, feeling slightly ridiculous that asking Brun to take her would essentially mean him walking her along the road, she had insisted that she could make her own way there. She actually felt fine about going by herself; the anxiety that she'd had every day so far had abated, replaced by thoughts of Brun. She was determined that things should not be weird between them, but as it was her first kiss with anyone for some time, many years in fact if you discounted Duncan's disinterested pecks on the cheek, it might be difficult to behave normally.

The bookshop was the flagship store of Penninn Eymundsson, and one of the oldest bookshops in Iceland. It was a glass-fronted building over four storeys, with a modern graphic of oversized book spines on the first floor windows, making it look like a gigantic bookshelf. It felt like walking into a branch of Waterstones, much different to the bookshop in Selfoss, but the staff were just as welcoming. Even though she didn't notice Brun arrive, she immediately felt comfortable, more used now as to what to expect and once she got going, managed to put Brun out of her mind while she did the book-signing. It was as much fun as it had been the other day and by the time she'd said goodbye to her last reader, she was feeling amazing.

As the shop cleared of people, she finally spotted Brun. He might have been there the whole time but now, she felt his eyes upon her and she was ridiculously pleased to see him.

Once she'd thanked the staff again, she headed over to him. He had his hands in his pockets and was wearing his hat with the earflaps, and a lopsided smile. Fliss grinned.

'Hi,' she said. 'I didn't see you arrive.'

'You were enjoying yourself. It looks like it went well?'

She nodded.

'I took some pictures.'

'Did you? I didn't see you. I also didn't realise you were in cahoots with my publisher on the social media stuff.'

'I thought you knew they'd asked me to do that,' he said, looking concerned.

Fliss shook her head. It didn't matter. 'It's fine, you did a great job.'

'So.' One of his hands emerged from his pocket and he tentatively reached for her hand, gently rubbing the tips of her fingers between his finger and thumb. 'Could we go for a coffee?'

'I'd like that.'

They strolled along the streets. Again, it was gently snowing and although not quite dark, the fairy lights on the trees twinkled in the dusk.

'It's so pretty everywhere,' Fliss said, feeling relaxed and dreamy as she walked along next to Brun, her arm tucked into his.

'More so today,' he said, flicking his gaze towards to her to see if she had picked up his meaning.

She had, and felt a blush creep into her cheeks. What had she been worried about? Being with Brun felt like the only place in the world she wanted to be. Obviously she caveated every thought like that with the fact that she would always want the children to be with her as well; it was impossible to allow herself to daydream entirely.

'How about here?' Brun asked, as they passed a cosy-looking coffee shop.

'Perfect.'

They ordered at the counter, Brun helping with her out with explanations of what some of the delicious pastries were.

'How do you feel about yesterday?'

It was refreshing that he didn't dance around the subject like she might have done. 'I was happy to see you today.'

'That is a good sign.' He smiled. 'I am worried that... the kiss,' he said awkwardly, 'it may not have been something you wanted.'

'It isn't something I *knew* I wanted, until it happened.'

'I am happy to hear that,' he said softly, exhaling in relief.

'I suppose the only thing I've been thinking about is that however we might be feeling, about each other,' she said, faltering as she struggled to string the right words together, 'we only have a few days.'

'And you are wondering whether it is worth starting something? Or if we should not because it might make us wish we had more than a few days together.'

'Yes, all of those things, and a hundred other things that I can't remember now.'

Brun laughed, making Fliss smile. She was beginning to love his laugh. And feeling more relaxed, she decided to share some of her background with him. Just because they only had a few days together, it didn't mean it wasn't important to get to know each other.

'I haven't had a relationship since I split up with my children's father. It's been a difficult few years and I couldn't even think about starting to see anyone new, mostly because I didn't have time. And then I came here and met you.'

'Maybe because there has been time.'

'I don't think that's the only reason. I wouldn't have ended up with whoever picked me up from the airport, just because it's the first time in years I've had a few minutes to myself to notice a man.'

He tilted his head to one side and smiled. 'I am pleased to hear that. And I am not in the habit of kissing women who come on my tours.'

They sat in silence for a minute, looking into each other's eyes as Fliss picked pieces from her pastry and Brun took great big bites of his, ending up with a few flakes caught in his beard. When Fliss reached over and brushed them away, he caught her hand and kissed her fingers.

'I am glad we have met. A few days is better than never.'

'Brun...' Her breath caught, his voice was so soft, it made her wish they were back in the hot pool in Akranes where it was so easy to sink into his kiss.

'Would you like to come back to my house for a coffee?'

She nodded, that was exactly what she wanted, even though they both still had coffee right here. She felt like a teenager again and it was exhilarating.

'I do not want you to think I am suggesting anything except kissing,' Brun said, pausing as they stood up to put their coats back on.

'Okay.' Fliss genuinely didn't know how she felt about what the kissing might lead to but she was determined not to overthink it. It was best to have no expectations. Equally, she wasn't sure how she felt about getting intimate with someone who had never seen her pre-baby body.

Brun's house wasn't far from the coffee shop. It was located off one of the side streets a few roads back from the main shopping street, Laugavegur. It was a small wooden-clad house painted blue, with a red corrugated roof. It had twinkling lights all around the edge of the roof and strung along the top of the sparse wooden fence that surrounded the house and tiny garden.

'This is gorgeous,' Fliss said, secretly excited to see what one of these houses was like on the inside. It looked tiny from the outside but in this weather, cosy was what you wanted.

'Thanks, it is small but it is in a good location for me. I prefer the old part of the city.'

Brun opened the door and stood aside to let Fliss in first. A tiny hallway was the transition between outdoors and in, signified by a few pairs of shoes that could only be Brun's, judging by the size. Fliss unlaced her boots and took them off, then stepped into the next room to make space for Brun to do the same. She was standing in a cosy living room. Two oversized armchairs which would each seat two very friendly people, were angled towards the chimney breast where a modest television hung on the wall. Underneath, tucked inside the hearth was a games console and an array of controllers piled next to it. Bookshelves to the one side of the chimney-breast held books and computer games and hung on the walls were framed posters of bands Fliss had never heard of.

'It's so cosy but I thought you'd have a real fireplace, or a wood-burning stove.'

'The energy in Iceland is from geothermal heat so it is very cheap. It is more expensive to buy wood or anything else like that.'

'You have underfloor heating,' said Fliss, noticing the warmth radiating through her feet in the most delicious way. 'I think I prefer that, actually.'

'Me too,' said Brun, moving towards her and helping her to shrug off her coat. He went through the only other door in the room, returning without the coat but with a bottle of whisky and two heavy glass tumblers.

'Can I tempt you?'

'Definitely,' Fliss said, settling herself into the corner of one of the chairs, tucking her feet underneath her.

Brun poured a small measure for each of them, and sat in the chair opposite.

'*Skál*,' he said.

Fliss said the same and they each took a sip, sitting in silence. Whatever had been beginning to happen at the coffee shop had fizzled out slightly on the way to Brun's. One of them needed to make the first move to get things back on track but she didn't know how, and neither it seemed, did Brun.

'How long have you lived here?' A boring question, but it was something.

'About five years. Rachel's husband, Jonas used to live a couple of houses away until they bought a bigger house further out of town. Now another friend of ours owns it but he doesn't live here all the time. Where do you live?'

'Just outside Oxford. I bought a house there about two years ago, once everything was settled with the divorce. I love it, I can have everything exactly how I like.'

'There is something to be said for that. When Kristin lived here, it was full of cushions that nobody needed. We had hundreds of candles everywhere.'

Fliss laughed. 'And now it's back to being a bachelor pad?'

Brun raised his eyebrows and smiled, shaking his head. 'Ah, I think your house is probably filled with cushions too?'

Emboldened by the whisky, Fliss stood up and went over to the chair where Brun sat. He watched her, his eyes full of appreciation as she perched on the small part of the chair that was empty, next to him. He put his glass down, put his hands around her waist and lifted her onto his lap. She tucked her legs either side of his and sat facing him. They both knew what was going to happen next.

The kiss was every bit as wonderful as it had been the day before. Fliss had worried that she'd elevated the greatness of it in her mind, as she'd replayed it over and over, but if anything, she hadn't remembered it well enough.

She cupped his beardy cheeks with her hands, making sure that there was no opportunity for him to pull away, take a sip of whisky, or anything else. She wanted him to kiss her endlessly.

After not long at all, their kisses became more intense and Fliss could feel Brun's hands making their way underneath the several layers she was wearing on top. She mirrored him by pulling his shirt out from his trousers, finding that he was also wearing several layers, burrowing her hands underneath them until she felt warm, bare skin.

The touch of each other brought an extra sensuality to what was already becoming a rather overwhelming experience for Fliss, in the best way possible. She could barely think of anything, except Brun and what he was doing to her. In the darkness of last night, when she'd wondered how she might feel if they took things further, she'd imagined that she would be checking in with herself at every moment, to make sure it was what she wanted, that she was doing the right thing and not setting herself up for regret or heartache. But now, in the thick of the emotions coursing through her, she was incapable of any kind of rational thought. And she was very happy with that.

12

Fliss had insisted on going back to her hotel afterwards. After they'd lain in each other's arms for the rest of the afternoon, she tried not to think about how she was going to have to leave this behind in two days, just as she'd discovered the most wonderful thing that had happened to her in so long.

She had promised to call Emma, which she did, biting her tongue as her daughter blamed Shona for her father's behaviour. To her, Duncan was the victim of a calculating woman who had brainwashed him, forcing him to leave his family against his will. Fliss knew it wouldn't help the situation to try and explain the facts to her, she'd tried before and only succeeded in pushing her away. She'd long accepted that there was nothing to be gained by stating the facts of the situation but it was harder to hear this time, when she already felt so angry with him for dumping the kids with Lily and Frank.

After the phone call, there wasn't much time left to get ready. She pulled the dress out of the wardrobe and held it against her as she looked in the mirror, seeing the face of a woman who'd had a very satisfying afternoon. She wanted to feel amazing tonight when she saw Brun again and this dress was going to help her do that. Lily had suggested it since it was possible to wear a long-sleeved vest underneath without it showing. It had a round neck, buttons down the front and blousy sleeves that came in at the cuff, matching the tiered skirt that came to her mid calf. It was slate grey with tiny flowers in all colours scattered across it. Best of all, it looked great with her boots.

She dressed, put on some mascara and a slick of lipstick that Emma had said was essential and looked "slay". A few drops of the hair oil that Emma had also recommended – or forced – her to buy did work wonders at calming her frizzy hair into a sleeker looking style. A spray of perfume and she was ready. It seemed a shame to cover up all her good work with a coat but she didn't want to freeze to death before she saw Brun again.

He'd said he'd meet her outside the hotel but in fact, he was waiting in the foyer. Looking up as she walked towards him, she saw the same look on his face that she knew was on hers. Rather than bother meeting his friends or going to the bar, all she wanted to do was grab his hand and take him up to her room. He stood and leant to kiss her, a nice lingering kiss that made her insides seize up with longing.

'You look amazing,' he said, his eyes shining.

'So do you.' His usual outfit of canvas trousers with pockets down the legs, a knitted Icelandic sweater and an insulated coat had been replaced by dark jeans, a checked flannel shirt over a black t-shirt and a well-worn black leather biker jacket which Fliss found ridiculously sexy.

'Ready?' He picked up a guitar in a case from where it had been resting against the wall and slung it onto his back.

'You're playing tonight?'

He looked bashful and nodded. 'I am not very good but it is a long-standing plan, so…' He shrugged. 'I thought you might enjoy it.'

'I definitely will,' she said, slipping her hand into his once they were walking along the street. 'What kind of music is it?'

'I think you would say folk or country, something like that. I have written some songs with my friend. He's playing tonight too.'

They headed towards the harbour, an area of town Fliss hadn't ventured to on any of her walks. The bar was a single-storey building that had no windows to the front but was, as everywhere else was, festooned with twinkling lights which made it look more welcoming than it otherwise would.

Inside, they were almost the first to arrive apart from a table of people over to one side and a guy who was setting up some equipment on a small stage at the front, in the corner next to the bar. Brun greeted the barman in Icelandic, then switched to English to introduce him to Fliss.

'This is FL Thorne, otherwise known as Fliss.'

'Oh, wow,' said the barman, raising his eyebrows in appreciation. 'Even I have read your first book. Good to meet you. Can I buy you a drink?'

Brun shook his head and smiled. 'Nice try, Thor, this round is on me.'

Fliss began to peruse the drinks on offer, keen to try something local, while Brun shouted over to the group of people asking for their orders. They shouted back and the barman nodded and began to assemble the drinks on the bar. Fliss settled on a pint of local beer that was light in colour and made with Icelandic spring water, then turned her attention to worrying about having to meet the group of people who were Brun's friends. They were all much younger than her, probably in their early to mid-thirties.

She and Brun carried a couple of drinks each over to the table. Now that she was closer, Fliss recognised Rachel who she'd sat next to on the plane.

'I had no idea that was you next to me on the plane. When Brun told me, I was so surprised you hadn't said. I was reading your book!'

Fliss laughed. 'It was a first for me, I didn't want to say, 'oh, that's my book, actually.' You might have thought it was rubbish.'

Rachel laughed and patted Fliss on the arm as if she'd told a joke rather than revealed her innermost fear. 'Well, I'm glad I get to finally meet you, knowing who you are. We all are, but we'll try not to ask you questions about Margot all evening.'

Brun, seeing that Fliss was in safe hands, returned to the bar to fetch the rest of the drinks while Rachel made the introductions.

'This is Anna, she lives here most of the time with her boyfriend, Ned, he's over there sorting out the amps or something. This is my husband Jonas, and this is Gudrun and her partner Olafur.'

'Great to meet you all,' Fliss said, sitting down next to Rachel.

'Have you had a book-signing today?' Rachel asked.

Fliss nodded since she was taking a sip of beer, then said, 'Yes, at the Penninn Eymunsson bookshop. I don't think it's far from here, actually.'

'We are coming to your signing tomorrow night at *Máls og Menningar*,' Gudrun said. 'I know the manager and she has already put books aside for us.'

'Oh, gosh,' said Fliss, suddenly feeling overwhelmed at the idea that anyone she knew would be willing to buy a book she was fairly sure they had already read. 'If you have the book already, I can sign it without you having to come to the actual event,' she said.

'Thank you, but they are for *Jolabokaflod* gifts and I love going to bookstore events for that. It's so much fun,' she said enthusiastically.

Brun came back from the bar with the rest of the drinks

and shortly afterwards, his friend Ned joined them too.

'Pleased to meet you, Fliss. I'm Ned.'

It was Ned Nokes. Not being across the world of celebrity gossip, even Fliss knew exactly who Ned was but had to drag from her memory what she knew about him. From what she remembered, he used to be in a boy band and left, maybe a year ago in the midst of furious press coverage. Emma would know.

'Great to meet you, Ned. You're playing tonight with Brun?'

'It's an open mic night so anyone can rock up and play but we have a regular slot. We like to get here early for the best table,' he said, waving his hand across at the rest of the virtually empty bar.

'It will be full in the next half an hour,' said Jonas, as if reading her mind.

'How long are you here for?' Olafur asked her.

'Only six days, altogether. I have the event tomorrow night and then the following day I have a signing in the morning and fly home after that.'

'We're flying back to London that day too,' said Anna. 'I'm going to subject Ned to his first Christmas with my family.'

Ned made a face, pretending to be terrified and they all laughed. What a lovely group of people. They all seemed so close, Fliss wondered how they felt about Brun bringing someone new with him. Someone who possibly they would never see again.

It was another couple of hours and some great music later before Ned and Brun took to the stage. By this time, the bar was packed to the rafters and the cheers that were readily forthcoming from the audience before they'd even started could only be a sign of how popular they were.

They settled on chairs which were angled towards each other with a couple of microphones between them, their guitars resting on their laps, ready to go. Ned nodded at Brun, who nodded back, then counted them in.

With the two guitars and the harmonies they were singing, as well as both of them drumming time with one foot as they played, they produced a sound that Fliss had never really heard before and she was captivated by it. It was a relatively-upbeat song and people started clapping along; they were doing a great job of taking their audience with them.

The cheering and applauding erupted at the end of the song and Ned and Brun smiled and nodded their thanks before they launched into the next one. This one was more lyrical but still a crowd pleaser.

'We'll be back later, thanks guys,' Ned said after that song had ended.

Fliss was beaming at Brun when he came back to sit next to her. She was so proud of him, and impressed, and desperate to tell him how impossibly sexy she thought he was.

'That was amazing,' she said, squeezing his hand. She wanted to kiss him but wasn't sure how he would feel about that in front of his friends. So when he did lean over to kiss her, she felt her heart bloom with affection for him. And no one around the table seemed to have batted an eyelid apart from Gudrun who was looking at them, saying, 'Awww, they're such a cute couple,' to Rachel.

'I am glad you enjoyed it.'

Now that she'd had a couple of pints of beer, Fliss found herself looping her arm around his neck and pulling him to her, whispering, 'You are so sexy when you play the guitar.'

He pulled back, with a grin on his face. 'And the music?'

'I loved it, especially the second song, the words were beautiful.'

'Those are Ned's words. The one we are playing at the end, those will be my words. And they are for you.'

Fliss pressed her mouth to his, unsure how it was possible

to feel this way about someone she had only known for four days. It could be the beer. It could be the thrill of being out. But at the back of her mind was Rachel's warning about falling under Iceland's spell. 'I'll be listening carefully,' she said.

There were a couple of singers who did cover versions of songs Fliss had heard before, then it wasn't long before Ned and Brun went up to close the show.

'This is a new song, written by my good friend here, Brun.'

Everyone cheered for Brun, who accepted the appreciation with a humble nod before he counted them in.

The song was beautiful with a melody that made Fliss's heart melt.

'I think this might be their best song yet,' Rachel whispered to her, before it had really even got going.

When they started singing, they were taking turns to sing the lyrics, with Ned singing in English and Brun singing in Icelandic. The languages weaved together to create something so special, that when Fliss glanced around the table, Anna and Gudrun had tears in their eyes. Although she couldn't understand what Brun was saying, she knew it was a love song and he was singing it to her, confirmed when he sought her gaze and looked at her as he sang, as if she were the only person in the room.

The bar was silent as they played, each strum of the guitar, each word adding more emotion to the song until by the time they finished, everyone was so stunned that it took a few moments for anyone to react and begin clapping. But when they did, it was an eruption. Everyone was on their feet, cheering, clapping, whooping. Fliss had never seen anything like it.

'It's because of the Icelandic words,' Gudrun said. 'He is falling in love with you.'

She said it as if it were a simple fact, something that she

was just passing along. But it floored Fliss. Mainly because she was starting to think that was exactly how she was feeling about Brun.

13

In a moment of tipsiness the night before, Fliss had accepted an invitation from Rachel to join her, Gudrun and Anna at Rachel's house to make *laufabrauð*. It had sounded exciting, a girls' day, making Christmas leaf bread together but in the cold light of day, Fliss was all too aware that she barely knew them. It was kind of Rachel to include her, although she worried that they might be reading too much into her friendship with Brun. But it was too late now, so she pulled her coat on and got ready to leave the hotel.

It was snowing yet again, which Fliss supposed was only to be expected in Iceland in the middle of winter and since it never seemed to concern anyone except her, she had gradually started to care less. Rachel had helpfully put a pin in Google maps the night before, so Fliss knew where she was heading but she didn't want to arrive empty-handed so she took a detour up to the shopping streets in search of inspiration.

She came across a shop called Snug, a branch of which she remembered seeing in London. She might even have bought a couple of candlesticks from there once. It sold homewares and had a tempting display of Christmas decorations, tableware and festive food and drink in the window. Surely there would be something perfect in there.

Fliss had a quick browse around the store, falling in love with several things she couldn't hope to fit in her case, but she did cave in for a set of shot-sized glasses that had been hand-blown somewhere in Iceland and looked as if they had lines of bubbles trapped inside the glass, and a beautiful woollen blanket that she could pass off as a shawl if it didn't fit in her case. Then she remembered that she was supposed to be on the hunt for a gift, and selected a couple of bottles of an Icelandic Christmas drink, *Jólaöl,* and some *Piparkokur* biscuits which looked similar to ginger nuts.

The woman at the checkout chatted as she wrapped Fliss's purchases, asking her if she was on holiday. It was tempting to take the easy option and say yes, but Fliss was enjoying the novelty of saying that she was a writer. If she couldn't announce herself as that while on her own book tour, when could she?

'Ah, you are here for *Jolobokaflod?'*

'Yes, I've been doing a few events.'

'I am going to an event tonight at *Bokabud Máls og Menningar.* It's not that one is it?'   T h e   w o m a n   w a s looking at Fliss with wide-eyed anticipation. Even if it hadn't been Fliss's event, she might have pretended it was, because it would be like kicking a puppy to have to say no.

'Yes, it is.'

'You are FL Thorne! I love your books. Margot is an amazing character. I am even more excited for tonight now!'

'Thank you. This a great shop, I wish I had more space in my case.'

'I will see you tonight, Miss Thorne.'

'It's Fliss. What's your name?'

'Svala.'

'Well, I'll see you later, Svala.'

In her dreams, the encounter with Svala was what she'd

imagined life would be like all the time when she'd become published and it felt amazing to have come to Iceland and find that this was how she was seen by people. It was funny to think that all this time, she'd had a fanbase that she was completely oblivious to, assuming that the lack of success at home had meant that would be the case everywhere. Admittedly, if she'd embraced social media for longer than the first three or four months after her books had been published, she might have noticed something happening but in some ways, it was quite nice to feel like an overnight sensation.

It was a half hour walk to Rachel's house. The wind was at her back, so the snow wasn't flying into her face, making it easier to see her phone when she periodically pulled it out of her pocket to check she was going the right way. She had followed the sea front road to the outskirts of the old town, and then the directions sent her inland for a short distance.

All of the houses on Rachel and Jonas's street were larger versions of Brun's house; all had red roofs, but only glimpses of the colour could be seen beneath the snow. Rachel had said theirs was the green house. It was pea-green, two storeys and had three steps that led up to the front door as most of the houses seemed to. Perhaps the snow really got that deep sometimes?

Fliss knocked and almost immediately, the door was opened by Anna.

'Morning,' she said, standing aside so Fliss could get in. 'That's good timing, Rachel's just making a cuppa.'

'Lovely. It's so cosy in here,' Fliss said, putting her bags down and taking off her boots and coat. The hallway led into a lounge which was painted navy-blue and had a couple of very comfy sofas facing each other across a large coffee table. There was a wood-burning stove which wasn't lit, perhaps because there was no need since it was already toasty warm.

They went through the lounge to the kitchen.

'You have been to Snug!' said Gudrun, seeing Fliss's bag of shopping. 'I'm the manager there.'

'I could have bought everything in there,' Fliss said.

'What did you choose?' Gudrun asked, reaching out to peek in the bag.

Fliss pulled out the blanket and everyone sighed.

'I saw those the day Hilde bought them in to the design call,' Rachel said, 'and I knew they'd be the bestseller. I used to work for Snug too,' she explained.

'They are the bestseller,' confirmed Gudrun. 'I think we all have one.'

'More than one,' said Anna. 'I seem to be able to get them under Ned's soft-furnishing radar, whereas if I bought a new cushion he'd complain straight away.'

'Brun has at least a couple, doesn't he?' Rachel asked.

Fliss kept quiet. She knew they had most likely belonged to his ex since his house was completely devoid of anything like that but it seemed too forward to make that observation to his friends when she had only been to his house once. And she'd been too busy to notice every tiny detail.

Rachel poured cups of tea from a large teapot and they sat on stools around the kitchen island.

'Oh, I brought some biscuits,' Fliss said, taking them out of the bag along with the bottles of drink.

'Yummy,' said Gudrun. 'I usually eat too many of these. It is very difficult when they are next to me every day at work.'

'Thanks, Fliss,' said Rachel. 'You didn't need to.'

'It's the least I can do. It's kind of you to invite me.'

'I get the sense that you might be good at this leaf bread,' Rachel said. 'We need all the help we can get, Gudrun's the only one of us who has made it before.'

'You are not even making it, Rachel,' said Gudrun. 'You have bought ready-made dough.'

'I thought the main thing was the cutting?' Rachel said.

Gudrun rolled her eyes. 'It is your first time with *laufabrauð*. It is important to have a good dough, it is probably good that you bought it,' she teased.

'Come on then, *laufabrauð* expert, what do we do?'

They finished their tea, then cleared the worktop so that they could lay out the thin circles of dough. There was no way they could have rolled it this thinly if they'd made it themselves, Fliss thought. Gudrun picked up one of the delicate copper knives and began making cuts in her dough. After she made a few marks, she used the tip of the blade to lift a small flap of dough and fold it back on itself, making a triangular hole and a triangular relief next to it.

'And you just carry on like that, whatever design you like.'

For a few minutes, they were silent as the three English women got to grips with the delicate cutting, periodically looking over to Gudrun's to see her progress.

'How long is this meant to take?' Anna asked.

'It can take a long time for an intricate design,' said Gudrun. 'It is traditional.' Her tone was a little on the fierce side but Anna grinned good-naturedly.

'Are you looking forward to tonight, Fliss?'

'I am, actually. I think it's a chat first and then a book-signing, a bit different to what I've done so far. I did a talk at the library in Akranes and signed a few books but other than that, it's been just signing at the other bookshops.'

'They have music at this place, and a bar,' said Gudrun. 'That is why they have you in the evening so that it will turn into a party.'

'That sounds good,' Fliss said.

'Is Brun coming?' Rachel asked.

'I think so. My publisher asked him to take photos for social media so he's been coming along even when he hasn't needed to drive me anywhere.'

'That's not why he's coming along.'

'Anna!' Rachel admonished.

'It's fine,' Fliss said. These were Brun's friends. They'd seen how he'd looked at her, how he'd sung to her, how he'd kissed her at the open mic night. 'I'm glad he comes even when he doesn't have to.'

'What are you going to do? Have you talked about it?' Anna asked.

Fliss knew exactly what she meant without her having to spell it out.

'Not really, but I think we both know it's something to savour over the next few days without thinking too hard about what happens after that.'

'That's what happened with me and Jonas,' said Rachel. 'And in the end I couldn't leave him.' She had a dreamy look on her face.

'Stop being so soppy,' Anna said. 'You're married now, how long is this honeymoon period going to last?'

'It's not a honeymoon period. Anyway, you're a fine one to be asking Fliss what's going on with her and Brun when you had no idea when you started seeing Ned.'

'That's different. He was hard to pin down. It was because he'd just left the band, he didn't know what he wanted to do about anything, let alone me,' she explained to Fliss, putting her knife down in a way that suggested she wasn't going to pick it up again. 'Brun is much more straightforward. Icelandic men are like that, you know where you stand. It's the English ones that are problematic.'

Fliss laughed. 'I have to admit, it's refreshing to meet someone who seems like a genuinely nice person and isn't afraid to be honest about how they feel.'

'That's Brun,' said Gudrun. 'He has a heart of gold and he was messed around by Kristin. He was too nice for her.'

'I think we need to open a bottle of wine,' Rachel said,

fetching a bottle from the fridge and glasses for each of them.

'So she broke things off with him?' Fliss's curiosity got the better of her.

'She started seeing someone else while he was working up in the north in the spring, but she didn't tell him,' Gudrun said. 'I saw her walk past the shop with the other man many times and hated that she was lying to Brun. In the end I told her she had to tell him or I would.'

'Yes Gudrun!' Anna said. 'And the heartache has been good for his songwriting.'

'Oh, Anna, you're awful,' Rachel said, rolling her eyes. 'She's really very sorry that he was heartbroken,' she said to Fliss.

'But now he's met Fliss and he's back to happy Brun. He's happier than when he was with Kristin.'

Fliss liked Anna's no-nonsense assessments of everything, but couldn't help wondering whether Brun was heading for another heartache.

'How about you, Fliss? Presumably you don't have a man back home?'

'Only an annoying ex-husband,' she said, making them laugh.

They carried on with their leaf bread cutting until Anna declared that they were pretty enough as they were and it was time to cook them before she died of hunger. Gudrun took charge of the deep-frying, expertly cooking the breads, one at a time, until they were golden.

'It's a shame to eat them, they look so pretty,' said Fliss.

'Sometimes people hang them in windows for decoration,' said Gudrun.

'Oh, they have them hanging up in the bakery near our house,' Anna said. 'I hadn't clocked that's what they were.'

Fliss took a photo of them before they started eating, resolving to do her own Instagram post about them later on.

'I'd better go,' she said, once they'd finished the bottle of wine and the bread. 'I need to get ready for later.'

'We'll see you there,' Rachel said, seeing her out.

'Thanks, Rachel, I've had a lovely time.'

Fliss was sorry that she couldn't be part of their group for longer than today. She had Abbie and Lily, but it wasn't the same. Ultimately it was because she'd lost a lot of friends when she and Duncan had split up. Couple friends who couldn't decide whose side to take had drifted away, and she didn't think they were Duncan's friends either now. Friends she'd known through work were still friends with Duncan through work because she'd been the one who had to leave the business; their loyalty still lay with him.

But there was still her event tonight which they were all coming to. As her friends. And she was quite surprised how much that meant to her.

14

Fliss arrived deliberately early, not wanting to walk into a bookshop-cum-bar full of people all by herself. It was better to assess the lay of the land before the place was busy. *Hús Máls og Menningar* was split-level over three floors, but the main space was on the middle floor which had a stage running along one side, with high bookshelves behind it, a couple of chairs in a similar set up to the library, and a table with a huge pile of her books on one side of it. The next floor was more like a large balcony that extended over half of the room, affording a good view of the stage since it overlooked the main shop floor. Fliss could see it was that which made it the perfect multi-purpose venue.

The manager, Erik, was thrilled to see her and immediately sat her down with a pile of books to sign for orders they'd had from people unable to attend. He offered her a drink from the bar, and feeling slightly unprofessional, she accepted, asking for a gin and tonic. It would help steady her nerves.

By the time she'd finished signing, people were beginning to arrive and the shop had closed to anyone but those customers with tickets. Erik shepherded her away to the staff room.

'We don't want you to get pestered before we start,' he said. 'Would you like another drink?'

'Better not, although a coffee would be great. My friend Brun is coming tonight to take photos for my publisher. If he lets you know who he is, I'd be really grateful if you could tell him where I am.'

'Ah, no problem,' said Erik. 'I know Brun. I'll look out for him.'

Fliss blushed, feeling embarrassed at having referred to Brun as her friend to someone who knew him. 'Thanks. He's been driving me all over the place. My publisher organised it.' And now that was a ridiculous amount of information to have told to justify something that didn't need justifying at all.

'I will get someone to bring you a coffee and then I will come back for you when we are ready to start.'

She should have had another gin and tonic. Waiting in the room was worse than milling around with everyone else, most people didn't know what she looked like so it wasn't as if everyone would be asking her questions before the event had even started. Still, it was a good opportunity to catch her breath and return a few messages. She'd had a couple of texts from Abbie asking how it was going and hadn't had chance to reply. But now that she was trying to compose a message that encompassed everything from the past couple of days, she found she couldn't put into words what had happened.

Last night, Brun had walked her back to her hotel, kissing her at the door with no expectation of being invited up to her room. It was just another thing that made her emotions soar with the tenderness he showed her. Having to suggest it herself made her feel bold; it felt dangerous and exciting all at the same time. Normally, she spent so much time doing things for everyone else, that she was enjoying having these few days where all of the decisions were just for her.

Decisions that would have no bearing on her life when she returned to England. As if it were that easy to compartmentalise everything.

Trying to write down the events of the past couple of days in black and white focused her thoughts on what was happening. She could dismiss the whole situation with Brun as a holiday romance but it was more than that. More than a kiss, more than an afternoon and a blissful night spent in each other's arms. It was him singing those words to her last night. It was the way he looked at her across a bookshop when he was watching her sign books. It was the way his friends accepted her so readily. It wasn't a holiday romance, it was something else. Something she had never had with Duncan. How could she reduce it to gossip to share with her best friend? How could she explain that she was starting to fall in love with a man who she had only met five days ago? How could she allow herself to be feeling like that about someone whose whole life existed in a different country to her?

There was a knock on the door and Brun stuck his head round, grinning when he saw her sitting there. All thoughts of texting Abbie were gone in favour of giving him her full attention because she hadn't seen him since he left her room that morning at five o'clock.

'How was the *laufabrauð* making?' he asked, taking a seat next to her. He wrapped an arm around her and drew her into him. He smelt amazing. It was the first time she'd noticed him wear aftershave and she liked it very much.

'It was fun, your friends are so welcoming.'

'Did they tell you all of my secrets?' He looked slightly worried.

'Of course they did,' she teased him. She took his beardy cheeks in her hands and drew him towards her for a kiss. 'I've missed you today.'

He smiled and leant in for another kiss. 'I would rather

have been with you than driving around the Golden Circle.'

That was the reason he'd had to leave so early. Since Fliss's event was an evening one, he'd been on the normal excursion rota for the day.

'I should have come with you,' she said.

'That would have been too distracting. The roads were not good, and with you next to me I would not have been able to concentrate.'

'I can't believe this is our last night together.'

'We still have tomorrow.'

A morning of book-signing and a drive to the airport via the Blue Lagoon didn't count in Fliss's mind as time spent with Brun, but it was all they had.

'I have told Jonas that I will take you to the airport, you will not need to go with the normal trip that we do. It will be just us.'

Fliss wasn't sure if that was better or worse. She was dreading the point at which they had to say goodbye to each other and was starting to focus on that instead of what time they did have.

'That's great, thank you.'

He shook his head. 'I do not like going to the Blue Lagoon but for you I will make an exception.'

'Why don't you like it?' Fliss couldn't imagine anything nicer than sinking into the steaming water together like they'd done in Akranes.

'It is too busy,' he said with a shrug. 'Although maybe not tomorrow, it is close to Christmas. There will not be so many tourists.'

'We don't have to go there. I'd rather have more time together tomorrow. Alone.' It felt bold to tell him that she wanted him. But she was so certain that they were feeling exactly the same, it didn't feel like a risk.

'Would you like to stay at my house tonight?'

Brun's house was more comfortable than her hotel and much closer to the bookshop. It might be nice to pretend that they were a local couple on a night out, then go home together and have a cup of tea before bed. Actually, tea was the last thing on her mind, but what she did want to do would be nicer to do at his house.

'I'd love that.'

There was another knock at the door and Erik came in.

'We are ready when you are,' he said.

'I will see you afterwards,' Brun said, giving her a kiss, not seeming to worry at all that Erik was right there watching.

Compared to when she'd arrived earlier, and indeed, compared to any of the other places she'd been, the noise level in the bookshop was overwhelming. Looking up at the balcony, Fliss could see rows of chairs filled with people who were busy chatting to the people sat next to them, waiting for things to start. The floor where the stage was had as many chairs again, all facing where she was about to sit, and there were even people on a floor level slightly lower down, who would be viewing the stage at a very odd angle. The place was heaving.

Thanking her lucky stars that she'd had the gin and tonic, even if it was unlikely that any of it was left in her system, she followed Erik up onto the stage. The crowd began clapping as they noticed them.

'I have put a gin and tonic here for you,' said Erik, 'but there is water as well if you prefer.'

'Thanks. A gin is exactly what I need,' she said gratefully. 'I can't believe how many people are here.'

'It has been one of our most popular events. You will be fine, Fliss. We'll have a nice chat, that is all,' he said reassuringly.

'Okay. Ready when you are,' she said.

As Erik introduced her in Icelandic, she allowed herself to

glance around at the audience and saw Rachel, Jonas, Gudrun and Anna in the crowd, a couple of rows from the front. Fliss smiled and Gudrun gave a small wave. Brun was standing to the side, his phone in his hand ready to record the evening. He had that look on his face; a mixture of pride along with something else that Fliss couldn't bring herself to identify for fear it would make everything harder.

She snapped back into the moment as Erik started to speak English, beginning their talk by asking her how she came to set her books in Iceland. That settled her quickly into the comfort zone she hadn't known she had before this week, and suddenly it didn't bother her at all that there were a couple of hundred people in the building all because of her.

They chatted about her inspiration, her route to publication and her beloved main character, Margot before Erik opened up to questions from the audience.

'Is Margot's character based any experiences of your own?'

'I wrote about Margot after my divorce. I was a single parent, I had to find a new job and a new house when I hadn't seen any of that coming. I think Margot came from a part of me that wished I could escape all of that and live life on my own terms. Margot has skills that she can use anywhere. I admire that in her.'

'You are perhaps more like Margot than you think,' Erik said, smiling.

Fliss blushed. She hadn't meant to compare her writing career to Margot's career. She hadn't even thought she could call it a writing career until a few weeks ago.

'I have two children, so not quite as able to locate myself anywhere as she is.'

The audience rumbled with a few laughs and Erik scanned them for the next questioner.

'Would you ever consider moving to Iceland like Margot?'

The question came from Gudrun, and Fliss's eyes

immediately flicked over to where Brun was standing. The morning they'd spent at Rachel's had been enough time for Fliss to realise that Gudrun was a hopeless romantic and was rooting for her friend to find love. She didn't blame her for asking but in this situation, she must know that Fliss couldn't give an honest answer. Even if she knew what the answer was.

'I love Iceland and I suppose if I were a full-time writer with no responsibilities, I could consider living anywhere.' She trotted the answer out, smiling as if the question didn't have any particular meaning behind it. 'But since you good people are the only ones so far to have embraced Margot, I think it might be a while before that happens.'

Everyone laughed and after a couple more questions, Erik called an end to that part of the evening and explained to people where to form a queue for the book-signing while Fliss took her place behind the table on the corner of the stage and began chatting to the first people in the queue. It wasn't that different to the bookshop signing in Selfoss, aside from there being more people and that most of them were drinking beer instead of coffee.   Gudrun, Rachel and Anna were right at the end of the queue and after a couple of hours of chatting, it was a relief to see friendly faces who didn't have any questions for her.

'Gudrun's sorry she asked that question,' said Rachel, holding her book out for Fliss to sign. 'Aren't you?'

'I am sorry, Fliss. It is only because I was not sure whether you had thought of staying here with Brun.'

'Everything you said after the sorry part cancels out the sorry part,' said Anna. 'They've only known each other a few days.'

Fliss gave Anna a grateful smile. 'Exactly. Just because we've hit it off, it doesn't mean we're ready to plan the rest of our lives together.'

'That is what these two thought,' Gudrun said, pointing at Rachel and Anna. 'They both came here and met the loves of their lives.'

'To be fair, I don't think either of us had made plans to stay after five days,' Anna said, taking her turn to present her book to Fliss.

'Look, enough of this. It's Fliss's last night, let's make sure it's a good one,' Rachel said. 'Stop going on at her about Brun. It's none of our business.'

'It's fine,' Fliss said. 'Come on, I'm ready for a drink.' They headed for the bar, making slow progress as people stopped her to chat. Eventually, Rachel came and pressed a gin and tonic into her hand as it was clear Fliss was never going to make it that far. Not long after, music started playing prompting some people to call it a night while everyone else took to the floor that had emerged once the chairs were cleared away. She saw Brun talking to Jonas, each of them with a beer, so she stuck with the women and began dancing. She couldn't remember the last time she'd been out dancing. Probably not since the children had been born. Where would she even go for that in Oxford without being amongst students twenty years younger than her? No, there was something about Reykjavik, Iceland really, that made Fliss feel very comfortable and if she was free like Margot, she might not hesitate to make it her home too.

15

It was well after midnight when the music finally stopped and everyone was ready to leave. Brun and Jonas had reluctantly joined them on the dance floor towards the end of the evening and Fliss had been surprised that Brun had moves. For such a broad, strapping man to have any agility when it came to dancing was unusual but it was probably because he was musical; the rhythm overriding his natural tendency towards large purposeful movements. Fliss couldn't resist dancing up to him, her eyes inviting him to take her in his arms, finding him almost as sexy as when he was singing to her the night before. She loved the feel of his hand on the small of her back as they moved, pressing their bodies together as they gazed into each other's eyes with meaning. Knowing, for at least that night, if not beyond, what was to come.

It was snowing when they emerged into the twinkling darkness of Laugavegur, but despite that there were a surprising number of people out and about, everyone wrapped up in hats, scarves and coats against the elements.

'What an amazing night,' she said as the group lingered outside the bookshop before splitting off to their own houses. 'Thanks so much for coming, it's been the best night out I've had in years.'

She was suddenly aware of how that sounded. This might be a regular occurrence for them, something they did that was so normal, that it would sound ridiculous for it to rank as the best night out in years for anybody.

'It is never like that,' said Gudrun. 'It really depends on who is there and tonight was the best.'

'Thank you.'

Gudrun pulled her into a hug. 'It has been so great to meet you, Fliss. I hope we see you again.'

'I hope so too.'

She said her goodbyes to Rachel, Jonas and Anna, hugging all of them as well, feeling immensely sorry to be leaving what felt like her friends.

'Do you mind if I walk with you?' Anna asked.

'No, of course not,' said Brun. 'Ned couldn't make it tonight?'

'You know how he is about crowds.'

Brun nodded. 'He worries that people will recognise him,' he explained to Fliss.

'People here are used to him being around so it's not as bad as it used to be, but he was worried that it might take the shine off you if he was recognised and obviously it is important that it was your night,' Anna said.

'That's so thoughtful of him.'

Anna shrugged, but she had a smile on her face. 'If you saw how some people react when they realise Ned Nokes is in the building, you would be pleased he didn't want to risk that tonight.'

'Can you thank him for me?'

'Course.'

They had reached the path that led from the road to the cluster of houses where Brun lived.

'It was great to meet you, Fliss,' Anna said. 'Have a lovely

Christmas.'

Anna waved and headed along a path towards her house, just a couple of doors away.

Brun put an arm around Fliss's shoulders and hugged her to his side. 'I have been waiting for this part all night,' he said, pulling his keys from his coat pocket and then letting her go so that he could unlock the door. They brushed the snow from their coats and stamped their feet before they went inside. It was as cosy as it had been the last time Fliss had been there, more so now that it was dark and the snow was falling outside.

He headed into the kitchen to make them a drink while Fliss curled up on one of the chairs, wishing that the throw she'd brought from Snug was hanging over the back of it ready to pull across her. Not because it was cold, but she wanted to get cosy and it would look really good in Brun's lounge. It was softly lit with a couple of lamps and aside from the sound of Brun in the kitchen, absolutely quiet.

'Here,' he said, handing her a mug of something that looked like hot, frothy milk but smelled of cinnamon, cloves and ginger, basically like Christmas in a mug.

'Thanks, it smells delicious.'

Brun sat in the chair across from her, 'You were wonderful tonight,' he said softly.

Fliss's heart skipped a beat. The look in his eyes was exactly how she'd always wanted to be looked at by someone she…loved.

'Thank you. I really enjoyed it.'

'Do you think it is crazy to think that we can have any kind of relationship after tomorrow?'

'I've tried not to think about what will happen after tomorrow. Once I realised how I felt about you, I tried to tell myself to take this chance to enjoy what we have without letting thoughts of afterwards change how that might look. I could have stopped myself, because if we never see each other again, it's going to hurt. But maybe it's worth it for what we have right now.'

Brun set his mug down on the table and came over to Fliss's chair. He hooked his arm underneath her knees and instinctively, she looped her arms around his neck as he picked her up and carried her through the kitchen to the bedroom.

He must have lit the candles while he was making the drinks. The flames flickered as they walked in. He put her down on the bed and lay next to her. They were facing each other, their hands resting onto each other, keeping the contact that they both craved and knew was not going to be possible for much longer.

'When Kristin left, I did not think that I would allow myself to love anyone again. It ended so quickly, it was hard to switch off my feelings for her. I did not want to be in a relationship again when I would always wonder whether the person really did love me. But now, with you, even in such a short time, I know I would never worry about that, Fliss. But I also know that I cannot ask you to return home to England carrying any promises for me in your heart.'

Yet again, Fliss thought her heart couldn't ache any more for Brun. This great, beardy, Icelandic man had the most tender of hearts. His honesty in telling her exactly how he was feeling took her breath away.

'I'm not sure my heart is giving me any say in what it wants to promise you. My head is saying we shouldn't wait for each other because who knows how long it could be before my kids are old enough that I don't need to consider them in every decision I make. And even then, I'm not sure whether I could move to Reykjavik. But I do know that a long-distance relationship isn't fair on either one of us.'

'I understand. I would like to offer to be the one to move

but I cannot force myself into your life because it is not just you. Your children might hate me,' he chuckled.

'They wouldn't,' she said, feeling certain that he would win them over as quickly as he had her. But with all the upheaval with Duncan and the baby, it wasn't fair to upset the only stable part of their lives by introducing someone else into their family. And it wouldn't be fair to Brun either to be put in the position of interloper, the person taking their mother's attention from them. 'But in a couple of years, they'll be that much older and what I'm doing won't seem as important.'

'I could wait, Fliss.'

'Two years is a long time for anyone to have to wait,' she said, saying what she knew was the sensible thing to say, rather than what her heart wanted her to. 'What if one of us meets someone else that we feel just as strongly for?' She didn't think that was possible for her and given how barren the past few years had been romantically, she thought it was entirely possible to wait for another two, in theory. In practice, if there was the possibility of Brun at the end of a two year stretch, the time would drag impossibly.

'That will not happen because there is no one like you.'

'I feel the same way.' She touched his face, cupping his jaw in her hand before leaning in to kiss him. All she could think about was how it was going to feel to leave him. Her feelings for him were increasing exponentially with every minute they spent together and tomorrow it would all come crashing down.

'So tonight is all we have.'

She nodded. 'But we have the whole night, Brun. Let's make it count.'

'It will break my heart to say goodbye to you tomorrow.'

'No, it won't,' she said gently. 'Because we will remember it as a beautiful moment in time where everything seemed possible. We won't dwell on what could have been because nothing can be.'

'If that is how it has to be, I would rather accept that and walk away tomorrow with the memory of the most wonderful woman I have ever met, than to not have had it at all.'

Fliss could hardly believe that she had not known this man for even a week and that they were having a conversation like this. But then, the whole trip to Iceland had seemed like the kind of thing that would happen to someone else, not to her. This week, she hadn't felt like a single mother of two teenagers, who normally struggled to cope with a life which was entirely different to the one she'd been living three years ago. Now, she felt like a character from a romance novel, who against all expectations, met the man of her dreams while on a book tour in a wild, snowy, romantic country. But that could only be her life this week. There was no happy ever after, although she would remember it forever.

Brun put his hand around her waist and pulled her closer, pressed together as if their lives depended on it. Fliss could feel the muscles that covered Brun's body rippling underneath his clothes. She had never found a man so physically attractive before. He wasn't clean-cut and handsome in the same way as her previous partners. She'd always gone for slick men in suits and had never thought that a more rugged-looking man would turn her on. And look where that had got her.

They gradually undressed, taking their time, as if they were committing every tiny part of each other, every touch, every moment to memory as they went along. It had to be enough. It had to sustain them through what they both knew would be hard days to come when they would question whether it had been a good idea to start anything that had no future. When they asked themselves whether it had been worth the heartache.

Fliss had all of these thoughts running through her head at the same time as trying to be as mindful as possible about savouring the moment, only truly able to give herself up to it at the hands of Brun's exquisite exploration of every last part of her. The feel of his hands wrapping around her hips, drawing her to him, the way he grazed his finger along exactly the right part of her thigh to make her insides melt.

How could she live without this?

They finally fell asleep in one another's arms, Brun spooning against Fliss's back, making her feel so safe and content that she didn't move, and was barely aware of anything, even when her phone pinged with a couple of alerts. When her alarm finally woke her in time for her to go back to the hotel and pack before her last book tour engagement - a simple book-signing - she could hardly believe that it was almost over. In just a few hours they would be saying goodbye to each other and it would be the end of one of the best experiences of her life.

Brun kissed her, then turned and reached for his phone while Fliss got dressed.

'Check your phone,' he said. 'I think your flight has been cancelled.'

She smiled. 'If only.'

'I am not joking,' he said. 'There is a big snowstorm on the way.'

Fliss picked up her phone and remembered the pings that she hadn't quite been conscious enough to bother about a couple of hours ago. There was an alert from the airline to say she should check with the airport about flight delays.

Christmas was in three days. She had to get home.

16

As soon as she read the alert, she switched from blissed-out, sex-drunk Fliss to someone more closely resembling Kevin's mother from Home Alone. After fruitless attempts to call the airline and the airport information number, she pulled on her clothes, ready to leave Brun's house and go back to her hotel. Maybe if she got to the airport right now, it wouldn't be too late.

'Fliss, wait,' Brun said, pulling his trousers on as he walked towards her. 'Let's find out what is going on before you rush off.'

'I can't get through to the airline or the airport.'

'So what is your plan?' He was looking at her with a smile on his face. It infuriated her. Didn't he understand how utterly disastrous this was?

'My plan is to get home. It's three days until Christmas. I have to get home. The kids can't go to Duncan's until Boxing Day. They need me.'

'I understand, but we need to calm down and make a plan together. I can help you, Fliss. There will be no taxis going to the airport now. But we have a jeep with tyres that can get through the snow. We may still be able to get there before it's too late.'

'What do you mean, too late?'

Brun gently pulled Fliss away from the front door and pushed it open. Now she saw why the doors all opened outwards here. There was snow piled up against it and he had to shove it hard to shift the drift. Actually, it wasn't a drift. It was simply the depth of the snow. Deeper than she'd ever seen before.

'Okay. I see what you mean. And you don't think it's already too late?'

Brun shrugged. 'Let's see. Come back in and I will make some calls.'

Fliss made coffee for them both while Brun rang a friend who worked at the airport and then someone called Siggi who he worked with. It was frustrating not to know what Brun's side of the conversation was, but he was asking plenty of questions which was good. Information was what she needed.

She couldn't imagine having to tell Josh and Emma that she wouldn't be home for Christmas. Even worse would be having to tell Lily. She and Frank always booked a couple of nights at a swanky hotel in London from Christmas Eve to Boxing Day. It wasn't out of choice that they had no children, and part of their acceptance of that was to live a life that wouldn't be possible if they did. They loved their Christmas trips, it was almost the only time that Lily spent the kind of money that some people would all the time if they earned what she did. But she was careful normally, and that was what made it special. Fliss couldn't take that away from them.

'The airport is open but there are no flights leaving now. There are still flights landing but my friend who works at the airport says that they are about to start diverting flights. If we went now, we could end up stranded there if the roads get worse.'

Brun walked the couple of steps it took to cross the kitchen and hugged her tightly.

'Let's go online and rebook your flight for a couple of days time. That way at least you will have a flight on Christmas Eve. You will be home in time.'

'But what if the flights are still cancelled in two days? What if it snows from now until January?' It seemed entirely possible that she might never leave Brun's house given the amount of snow outside.

'It is unusual for the airport to be closed for more than a couple of days,' Brun said, soothingly. 'We will book a new flight and then you can call your kids and let them know.'

'My sister's going to go mad.'

'They are not with their father?'

'No. It's a long story but she will kill me if I'm not home on Christmas Eve. I should have kept an eye on the weather and left yesterday instead.' She'd been so busy having a nice time, that she'd slipped into thinking of the snow like an Icelander would; an everyday occurrence that didn't interfere much at all with anyone's day-to-day existence. Until now.

'I am not sure this storm was forecast to be so severe. I know that Jonas did not cancel the excursions for today so it must not have looked like it would be such heavy snow.'

That did make her feel a bit better. She had picked up that they were constantly watching the weather so the fact that they didn't see it coming either meant there would have been no chance for her.

'Okay,' she said, 'I'll have a look at the airline website and see if I can change my flight and then when I know what I'm doing, I'll ring Lily.'

The website confirmed that her flight had now been cancelled which validated Brun's advice not to travel to the airport. They were already expecting no flights to be leaving the following day and all the flights on Christmas Eve were full. Remarkably, there was one direct flight early on Christmas Day but that was also already full. She checked everything twice before she put her phone down, struggling to keep the tears at bay as she came to terms with the fact that she was going to have to spend Christmas away from her children.

'I am so sorry, Fliss.' Brun said, coming to sit next to her and pulling her onto his lap so that she could cry into his chest. 'I am sure that as soon as flights can leave, they will put more on to try and clear the backlog. They have done that before. It might not be too late.'

'I have to tell them that I won't be back,' Fliss sniffed. 'I can't let them think there's a chance. Lily and Frank need to change their plans, at least.'

'I will leave you to call them.'

'Wait for a minute.' Fliss snuggled further into Brun's embrace. At least there was one upside to being stranded in Reykjavik. She wasn't quite ready to be overjoyed but once she'd spoken to Josh and Emma, she might be ready to accept the situation.

Brun disentangled himself from her after a couple of minutes and she picked her phone up and called Lily.

'Don't worry, I've already seen it on the news,' Lily said. 'It's fine. We've pushed our hotel booking by a few days. You'd better be back before the twenty-eighth or Frank will never speak to you again.'

Fliss smiled. Frank would never not speak to her; he was a softy. 'Thanks, Lil. I'm so sorry for ruining your Christmas.'

'It won't be ruined,' her sister said, in her usual forthright manner. 'It'll be different, but in a good way. Your kids are great, we'll make sure it's a Christmas we all remember.'

'I know you will. Are they around? Might be best if I talk to Josh first.'

'Do you want me to prime Emma for you?'

'No, it's okay.' Her sister had done enough. 'I'll offer her extra Christmas presents, she'll get over it pretty quickly.'

Lily laughed. 'But what about you? Are you going to end up having Christmas alone in a soulless hotel room?'

'I don't think so. I've made some friends so I think I'll have somewhere to go.' She had no idea what anyone's plans for Christmas were, apart from Ned and Anna who were going to be in the same boat as her since they were supposed to be flying back to England today too.

'People you've known for five days are going to invite you to spend Christmas with them?'

Fliss couldn't blame Lily for thinking that. She'd have thought the same a week ago.

'It's that kind of place. I've already been round to someone's house to do Christmas baking.'

'Good for you. Try and enjoy it, Fliss, and don't worry about Josh and Emma, they'll be okay.'

'I know. Thanks Lil, I owe you.'

'I'll put Josh on.'

Fliss could hear her sister's smile in her voice and was so grateful that she had stepped in to help. If the children had been staying with Duncan and he'd not been able to dump them with Lily, who knows what would be happening to them now.

'Hi Mum.'

'Hi Josh.' There was no easy way to say it. 'I'm stranded in Iceland because of a storm and I'm not going to be able to get back for Christmas.'

'Oh. Are we going to Dad's then?'

'No, Auntie Lily and Uncle Frank are going to London a few days later than normal so you can stay with them. I'm so sorry.'

'It's okay, it's not your fault. Do you want to tell Emma?'

'Okay,' Fliss said, bracing herself for an onslaught of self-centred teenagerness from Emma that Josh never seemed to have had. 'We'll have our Christmas when I get home, Joshy.' She had tears in her eyes at the thought of them celebrating without her, but Lily was right. It would be a different kind of Christmas for all of them and she would still do a Christmas Day when she got home, whenever that might be.

'What about my presents?' Emma said.

Fliss tried to think kindly of her daughter. It was perhaps the first thing she would have thought as a fifteen-year-old, but it stung that it was Emma's main concern.

'We'll have our Christmas when I get home. You'll have presents there from Auntie Lily and Uncle Frank and having to wait a few extra days gives me a chance to buy a few extra things.' It was pure bribery but Fliss didn't care. She knew what made Emma tick and it would make everyone's lives easier if she was happy.

'I suppose that's okay. Are we still going to Dad's on Boxing Day?'

'I don't see why you wouldn't be,' Fliss said. She'd forgotten that they'd be with Duncan for a couple of days. 'I can't imagine I'll be able to get a flight home before that anyway. I'm sure Dad's looking forward to seeing you.'

'I wish we could see Dad on our own without Shona and Dylan.'

'I'm sure he'll take you and Josh out somewhere, just the three of you,' she said, although she was about as sure of that happening as she was of getting home by Christmas. 'Perhaps ask him if you can spend some time with him by yourselves. I'm sure he'd enjoy that too.'

'Mmm. Maybe. What will you do, Mum? Will they do Christmas lunch in your hotel?'

Fliss knew that her lovely Emma was still somewhere inside the moody teenager and this was the proof.

'I've made some friends, so I'm hoping I'll get to have an

Icelandic Christmas with them.'

'Are you doing the yolo bokky flot thing?'

Fliss laughed. 'I might do. Perhaps we can do it when I get home. Oh, I did make some bread which I think we should try at home when I get back. I'll send you a photo of it.'

'Bread? That's so random.'

'Well, yes. But it was fun.'

'I need to go. Do you want to talk to Auntie Lily again?'

'No, that's okay. Love you Em. Give Josh a hug from me.'

'Eww. I'm not doing that. Love you, Mum. Bye.'

Fliss felt so much better about the whole situation now that she'd spoken to the kids and to Lily. It was going to be fine.

'Everything alright?' Brun asked, coming into the lounge from the kitchen where he'd been loitering to give her some privacy.

'Yes, it's all sorted.' She smiled, and stood up to give him a hug. 'How do you feel about having a Christmas interloper?'

'I think that sounds wonderful. But before that, we have a book signing to go to.'

'Don't you think it will be cancelled because of the weather?' If there was this much snow at home there was no question that everything would be cancelled.

'I do not think so. People will still go out, the shops will be open.'

'Really? Perhaps I should call and check.'

'Would you like me to, in my role as your book tour assistant?' he asked, raising a suggestive eyebrow.

'That would be great. I always worry that people won't speak English, even though everyone does.'

A couple of minutes later, it was confirmed that it was going ahead which sent Fliss into a spin because she needed to get changed out of her party dress and clean her teeth.

Calmly, Brun went to a cupboard and pulled out an assortment of outdoor clothing and two pairs of snow boots.

'We will dress in this and go to your hotel together. We will collect all of your things and bring them here and you will stay with me.'

Brun being so masterful made Fliss a little weak at the knees. It was very sexy and a shame that the book signing was going ahead and they had to leave his house at all.

17

'What are you doing for Christmas?' Fliss asked Brun later that morning as they made their way from his house to the book shop. Even shouting, she could barely hear herself speak since the wind was strong enough to whip her words away. The snow was like pinpricks on her face as the wind relentlessly blew the flakes along at a hundred miles an hour. Her hood was done up so tightly around her head that she could hardly see out. And she didn't hear Brun's reply even if he had heard her in the first place. Deciding that it was too much trouble to pursue a conversation, they walked in silence, holding hands. Fliss felt as if Brun was having to drag her along, the wind determined to try and stop them in their tracks. She was cosy though, in her own multiple layers of clothes which now were covered by Brun's seriously practical outdoor clothing. She didn't imagine it was actually his since it wasn't huge on her. And she preferred not to know whether it had belonged to Kristin.

The bookshop was the wintery equivalent of seeing an oasis in the desert. It felt like they'd traversed miles and miles of snowy wilderness when actually, it was only a couple of streets away from the Harpa, Reykjavik's huge concert hall on the edge of the harbour. In normal weather, it might have taken them fifteen minutes but today it felt like it had taken hours. On top of already having been to the hotel and back, she felt physically exhausted. Given the weather, Fliss was surprised at how many people were out and about. It looked like her book signing at *Iða Zimsen* might be just as successful an event as the others had been.

'I would usually have Christmas Eve lunch at my parents' house and then I would go to Jonas and Rachel's in the evening, probably,' Brun said over a coffee once they reached the book shop. They had an hour before Fliss was expected to do anything and it was nice to have the chance to relax after the intrepid journey they'd had.

'What about Christmas Day?'

'The family celebration is on Christmas Eve so Christmas Day is a quiet day for lazing around at home. Or seeing friends,' he said. 'If you are still here on Christmas Eve, you are very welcome to come to dinner with my family.'

'Thanks. You don't think they'd think it was weird?'

'They would not want someone to be away from home at Christmas and have nowhere to go.'

'So it would be weird but they'd do it anyway?'

Brun laughed. 'No one would think you are weird, Fliss.'

She wondered whether Kristin had been to his family for Christmas. Would they think it was strange that Brun was bringing someone they'd probably never even heard him mention before? She wanted to know more about Kristin but on the other hand, it wasn't any of her business. If she and Brun were planning a future together, then that would be different but they couldn't and this extra couple of days didn't change that.

'And who else is there in your family apart from your parents?'

'My grandparents, my mother's parents, my brother and his wife and their children. It will be quite a houseful.'

'It sounds great. We've always had Christmas with just our family since my parents passed away. And the last few years it's just been me and the children until they go to their dad's on Boxing Day.'

'And then it is just you?'

'By then I'm glad of the peace,' she said, smiling. But it had been hard being alone on Boxing Day. She was welcome at Lily and Frank's once they were back from London which was lovely but as a grown-up, it had never been the same as the family Christmases they'd had when she was young and they'd had every single relative possible round at their house. She had always been sad that her children didn't have memories like that. And now they had this horrible disjointed Christmas of two halves, exacerbated this year by her not even being there.

Perhaps Brun picked up on the melancholy feeling that was threatening to overwhelm her because he said, 'These extra days, however many there are, are a Christmas gift to us both.'

Fliss reached for his hand and squeezed it, with tears in her eyes. How was she ever going to say goodbye to him? This stay of execution was a gift, he was right, but it was also delaying the inevitable and the moment when they would part was still lurking at the back of her mind.

'If it wasn't for you, being stuck here would be much worse. And now I know the kids are alright, I'm quite looking forward to it.'

'We had better make it memorable then. Leave me to think about it.'

Fliss wasn't sure what they could do in a snowstorm, apart from hanging out at Brun's house, or with his friends, both of which would be perfectly enjoyable.

The turnout for the book signing was good. Not as frenetic as the night before but a few more people than there had been in Selfoss or Akranes. Everyone was togged up in snow boots and there were lots of Icelandic sweaters on show. They were a mixture of what she assumed were traditional ones in variations of brown and cream, and some that were more vibrant. A woman who was waiting in the queue to see her had a beautiful dark navy blue one with a red, green, pink and cream pattern.

'I love your sweater,' Fliss said.

The woman smiled and flushed with pride. 'Thank you. I knitted it.'

'Oh my goodness, it's beautiful.'

'Do you knit?'

'Not really but I did when I was younger.' She'd had a phase of knitting oversized jumpers when she was a student. They weren't very accomplished and she'd only been able to afford acrylic yarn, but she'd enjoyed the process and had lived in them at the time.

The woman pulled her phone out and tapped for a few seconds. 'Can I airdrop this to you?'

'Yes,' Fliss said, grabbing her phone and hoping she could manage to accept an airdrop without a teenager next to her to advise. 'Thank you,' she said as a PDF of a knitting pattern popped up.

'There is a yarn shop on the road to the cathedral. It will be open today because people knit more when it snows.'

'Thank you so much. I might pop in later.'

'It would be a good souvenir of your trip. Thank you for signing my book.'

'No problem. Thank you for coming, and for the inspiration.'

By the time she'd finished signing, she was inexplicably desperate to buy some yarn.

'Do you know where the wool shop is?' she asked Brun when he came over carrying their huge bundle of outdoor clothes as they got ready to leave.

'I do. Are you asking me to take you there?'

'Yes, please. I can't really explain it, but I need to knit a jumper.'

'You are turning into an Icelander, Fliss. Every Icelander has three sweaters. One that their mother knitted, one from their girlfriend and one that someone left at their house after a party.'

'I've only seen you wearing one.'

'I do have several but my favourite is the one my grandmother made.'

'They must be perfect in this weather. They look so cosy.' Fliss was wondering how long it would take to knit one.

'I think you are going to get on well with my mother and grandmother. If you bring the knitting with you, even better.'

The wool shop was open and since it was lower than ground level, with a couple of steps down from the street, it was like walking through a snowy tunnel to get inside. It turned out that Brun knew the woman in there, Katrin. It also turned out that there were many ready-knitted sweaters for anyone not keen to knit their own. Fliss was torn. The idea of knitting one was appealing but she did want to wear it now.

'How much is the yarn to knit one, Katrin? Brun asked.

'Around six thousand Krona,' she said.

'But that's only about thirty pounds,' Fliss said.

'The cost is in the knitting,' Katrin said, reading Fliss's mind about the price difference between the ready-made and buying the wool to knit one.

Brun began chatting to Katrin in Icelandic while Fliss started to pick out the wool according to the pattern that the woman in the book shop had sent her. The colours available in the knitting yarn were so bright and vibrant compared to the ready-made traditional Icelandic sweaters, but then again, she could wear it now if she bought one of those.

'I think I'm going to buy one to wear now and I'll buy the wool to knit one too.' Why not? She deserved a treat from the royalties and this could be her Christmas present to herself. Why was she justifying it anyway? It wasn't a fortune and the ready-made jumper would be a great souvenir, even if the one she knitted might not be up to actually being worn by anyone.

She put her wool on the counter in a glorious pile of colour, and then began instructing Brun to reach for various sweaters from the high shelves that lined the shop, so that she could try them on. She chose one in a soft grey with the pattern on the yoke and cuffs in darker shades of grey. The yarn itself wasn't as soft as the colour but Katrin assured her that it would soften with wear.

'I'll wear it now,' she said, tucking her own thin wool sweater into the bag with her yarn. 'Can I buy some needles too, please?'

'I think you are going to lose your friend to this sweater,' Katrin said to Brun with a grin.

He laughed. 'I would not try to compete.'

'He can knit, you know,' Katrin said.

Brun sighed and shook his head.

'Why don't you get some yarn and knit one too?'

He said something to Katrin in Icelandic that made her laugh, then leaned close to Fliss and whispered, 'There are other things I would like to do with you than knitting.'

She put her arms around his neck and kissed him. 'We have time to do everything. What else are we going to do in weather like this?'

'You might be surprised,' he said, raising his eyebrows.

Fliss paid, then they gathered up all of their things and pulled on their gloves and hoods ready to go back outside. A couple of other intrepid knitters came in as they were leaving, greeting Katrin and pulling off their coats as if they were planning on staying. It really was more like a village than a capital city in many ways.

The storm had not abated at all while they'd been at the book shop and wool shop and the prospect of the trek back to Brun's was a pretty grim one. He took her bag from her and held her hand, heading down the hill when Fliss was sure that his house was the other way.

'Are we going home?' she shouted into the blizzard.

He shook his head in reply and started down the road. What else was there to do but follow him?

Another few minutes in the snowstorm was all it took for Brun to lead her to their destination. It was a white building that looked like it ought to be a hotel but which had nothing on the outside to suggest that. Brun tapped a code into a number keypad next to the door and pushed it open. They both fell inside, grateful to be out of the wind.   F l i s s unzipped her coat and pulled down her hood to take a better look at where they were. It did look like the foyer of a hotel but it felt strangely empty.

'It is not open yet,' Brun said, without her needing to ask the question. 'It belongs to a friend, he is letting us use it today.'

Fliss wasn't quite sure why they needed a hotel since she had just vacated one and they had all the privacy they needed at Brun's house. But she went along with it.

It was shaping up to be a very nice hotel. The foyer was painted white, with the reception desk in a pale oak. The floor was dark grey flagstones and in the centre there was a pile of black rocks that Fliss recognised as lava from her geography field trip memories, encircled by a low plinth that created a pool around them. It looked as if it might be a water feature eventually. There were a few other things that told her this was still a work in progress, making her even more curious as to why Brun had brought her here.

He led the way to a staircase where they climbed at least four flights, emerging onto a large landing with two doors. The window light above one of them showed that it led to the outside, maybe to a roof terrace. But Brun took her through the other door into a small room clad with smooth wooden planks, like a sauna, with a bench seat running around three walls with cubbies underneath. Hooks were spaced evenly above the seats and there were a few robes hanging on them, with the waist ties coiled around the middle, showing in a universal language that they were freshly laundered. A pile of fresh towels sat in one corner and there was a laundry basket behind the door which had a few discarded robes and towels in it already.

'I'm intrigued,' Fliss said as she watched Brun begin to undress. 'But I didn't bring any swimming things.'

'We're not going swimming and you do not need to wear anything.' He said it as if it were the most obvious thing in the world but Fliss needed more information before she stripped off.

'What if someone else comes?'

'No one else is here, apart from Anders and he knows we are coming, he won't come up here.'

'Okay. So you want me to just… be completely naked?'

'Yes,' he said, laughing at her innate British prudishness.

Still slightly worried that Anders, whoever he was, might walk in on them, Fliss began to undress. By this time Brun was wearing a robe which was far too small for him, had a couple of towels under his arm and his hand on the doorknob.

'There is nothing to worry about,' he said, planting a kiss on her forehead. 'You will love this.'

Fliss tied her robe tightly around her and followed Brun back into the hallway.

He opened the door and the cold hit Fliss straight away. Although, miraculously, the wind was blowing the snow away from the door.

'Quick, or our feet will freeze!' Brun said, pulling the door closed behind them. The floor was wooden, like a deck and where there were a few snowflakes, it wasn't too cold but after a couple of steps, there were more and it was freezing. What was worth this?

Her eyes half-closed against the wind, now that they had left the shelter of the building, she followed him to the left, where there was another door. The warmth hit her as soon as she stepped inside. It was a sauna. The front was glazed, and in clearer weather, Fliss imagined there would be a wonderful view across the rooftops, probably to the sea. Today, it was a whiteout as snow whipped across the rooftop but now that they were inside, she didn't mind that at all.

'Wow, this is amazing. Is it a rooftop spa or something?'

'Something like that. So far there is just the sauna and a hot tub but Anders is planning a bar for the summer months so it will be a cool place to hang out.'

'And he's living here by himself?'

'Yes. He has had some parties up here already.'

'I would too if I lived here. It's amazing. Can you see the sea usually?'

'Yes, and the Harpa. It is pretty at night with the lights.'

The smalltalk was delaying the inevitable unrobing but Fliss was starting to get hot. She looked at Brun and he smirked at her.

'Shall I go first?' he said.

She nodded, feeling ridiculously shy since she had already seen him naked, and he her. But this was literally the cold light of day and felt very different to stripping off in the bedroom where it was darker and they were less inclined to scrutinise each other. Now, she felt every bit as if she were about to get naked with someone she hardly knew.

He took his robe and hung it on a hook near the door before sitting down on the bench seat that faced the window. He leaned across to the opposite corner from the door, reached for a ladle of water from a bucket, and threw it on the sauna coals which made the room fill with steam.

'Now is your chance,' he said.

And Fliss took it. By the time the steam cleared she was sitting on the bench next to Brun, staring out at the snowstorm through the window.

He turned his head to talk to her.

'Don't look at me,' she said. 'Not yet.' She giggled at the ridiculousness of it and this told Brun that she only half meant it.

'Really, Fliss. I have seen it all and even touched most of it. You don't need to hide from me. You are beautiful.'

She didn't feel beautiful, sat there with her thighs spreading across the bench and her boobs sagging down towards her stomach, which was best not mentioned at all.

Without looking at her, Brun ran a finger down the side of her thigh. It wasn't going to take long for him to break her.

'You're going to make me overheat more quickly than the sauna will,' she said.

'Is that a problem?'

'I suppose not, I can always run out into the snowstorm to cool down.'

In the end that was exactly what she had to do. As inviting a prospect as it had seemed after kissing Brun to the point where she thought she might pass out, it was instantly so unpleasantly cold that she had barely opened the door before she changed her mind.

'Put your robe on,' he said, as he stood up. 'If you are getting too hot in here, let's try the hot tub.'

Getting to the hot tub entailed a more lengthy dash

through the snow to the other side of the sauna where it was housed in a three sided gazebo with a roof, giving them some shelter from the storm but also the experience of being more freezing than Fliss could imagine as she took her robe off, to the most blissful feeling of warmth as she sunk her shoulders under the water. The cold air on her face was enough to keep that feeling going as they sat there together, watching the blizzard rage just a metre or so away.

'If the wind was blowing the other way this would be horrible,' Fliss said.

'Yes, I did call Anders when you were signing books to get him to have a look,' Brun said.

'Thank you. Any chance Anders has a room that's made up and ready to go or are we going to have to trek through the snow for me to show you how happy you've made me?'

'Do we have to wait until we're indoors?' He kissed her, slowly, in the exact way that made her care a lot less about needing to be in a bed.

'I can't do it in a hot tub,' she managed to say between kisses. 'It's not a good idea. For a woman.'

'Mmm. In the sauna then?'

What was happening? Was she seriously about to have sex with someone in a sauna on a rooftop in Reykjavik? It seemed so, and she felt powerless to do anything to stop it happening. In fact, she felt very happy to let herself give into this version of herself who was apparently a sex addict who needed to tend to her desires wherever the mood struck her. She wasn't sure if it was because of the way Brun made her feel or whether it was more to do with her new-found freedom but either way, it was something she hoped stayed with her when she finally left Reykjavik.

18

The walk back to Brun's was nowhere near as bad at the walk into town had been that morning. It wasn't that the storm had died down at all, if anything the snow was deeper than ever and more difficult to tramp through, but the wind was at their back so there was no snow flying into their faces and they could attempt conversations with each other. In fact, the wind was so strong that Fliss was forced to break into a run now and again for fear of getting blown over. Brun's house was a very welcome sight indeed.

Once they'd taken their snow-covered outdoor clothes off, they retreated to the bedroom to finish what had been started in the sauna. It had simply been too hot and practicality had won out over desire. But the desire had been bubbling all the way home and Fliss silently thanked the weather gods for making it impossible to leave Iceland because otherwise she'd never have known the heights her feelings for Brun could rise to.

When Duncan had left, sex had been the last thing on her mind. Obviously she had dwelled on the fact that maybe that was why he'd strayed, since their sex life had been lacking somewhat while the kids were growing up. Neither of them could relax knowing that a child could walk through the bedroom door at any time of the day or night and there were precious few times that they found themselves at home alone. It was what happened to all parents, Fliss thought. Their time would come again when the children were older. Of course they never made it that far and then any thoughts about having sex were addled with anxiety around having to be naked around a man who wouldn't be very sympathetic to the fact that pregnancy had ruined her body, because they weren't his children.

None of this mattered to her when she was with Brun. Any hang-ups she had about her body were dismissed purely by the way that his eyes appraised her. She knew he thought she was sexy and even if she didn't agree with him, it was the most empowering thing in the world.

Fliss borrowed one of Brun's sweatshirts and paired it with some leggings that she'd brought with her to wear under her jeans if it was cold. She pulled on some thick woolly socks that she found in his drawer and wandered into the kitchen where he was making some food for them.

A bottle of red wine was open on the table and there were two glasses waiting to be filled.

'What are you cooking?' Fliss asked as she poured wine for each of them and sat down to watch him.

'It is some lamb steaks, vegetables and fries.'

He was cutting potatoes into chips. Homemade fries were quite impressive in Fliss's book.   'Sounds delicious.'

'I checked with Henri when you were in the shower and he says there will be no flights tomorrow.'

'Thanks. The storm is as bad as ever, so that's not a surprise.'

'You haven't had any emails from the airline?'

'I haven't checked.' Fliss went to fetch her phone from her bag. She hadn't looked at it since the book shop. There were a couple of missed calls from Duncan but no other news.

'No, there's nothing new about the flight. I just need to call Duncan.' She walked into the lounge and curled up in one of the chairs, pulling the throw that she'd brought from Snug over herself. She'd put it on the back of the chair when they'd got back from fetching her things from the hotel because it seemed a shame not to use it in its natural habitat.

Duncan picked up straight away.

'I suppose you're caught up in the bloody snow storm in Reykjavik?'

'Yes, my flight's been cancelled,' she said, trying to keep calm even though he wasn't.

'Well, that's perfect, isn't it?' he said with an unpleasant sarcastic tone that Fliss hadn't heard in a while.

'I didn't want to be stuck here and miss Christmas with the children. Now that you've dumped them at Lily's I don't really know why it's an issue for you.'

'Because I can't have them on Boxing Day.'

'Why not?'

'I have plans.'

'Your plan is to have the kids. How is it that you already know this on the twenty-second? Has something come up or was this always your plan, to back out of having them?'

There was a moment of silence.

'Things are different now, Fliss. I can't be dictated to by you any more.'

'It's a long-standing arrangement. We decided that I would have them for Christmas and you'd have them on Boxing Day. We've done this for three years and now suddenly it doesn't suit you anymore?'

She heard an exasperated sigh.

'Look, Duncan. If you don't want to have them, you have to have the decency to explain that to them and to me, ahead of time. I find it hard to believe that with a baby, you are making plans on the fly.' She knew she was right about this.

He was being dictated to by Shona and didn't have the nerve to tell her he couldn't go along with her plans because of his arrangements with his old family.

'We have to stay at Shona's parents because they're having a New Years Eve party for us. It's nothing to do with Shona, she doesn't know yet,' he said sheepishly.

And then Fliss knew, before he'd even started to explain it all to her, that he was going to propose to Shona at Christmas. He'd asked Shona's parents for their blessing, hence the party.

It hurt. Not because he was moving on from her but because he was moving on and didn't want to involve Josh and Emma in any of it.

'Everything alright?' Brun asked, coming into the lounge with his own phone in is hand.

'Duncan's not having the kids now on the twenty-sixth. I have to hope I can get home by then or my sister is going to kill me.'

'There is nothing you can do,' Brun said with a frown. 'He will not change his plans because of that?'

'No. He's doing exactly what he wants regardless of anyone else. But you're right. There's nothing I can do.'

'Ned just called. They're at a loose end and wondering if they can come round tonight? I said that was okay.'

'Of course that's okay.' Fliss liked Anna with her straightforward manner and she knew Brun loved hanging out with Ned.

'I told them to come after dinner since we don't have enough to share,' he said with a grin. 'I also told them to bring more wine.'

Ned and Anna were down in the dumps after their flight to the UK was cancelled too.

'I tried to get us a private jet but that was too late as well,' said Ned.

'I wasn't really interested in that option,' Anna said. 'Why would it be any safer to travel through a storm on a private jet?'

Ned shrugged. 'Sometimes throwing a bit of money at it can get you in there before everything grinds to a halt.'

Fliss marvelled at how much money he must have to be able to do something like that without even having to think about it. She knew he'd been in that boy band but he seemed so normal, it was easy to forget he was a celebrity.

'Anyway, I am first on the list for a private jet as soon as the storm lets up. You're welcome to join us Fliss, if you still want to get back to the UK for Christmas. If we can't leave by Boxing Day I think we'll stick it out and go in the spring because the moment will have passed.'

'I'd love that, thank you. I'm really hoping to get back before Boxing Day.'

'Or her sister will kill her,' Brun added.

'She hates looking after your kids that much?' Anna said.

Fliss laughed. 'God, I hope not. No, she has a romantic getaway with her husband booked and she's already had to change the date because of me.'

'My family is going to go bonkers if I don't finally take Ned home to meet them. We had our first Christmas together here last year and we've both been too busy to visit them since. Also, I just don't think they'll be able to be normal around him. My mum is so weird on FaceTime, isn't she?'

Ned shrugged and smiled. 'It's fine. She doesn't know me yet, it won't be weird like that forever.'

Anna rolled her eyes. 'You don't know my family. They can't stop telling me how they can't understand how I managed to bag you.'

Ned laughed. 'My family say the same about you.'

'Oh, shut up,' Anna said, laughing along with him. 'So you two must be happy to have an extra couple of days together.'

'That we're ruining for you,' Ned said. 'Sorry, we needed some company, we were going stir-crazy in the house by ourselves.'

Brun and Fliss shot each other a knowing look.

'We've been out and about. Fliss had a book-signing this morning.'

This was the catalyst for a very English conversation about how everything in the UK ground to a halt when it snowed. Brun looked on, sipping his wine, grinning at their snow stories.

'Although last year, I did still run an open mic night in the snow in London and it was very successful. Perhaps there's something to be said for soldiering on in adverse weather conditions,' Anna said.

'It depends how adverse the weather is,' Brun said.

'There were at least a couple of inches of snow.'

'I think I am coming to realise that almost doesn't count here,' Fliss said. 'I've never seen snow like there's been today.'

'This is the most it's snowed since I've been almost-living here and if it wasn't for Ned, I would have been gone at the sign of the first flakes,' said Anna. 'I just can't get used to the cold.'

'I bought an Icelandic jumper today,' Fliss said. 'It's made all the difference.'

'Rachel loves an Icelandic jumper. She started knitting when she moved here. I've got a couple of hats but they make my forehead itch like mad.'

'Katrin in the wool shop said they soften up with wear.'

'Oh, god. Are you knitting one as well?'

'Yes, but I haven't started yet.'

'If you get stuck, Rachel will help you. She's evangelical about knitting.'

'Are you guys going over there for *Jolobokaflod* on

Christmas Eve?' Brun asked.

'If it's like last year, yes. If it's seriously reading books all evening, no,' said Ned. 'No offence, Fliss.'

'Writing books doesn't make me the reading monitor,' she said. 'Anyway, my ex-husband's partner does *Jolobokaflod*, which puts me off straight away.'   'I'll support you a hundred percent,' said Ned. 'Me and Fliss are only coming if there's no reading involved.' He held his glass out for Fliss to cheers.

'Just to clarify, I do like reading,' she said, clinking her glass against Ned's.

'We all like reading,' said Anna. 'We just don't want it forced upon us on Christmas Eve when we could be having fun and drinking.'

'So what did you do last year that was so much fun?' Fliss asked.

'Mmm, mainly drinking,' said Anna.

'And Brun sang a very funny song in Icelandic about the Yule Lads,' Ned said.

'Was it funny?' Brun said.

'We laughed a lot,' Anna said. 'But it might have been Jonas trying to simultaneously translate the lyrics that made it funny.'

'The Yule Lads are no laughing matter,' Brun said, and then proceeded to explain to Fliss the Icelandic tradition which happened in the run up to Christmas.

'You could be on your own, Brun, if we get a flight out before that,' said Ned. 'In fact we were going to suggest getting Rachel, Jonas, Olafur and Gudrun over here for breakfast in the morning. The forecast says the storm won't have cleared tomorrow. What are you guys doing?'

'Nothing planned,' said Brun 'Breakfast sounds good. Are you thinking about going to the bakery?'

'I'm guessing you haven't had chance to introduce Fliss to

the cinnamon buns yet?'

'That is true,' Brun said with a grin. 'We must go to the bakery, then.'

Later that night, they lay in bed beside each other, holding hands.

'Thanks for today. I think it's been my favourite Iceland day so far.'

'And we would not have had this day if it wasn't for the storm.'

The wine and the darkness made it easy for Fliss to say, 'I don't know how I'm going to leave you.'

'Today has made things harder.'

'Every minute we spend together makes it harder but at the same time, I want every minute I can get with you.'

'And it's okay if lots of the minutes are with my friends?'

'I love your friends.'

He squeezed her hand. 'Rachel especially will love you when she finds out you are going to knit.'

'Isn't it weird how I never had any inclination to knit until today? There's a really good yarn shop in Oxford that I went to with a colleague one lunchtime and even that didn't tempt me like it has here. And I have to say, the yarn at home is softer.'

She heard Brun exhale with a laugh. 'I think Iceland has you in the grip of its magical forces.'

'That's what happened to Rachel and Anna.'

'Yes, but it was different for them. They didn't have lives to leave behind like you do.' He paused. 'We will keep in touch though.'

The answer to that wasn't straightforward. In the long-run, surely it was best to keep the memories, as they'd said before. Not run the risk of their relationship gently diminishing with every missed phone call, every unanswered text message, until they just didn't feel the same way anymore and had to conclude that it had been nothing more than a holiday romance that should have ended at the end of the holiday. It would be hard to call it a day whenever Ned got the call for the plane or whenever Fliss managed to get a seat on a regular flight. But that was what they'd been going to do before the storm.

Now, lying in Brun's bed, feeling him next to her, Fliss couldn't imagine the idea of this never happening again.

19

As Ned had predicted, the storm showed no signs of abating by the following morning but Fliss had been prepared for that and it was nice to wake up knowing that they had the day together.

'We don't have to go for breakfast if you would rather stay in bed,' said Brun, lazily.

That was a tempting prospect. The idea of leaving the cosy warmth of the house, let alone the bed, seemed less attractive than it had done last night. 'No, we should. If Jonas and Rachel are walking all the way from their house, we can make the effort.'

'Can we? I am not so sure.'

Brun turned onto his stomach, pinning Fliss into the bed by slinging his arm over her. He buried his face into her neck and pretended to munch her. His beard tickled and made her giggle. She threw her leg across him and turned him onto his back, gaining the upper hand. He was playing along, otherwise she'd never have managed that and it was another half an hour before either of them mentioned getting up again.

'We're going to be late,' Fliss said, her usual anxiety about being punctual and not letting anyone down outweighing the temptation to stay in bed any longer.

'Ned and Anna are always late. We will still be there before them.'

The bakery wasn't far from Brun's house and even with the wind and snow, the smell of freshly baked pastries was wafting out into the street. If there was a good reason to have left the house, Fliss's stomach rumbled in agreement that this was it. They were indeed there before Ned and Anna but Rachel and Jonas were already sat at a table with coffee and pastries in front of them.

'Sorry, we couldn't wait, we were starving,' Rachel said.

'I'm not surprised after that walk,' said Fliss. 'We walked into town yesterday to the *Iða Zimsen* bookshop and that was exhausting enough.'

Brun offered to order the coffee and cinnamon buns that they had decided on while Fliss sat and chatted.

'So Anna told me that you went to the wool shop yesterday,' Rachel said. ' Have you cast on yet?'

'Not yet. I can't quite remember how so I was going to watch a YouTube video but haven't had chance.'

'I could get you started later, if you like?'

'Fliss and Brun might have plans today,' Jonas said, which gave her an out if she wanted it.

'You should do the knitting if you want to,' Brun said, hearing the tail end of the conversation as he came back to the table. 'We have all day.' He reached for her hand and gave it a gentle squeeze.

'I would like to start it off while I'm still here,' Fliss said. 'Perhaps you could come back with us after this?'

'I'd love that,' said Rachel, beaming. 'I've tried to get Anna interested but she just bangs on about how the wool is too itchy, which is missing the point really.'

'Oh, god. Are you talking about knitting?'

Anna and Ned came into the shop bringing a blast of cold

air with them that seemed to linger around them as they took their coats off.

'We're going to start off Fliss's knitting after breakfast,' said Rachel.

'I'll come,' Anna said, sitting down while Ned went over to the counter to order for them, testing out his Icelandic at the same time, it sounded like to Fliss.

Rachel rolled her eyes, presumably because she knew Anna wasn't interested in knitting.

'It's so boring when it snows like this, what else is there to do?'

The men decided to head to their favourite bar for a festive post-breakfast pint and to give the knitters a bit of space since Brun's house wasn't huge.

'See?' Rachel patiently demonstrated the casting-on to Fliss.

It looked straightforward enough but when she took the needles for herself, she wasn't sure she had enough hands to do what Rachel had shown her.

'That's it, you're getting it.'

'Are you, Fliss?'

'Anna! Be encouraging.'

'Sorry. It looks great. Seriously, I love the colours you've picked.'

'Thanks. I've copied one that I saw yesterday.'

It was hard to believe that it was only yesterday when she'd done her last book tour appearance. Such a lot had happened since then but she had to admit, she felt an enormous weight had lifted off her since she'd left *Iða Zimsen*. Not because she hadn't enjoyed it but because that was the end of any obligations she had to anyone but herself for the next few days. In fact, she couldn't remember the last time that had happened. Even when the children were with Duncan, she always had a nagging feeling of anxiety and there were always things to be doing when she was at home.

'How does it feel now that the book tour's over? Will you be able to go back to your normal life now you've had a taste of stardom?' Anna asked.

'It's been amazing. It does feel like I've taken over someone else's life for a few days. I'm sure it'll all be forgotten the minute I get home.'

'All of it?' Anna asked quietly, with a pointed look.

There was no reason to be anything except honest. 'No, not all of it. I don't think I'll be able to forget Brun.'

'I knew it!' said Anna. 'So you've talked about seeing each other after you leave?'

'We haven't discussed details, how it would work or anything but I don't think either of us want it to be over when I go home.'

'It doesn't have to be, does it? It feels like more than a holiday romance to me, Fliss. It's like you've always been part of the gang,' said Anna.

'Thanks, I feel the same way. I have the kids to think about though, and that makes things more complicated. If it was just me, I'd carry on and see how things went.'

'You'd move to Iceland, wouldn't you?' Anna pressed.

'I do love it here, but that's a huge step. Even without the children, I have other things I would find hard to leave behind. Like my sister, my house, Waitrose.'

They both laughed.

'Oh, god. I miss Waitrose,' Rachel said. 'There was one on my way home from work in London. It was so easy to pop in and buy dinner. But then I wasn't living with someone who worried that much about what they ate. Jonas likes to cook from scratch.'

Fliss handed her knitting to Rachel for her to check. 'That looks great, keep going.'

'So what's the answer for me and Brun, if you had to

decide how it was going to work out for us?'

'Oooh, this is the kind of conversation I came for,' Anna said. 'I think the only answer is to break things off, in the nicest way possible, when you leave. Don't make any plans, just see how things go.'

'Why wouldn't you carry things on if you felt like that about each other?' Rachel said. 'I'm only saying this because Jonas and I decided we weren't going to carry things on after I left and just the thought of that made us both miserable.'

'You have to be so committed to make long-distance work. You'll automatically expect each other to use any holidays to visit each other and it just ends up being a drag. Takes the romance out of it,' said Anna.

'See? There is no good answer,' Fliss said.

'Basically it depends on whether you think he's the one because then you do whatever it takes to be together,' Rachel said with a romantic look in her eyes.

'Well, not *anything* to be together,' Anna said. 'She can hardly haul her kids to Iceland or just rock up back at home with Brun in tow. It's tricky.'

Fliss had been carefully counting her stitches throughout this last exchange. 'I'm there.'

'Right, so now you need to start doing one stitch knit, one stitch purl,' explained Rachel.

'Oh, okay. I can remember how to do that.'

'Is Brun anything like your ex-husband?' Anna asked.

'No similarities whatsoever,' Fliss said, laughing. 'Doesn't look like him or behave like him. Even before the divorce, I don't think Duncan ever saw me in the way that Brun does. He's been there for all the events I've done here and he looks at me like he's proud, or something. And that makes me feel really special. No one at home respects my writing career like everyone here does.' Fliss squirmed slightly at hearing herself refer to it as a writing career but that's what it was and she was starting to get used to thinking of it like that, rather than as a hobby that no one took seriously.

'I've seen him, Fliss,' Rachel said. 'You're exactly right about how he looks at you. He never looked at Kristin like that. And she never really hung out with us like you have. It's altogether different.'

'I don't want to break his heart by promising him anything when I don't know what's going to happen.'

'Your heart's involved too,' Rachel pointed out. 'You're not the one who has to decide all of this for Brun's benefit. There might be other options if you talk to him. He might want to live in England.'

Anna raised her eyebrows but said nothing.

'Did you ever think Jonas might leave Iceland?'

'Well, no. He did offer but I couldn't imagine him in London and I loved it here straight away. Also, by the time we knew how we felt about each other I didn't have much to go back for.'

'I can't see Brun in Oxford with me. This place is part of him, the same as it is with Jonas. What's he going to do in Oxford?'

'It's a good point. But it's up to him. Don't assume he wouldn't want to. He might have secret desires to become an academic or something,' Anna said.

Talking things through was quite helpful and made Fliss realise how much she'd been mulling over all of the possible options without discussing it with Brun. Talking to him about it meant putting herself out there. Admitting that she thought things were serious enough that they needed a plan for the future. But sitting down and discussing it might take the magic away. They'd been swept along by their feelings for each other, able to leave any thoughts of practicality to one side, as if it was just a holiday romance. But if it wasn't that, if it was something else, then they needed to give it a chance and they could only do that by having a proper discussion.

'That's looking really good,' Rachel said, inspecting Fliss's stitches.

'Thanks. I might have a jumper in about five years.'

'You'll speed up in no time. I knitted my first jumper in the couple of months after I moved here because I had nothing to do and Jonas was really busy with work. It kept me going, having a focus like that.'

'I might have to commit to making sure I knit an inch a day otherwise it'll never grow,' Fliss said. 'Perhaps I could take it to work and knit in my lunch hour.'

'What is it with you two and the knitting? I really don't get it,' Anna said, looking genuinely bewildered.

The front door burst open, signalling the return of Brun, Ned and Jonas and once they'd taken their boots and coats off, the lounge was suddenly full of people.

'Ready to go, Rachel? We have to start on the food for tomorrow.'

Rachel rolled her eyes at Fliss and Anna. 'We're going to Jonas's parents for lunch tomorrow and I have to take a traditional English dish. The pressure.'

'What are you taking?'

'Roast potatoes and parsnips.'

'That is literally the easiest thing you could have picked. I don't know why you're worried,' Anna said. 'Even I could make that.'

Ned solemnly shook his head behind her back, making everyone laugh.

'Oh, shut up, Ned!' she said, getting up and throwing her arms around him.

'Come on, let's leave these good people to it,' he said. 'I'll text if I hear anything about the plane.'

'Thank you. I'm torn between hoping for a flight tomorrow and not wanting to miss tomorrow night,' Fliss said.

They all said their goodbyes, Fliss conscious that it could be the last time she saw Rachel and Jonas but not wanting to make a big thing of it.

'Ah, you started the knitting,' said Brun, picking it up to have a closer look. 'It is very even.'

'Thank you. I think I've got it out of my system for now.'

'Good because we need to make the most of today.'

He took her hand and pulled her up and into his arms. His face was cold against hers and she could smell the outdoors on him. The conversation could wait. At the moment, there were more important things to do.

20

Brun was finding it increasingly difficult to hide his pleasure at the fact that the airport was still closed. He knew Fliss was desperate to get home for Christmas, and he completely understood. Her children were everything to her, and if there was anything he could have done to get her home, he would have done it. But these extra days with her were one of the best things that had ever happened to him.

He was deliberately not thinking about how heartbreaking it would be when she left. If anything, these days of waiting for the storm to abate had made that prospect much harder to consider than it had been before. As yet, neither of them had broached the subject of what would happen between them, how they might navigate a relationship or whether that was even possible. Brun wasn't sure that he could let Fliss leave without some idea of what to expect. If this was to be all that they had, he would have to deal with it but he needed to know that when she left, however hard. He hadn't forgotten his pledge to himself a few days ago that she ought to be the one to call the shots.

Right now, she was sat in his lounge, knitting. Very slowly. She seemed so at home here, it was hard to remember that she had only been there a couple of days and he knew that the void she'd leave would be far worse to bear than when Kristin had left.

He shook his head, to dislodge thoughts of how it was all going to end. It was important to concentrate on the fact that they were together now. He was making tea for them both when his phone rang. It was his mum.

'Hi Mamma.'

'You cannot leave a message with your father to say you are bringing a friend to lunch. I need the details. Who is it?'

He smiled to himself. His mum loved to know everything.

'She is an English author and she is stuck here because the airport is closed.

'And you have taken her under your wing?'

'Yes, I was driving her around, so now she is stuck here I am still looking after her.'

'And she managed to get a hotel booking? The hotels are full of tourists who can't get home.'

He sighed. His mother knew exactly what she was doing.

'She is staying with me, Mamma. We are friends now.'

He could almost hear the smile through the phone. He knew his mother had been worried about him after Kristin left so the very first sign of a new girlfriend was bound to elicit this strange mix of over-interest and glee.

'Will she eat the lamb?'

'Yes, of course.' He said it not knowing whether Fliss would eat the traditional smoked lamb that would be served tomorrow but sure that his mother would be too busy feeding the other nine people to notice if she didn't.

'Make sure to come well before we eat so that I can meet her properly.'

'Mamma, she lives in England. You'll probably never meet her again. I might not ever see her again.'

'Brun. If you like someone enough to bring them with you tomorrow, I know we will see them again.'

He could understand how she might think that because Kristin had never been for the Christmas Eve meal to his family. She had never wanted to. That seemed like an obvious sign of incompatibility now that he thought about it. But equally, he didn't want his mother getting attached to the idea of Fliss being anything other than a one-off visitor because of a Christmas storm.

'Okay, Mamma. We will see you bright and early tomorrow.'

'Was that your mum?' Fliss asked, wandering into the kitchen and taking over the tea-making. Brun loved that she felt so at home.

'Yes, she was just checking whether you're a vegetarian.'

'Are you sure it's okay for me to come?'

He took her in his arms, loving the way she nestled her head into the top of his chest, fitting perfectly into his embrace. 'Of course. They are all looking forward to meeting you.'

She groaned into his sweater. 'I'm scared. Do they know we've kissed?'

'Do you think that is all we have done?' he said with feigned shock.

'Seriously, what are they going to think? We've only known each other a few days.'

'Fliss, please don't worry about anything like that. They will not be thinking anything. I have not told them anything.'

It was a small white lie but in his defence, his mother had guessed.

21

Although she hadn't heard from Ned about a flight home, Fliss checked the airline's website anyway, just in case, but nothing new had happened. Brun was outside clearing snow from the path again in preparation for their trek to his parents' house which was closer to where Rachel and Jonas lived.

She was sat in one of the chairs in the lounge, her cosy blanket wrapped around her, with a cup of coffee and nothing to do. If she was at home now, her Christmas Eve would be nowhere near as relaxing as this. She'd be heading to Waitrose with the rest of Oxford to collect her turkey crown, hoping that there were some pigs in blankets left in stock because every year she promised herself that next year she'd buy them in advance and freeze them, and she always forgot. She'd gifted her turkey crown to Lily who hadn't done any Christmas food shopping, and invited her to raid the house for all the bits and pieces of food that she had bought in advance, like Twiglets, Cheeselets, nuts and an assortment of biscuits for cheese. She'd had to tip Lily off about the cunning hiding places she used so that the kids didn't find it and snaffle it all before Christmas Day.

Her phone rang with a FaceTime call from Emma.

'Hi Mum, Happy Christmas Eve!'

She sounded in good spirits which made Fliss happy, and grateful to Lily and Frank.

'Happy Christmas Eve, Em. What have you been up to?'

'Auntie Lily got tickets from her work and they took us to the Winter Wonderland in Hyde Park last night! We went on the train and had such a good time. Uncle Frank went on all the rides with us and we went ice skating and had hot chocolate with massive marshmallows.'

Her sister had really hit the nail on the head with that, something that Josh and Emma would love. Fliss had always said no because it was so expensive and crowded.

'Wow, that sounds amazing! Was it all Christmassy and magical?'

'I suppose so,' Emma said with a shrug. 'Anyway, Josh saw a girl from his school and they went on the Ferris wheel together.'

'Shut up, Emma,' Josh said from out of the camera's view.

'That's nice, Josh.' Fliss said, beginning to feel like she was missing out.

'How about you, Mum? What have you been doing?'

'I went out for breakfast yesterday and then started knitting a jumper and today I'm going for Christmas lunch and then to a *Jolobokaflod* thing with some friends.'

'You're knitting a jumper? That's so random.'

'Well, I suppose it is.' She hadn't knitted for years so it was bound to be a surprise. 'It's navy blue with a coloured yoke.'

'That sounds nice. Is it still stormy there?'

'Not so bad today,' Fliss said, looking out of the window. 'It's still snowing but the wind has died down. Are you two doing anything today? If I ping you some money will you have time to walk to the shops and buy something nice for Auntie Lil and Uncle Frank?'

'Okay. What like?'

'You could perhaps get a big box of chocolates from Hotel Chocolat?' Fliss suggested, feeling like it was a boring suggestion but the best she could come up with since they couldn't buy alcohol.

'What about if we get them one of those hot chocolate makers?' Emma said, enthusiastically, obviously hoping that it would be of benefit to her as well.

'If you like. I'll leave it to you two.'

'Okay,' Emma said with a huge grin on her face, presumably imagining the endless hot chocolates she'd be getting Lily to make her.

'And you're both okay?'

Josh popped his head into view. 'We're fine, Mum. Miss you though.'

'I miss you too, Joshy. Hopefully only a couple more days and I'll be home. I'll ring you in the morning. Love you both.'

'Bye Mum, love you,' they said together, Emma waving as well.

She hung up and texted her sister to say thank you.

'We will need to go soon,' Brun said as he came back inside, reminding Fliss's stomach to turn back into a ball of anxiety at the thought of going to meet his family when she'd just managed to forget about it for a few minutes.

'Okay, I'll get dressed.'

Her nerves had begun the previous afternoon after Brun had had a lengthy phone conversation with his mother in Icelandic about what Fliss would eat or not eat. With his mother going to so much trouble to make sure she was happy, she suddenly realised that she ought to take a gift. She'd announced to Brun that she was going shopping and fought her way through the snow back into town. She headed to Snug, where she bought a beautiful candle and some of the biscuits that she'd bought before. She also picked something out for Brun which she hoped would remind him of her after she left. Then she carried on to the nearest bookshop which happened to be the one where they'd had the dancing after her book signing, and spent a very pleasant hour choosing books for Brun's friends just in case the *Jolobokaflod* evening ended up being more traditional than they'd made out it would be.

'Are we going straight to Rachel and Jonas's when we leave your parents' place?'

'Yes, they are not far from each other.'

She wore the dress again since it was the only one she'd brought with her, but she wore a cropped round-necked jumper over the top which made it look less like a party dress, and was also cosier. She pulled a pair of socks on over her tights. Not the sexiest look but she'd have to wear snow boots to walk over there. The gifts and books were packed into a rucksack that she'd borrowed from Brun and when they were ready to go, he added a couple of bottles of wine and a few bottles of beer to the bag and then insisted on carrying it.

It reminded Fliss of a holiday when she and Duncan had cycled along the Loire valley in France. He'd insisted that they take turns carrying the tent, even though he had panniers on his bike and she had everything in a rucksack. He had sailed along quite happily with nothing to encumber him while she had her rucksack with the tent strapped to the top, and a much ropier bike than him. Why hadn't she thought anything of that at the time? It had definitely been a sign of things to come. But Duncan was nowhere near as strong or tough as Brun. He'd have as much trouble carrying that rucksack with the books and booze in it as she would.

The lunch with Brun's family was wonderful. They made her so welcome and she felt at home straight away. The glass of wine she almost downed as soon as it was poured for her when they arrived probably helped, but she thoroughly enjoyed herself.

Thankfully, aside from his grandparents, everyone spoke very good English, even Brun's two nephews who Fliss guessed were around ten and twelve, and no one minded having to make the effort to speak it all the time just for her. The only exception was when they spoke in Icelandic to explain English words that the boys didn't know, but there weren't many of those. His grandparents said very little but his grandmother sat listening with great interest as she knitted, barely looking at what she was doing which Fliss found mesmerising to watch. She would have loved to talk to her about it but felt too shy and worried about the language barrier.

The meal was along the lines of an English Christmas dinner but with a ham, and smoked lamb as the centrepiece instead of turkey. Brun's mother had made three different kinds of potato and there were a variety of vegetables including cabbage, peas and beans. They also had the most delicious gravy. Fliss and Brun sat along one side of the table with his grandparents, and his brother, sister-in-law and the nephews were opposite, with his parents at either end. As soon as they had finished their meal, the boys were excused and allowed to go and play while the grown-ups sat and chatted over more wine.

Brun's brother, Sven, worked for the Bank of Iceland and the difference in their jobs wasn't the only thing that set them apart. His brother was slighter, whereas Brun took after their father, even down to the facial hair. Fliss could tell that Sven was serious about almost everything, nothing like his brother who was easy-going and relaxed.

'Brun says you have had a very successful trip,' Sven said.

'Yes, it's been amazing. I don't even mind being stuck here over Christmas.' She flicked her gaze to Brun who was smiling at her.

'Do you think you will visit again? Perhaps for more inspiration for your books?'

'I hope so,' Fliss said, feeling that Sven was moving from chatting to interrogation quite quickly. 'Have you ever been to England?' She addressed the question to the whole table but it was Sven who answered.

'I often go to London for work. We take the boys if it is in the school holidays. Do you live in London?'

'Oxford. So not far away.'

'Oxford is beautiful,' Olga, said. 'We took the boys to the Natural History Museum. I think we enjoyed it as much as they did.'

'It's amazing, isn't it? Did you find the dodo? My children loved that.'

'Yes! The boys were more excited about the dinosaurs though. You must go, Brun.'

Brun looked at Fliss and raised his eyebrows. 'Perhaps I will.'

She grinned. She'd love to show him around Oxford. Whatever happened between them, hopefully she could do that one day.

'Are you all doing *Jolobokaflod* today?' she asked.

Brun's mother nodded. 'When Sven and Brun were small we used to meet with the rest of the family at their grandparents' house and spend the afternoon and evening reading. There were a few years when they started going out with their friends instead and it was my parents and me and Thor. But now Sven and Olga bring the boys and we will read with them later.'

'They will only manage an hour or so,' said Olga. 'Are you going to Jonas's?'

'Yes. Although there is never any reading,' Brun said.

'I might start having a reading hour at home with my kids if I can pin them down. I love the thought of sitting by the fire with a cup of hot chocolate, reading together.'

'That is what it will be like here,' Olga said. 'You are welcome to stay if you want the authentic experience and not just an evening of drinking.' She was teasing Brun, and Fliss could see the affection she had for her brother-in-law.

'Thank you but I'm hoping to catch a flight home with Ned and Anna so I probably need to be wherever they are now that the storm has died down.'

After another hour or so, Brun announced that they ought to think about leaving. Fliss offered to help tidy up but Brun's mother wouldn't hear of it and Olga insisted that Sven and his father would be doing it.

'Thank you so much for inviting me. It's been lovely to meet you all.'

Brun's mother hugged her and whispered in Fliss's ear, 'My boy is very fond of you.'

Fliss gave a small nod and what she hoped was a reassuring smile. It could have sounded like a warning but Fliss didn't take it like that and she didn't think Brun's mother had intended it to be.

They pulled on their outdoor clothes while Olga called the boys into the hallway to say goodbye.

'What did Olga say to you?' Fliss asked Brun once they'd left.

'She told me she liked you.'

'Is that all?' It had been more than a couple of words of Icelandic that Fliss had overheard while she'd been thanking Brun's parents.

'That is the gist of it,' he said grinning. 'I can't tell you exactly because it does not come out very well for me.'

She looked at him, wordlessly enquiring, until he caved in.

'She said I would be an idiot if I let you go.'

'I can't disagree with her.' She hoped her light-hearted tone would mean they could save this discussion for later. There wasn't time to get into it all now, even though she knew it was a conversation they needed to have before she left.

'Neither can I,' Brun said, squeezing her hand.

22

The evening at Rachel and Jonas's was nothing like Fliss was expecting from *Jolobokaflod* but it did run along the lines of how they had all described the previous year to her. It may not have been the authentic experience, given that once they had exchanged their books, they were cast aside in favour of beer, wine, chatting and eventually singing and guitar playing from Ned and Brun, but the atmosphere was definitely festive.

'There are more English people here tonight than Icelanders,' Anna pointed out. 'Why are we even doing *Jolobokaflod*? We should be doing English Christmas things.'

'What would you normally do on Christmas Eve?' Rachel asked her.

Anna shrugged. 'I don't know. Depends.'

'The year before last, for example,' Rachel said. 'Before you met Ned.'

'I had a VIP pass to a corporate do at the Harry Potter studios where they'd recreated the Yule Ball from one of the films.'

'Oh my god,' Fliss said. 'I spend every Christmas Eve prepping the food for the next day and then watching films until the kids go to sleep and I can sneak in and fill their stockings. Last year I had to stay up until two in the morning because Josh had been round to a friend's. If I had to stay up until two in the morning, I'd rather it had been for a party.'

'It's only because she used to work in PR. I used to stay in and watch Christmas films too,' said Rachel.

'Me too,' said Ned.

Anna snorted. 'Really? An international pop star stays in on Christmas Eve and watches films?'

Ned tipped his head to one side. 'Okay, not every year.'

'Year before last?' Rachel asked him.

He grimaced which made them realise it was going to be something juicy. 'I was at a party.'

'Whose party?' Rachel looked like she was going to burst with excitement.

'Excuse her,' Anna said to Fliss. 'She's obsessed with celebrities, even though she can see from Ned that it's all smoke and mirrors.'

'Thanks, my love,' he said. 'I'm glad I've got you to keep me grounded. It was the Kardashian Jenner party.'

'What? The actual Kardashians?' Rachel was wide-eyed.

Ned nodded. 'It's not like I know them very well. They just invite the people of the moment.'

'Knowing them not very well isn't not knowing them,' said Rachel. 'I can't believe I've known you for a year and you've never mentioned that before.'

'And you didn't see it in Hey! Magazine, Rach?' Anna asked, winking at Fliss.

'I can't afford to buy it every week, you know that. It's imported, Fliss, so it costs a fortune.'

'Come on Brun,' Ned said. 'Let's diffuse the situation with some music.'

'Can I come with you if you get invited again?' Rachel asked Ned.

'Sure. I won't, but yes. I'm sure Anna would be glad to

offer you her place.'

'Normally I would, but it is the Jenners.' Anna gave Rachel a sympathetic look.

'Anna, stop teasing your friend. Trust me, Rachel, since I left the band, those kind of invitations have dried up.'

Ned and Brun got their guitars out and began strumming, seeming so tuned into each other that they needed no discussion as to what they were playing, one of them joining in with the other after a couple of chords. After a couple of Christmas songs that everyone joined in with, Fliss begged them to play the song from the open mic night that was in English and Icelandic.

Jonas nodded. 'That is one of the best songs I have ever heard at the open mic night.'

Brun looked at Fliss the entire time they played, just as he had in the bar that night and afterwards when Rachel and Jonas went into the kitchen to organise more drinks, he took her hand and led her outside.

Jonas and Rachel had a back porch which was a decked area covered with a roof, so it was largely free of snow, and had a wooden swing suspended on chains from the roof. A brazier was laid with wood and Brun went back into the kitchen to get some matches and then lit it. It sprang into life, quickly warming them against the cold of the night.

'Won't they mind that we've lit it?' Fliss asked.

Brun shook his head. 'I expect they will all be out here later with their hot chocolate watching for the Northern Lights, even though it is too cloudy.'

'I love that song, Brun.'

'I will only sing it for you, whatever happens.'

'I feel as if we should make a plan about what happens next. I know when I should have left the other day, we had decided not to wait for each other but I can't just leave you behind.'

'I meant what I said. I will wait for as long as it takes.'

These three stolen days together had given her an insight into what life would be like with him and she wouldn't have had that if not for the storm.

'Practically speaking, if we did want to carry on seeing each other, when could that be? I don't get any time off now until Easter and both of the children have exams this summer so I can't bring them here on holiday or anything like that for ages.'

This was what they'd be up against. This week together was never going to be repeated because her normal life was full of immoveable commitments. A book tour was an extraordinary thing that might never be repeated.

'I could come to you. Stay somewhere close by and we could see each other. I am not so busy with work in the winter. February would be a good time for a visit, if you wanted that.'

'I do want that, more than anything. I don't know what's stopping me from saying yes.'

'Because it is saying yes not to a visit in February but to a relationship that maybe you are not ready for.'

Was that it? She hadn't considered a relationship as part of her future but not because she wasn't ready. It was because she didn't have the time and energy. Wasn't it? And who had the time and energy for a long-distance relationship apart from people who were much younger with no baggage and no experience of how heart-breaking it could be to have to end a relationship that wasn't working. And Fliss knew they both had experience of that.

'I didn't come to Iceland expecting this. Even if you lived in Oxford, I might have the same doubts.'

'I don't have any doubts about how I feel about you. Is that what you are worried about?' The light from the fire flickered on his face and Fliss could see the depth of his feelings right there in his eyes.

'No, I've never been more sure about how I feel. I'm falling in love with you. Any doubts I have are nothing to do with how I feel.'

He pulled her towards him. 'We have to see what happens, Fliss. No promises, but we have to give ourselves the chance to love each other. I believe love like this is a rare thing.'

Fliss thought her heart would melt and suddenly she knew what to say.

'It is rare, and we shouldn't let it pass us by just because it's bad timing. Let's plan the next time we'll see each other. How about we aim for every couple of months, and never say goodbye without knowing when the next time will be.'

'That sounds perfect.' He pulled her closer and they sat watching the fire together. It wasn't long before the door opened and everyone else came outside. Rachel was carrying a tray of hot chocolates and Jonas had a huge pile of blankets, which Fliss was grateful for since there was only so much the fire could do against the December cold.

As they sat on the deck, chatting, throwing logs on the fire, and eventually toasting marshmallows on very pretty metal skewers that Rachel had got from Snug, Fliss found herself wondering whether this group of people could actually become part of her life. Brun was so interconnected with them that it wasn't hard to imagine how it could be if she and Brun were together all the time. It was easier to imagine that than it was to imagine him in Oxford. She could picture her kids in both places but at the age they were, she could never contemplate moving them to another country and as flakey as Duncan was, it wasn't fair to take them away from him.

At the back of her mind, she was also wondering how she was going to afford possibly three trips a year to Iceland. Even with more royalties than she'd expected, she still only had two books out and there were only so many people in

Iceland to buy them; she was hardly a global sensation. Although she knew next to nothing about Brun's finances, she didn't think being a tour guide was a career that could finance that amount of travel. Was it crazy to be worrying about all of this when the fact remained that they were planning on starting a relationship based on a week of knowing each other?

Later, after they'd said good night to Ned and Anna, once the four of them had walked back from Jonas and Rachel's, they were lying in bed, facing each other.

'How about we take a breath once I go home?'

Brun's face fell. Fliss reached out and laid her hand gently on his cheek.

'To see how we feel once we're apart. I'm expecting to miss you like mad. I hate the thought of not waking up next to you even though I've only done it three times but if we're going to do this, I need to be sure that I can't live without you. That's what I feel like now, when we're lying here like this. I feel like my heart might break when I leave you. But when I get back to Oxford, I might go back to being the Fliss I was before I came here and I don't know how these feelings fit into that life.'

'I see that,' he said, taking her hand and holding it to his lips. 'I want to be sure that this is what you want and I know that you have more at stake than I do. I understand.'

'Can we do a couple of weeks? Is that okay? And then after that we'll make plans to meet in February if we still feel the same.'

'Two weeks? I can do that. It is a drop in the ocean compared to the rest of our lives.'

They fell asleep in each other's arms until Fliss's phone pinged at five o'clock the next morning.

'Sorry,' she mumbled as she reached for it. 'The kids must have got up early.'

It wasn't the children, it was Ned. He had a flight home but they had to be at Reykjavik City airport within the hour.

'You're leaving now?' Brun said, rubbing his eyes as he sat up in bed.

Fliss had sprung to life the moment she had put the phone down, excited about the fact that she might make it home for Christmas after all. Yes, it was bittersweet to be leaving Brun but she had never been away from her children for this long. Now that she knew she would be on her way, it felt safe to allow herself to break the protective coating she'd built around the whole idea of missing Christmas.

'Yes, Ned's booked a plane that needs to go to London to pick someone up from there so we have to go now. He has a car coming to collect us in ten minutes.'

'It's great that you will be with your family today.' He pulled some clothes on and began helping her to collect her things together.

'What will you do?'

He shrugged, 'I will probably meet up with Siggi and go to the bar. Maybe see my parents and everyone again before my brother leaves. Don't forget your knitting.'

It was the only thing she hadn't packed. Fliss grinned and took it from him. 'Thanks. I've had the best time with you,' she said softly.

He took her in his arms. He smelled of sleep and warmth and Fliss couldn't believe it was time to leave. These were the last moments they would share together for a while.

'Until next time,' he whispered into her hair.

'I love you, Brun. Whatever happens, that will always be true.'

'*Þú ert mér allt.*'

Fliss didn't need a translation to know what he meant.

He pulled on his coat and boots as she pulled her own on. 'I'll help carry your things to the car.'

They left the house in silence. There was nothing else to say for now, and when they reached the car he helped put her things in the boot, embraced her hard and then turned without looking back.

She couldn't watch him walk away, and climbed into the back of the car, hoping she would be able to hold the tears back in front of Ned and Anna.

'Merry Christmas!' Anna said, getting in next to her while Ned sat in the front next to the driver.

'Merry Christmas,' Fliss said with as much cheer as she could muster, which wasn't much.

Anna squeezed her hand. 'He'll wait for you, you know.'

Fliss gulped down a sob. 'I know,' she managed to say.

'It'll be okay. Concentrate on what you're going home to,' she said quietly. 'Put this week in a little box that you can open occasionally when you want to be reminded that someone loves you but don't let it weigh you down. Dwelling on it will make you sad and you don't want that when you already have so much going on in your life.'

It was the voice of experience. Fliss had gleaned from the past week or so that it hadn't been plain sailing for Anna and Ned in the beginning and that they had been apart for a while. She could take comfort in Anna's words. It was good advice because she didn't have the luxury of time to wallow in her lost love. She was going home to be with her children and for the moment, this week needed to be nothing more than a wonderful memory.

23

Fliss couldn't help but enjoy the flight home. After a quick drive across town to Reykjavik City Airport, they boarded the tiniest but most luxurious plane for the flight to London. Despite it being early in the morning, they were offered champagne by their flight attendant and since it was Christmas Day, they all accepted.

'I've booked a car to take you to Oxford,' said Ned. 'And don't say anything except thank you because how else are you going to get home on Christmas Day.'

'Thanks, Ned. I really appreciate that but I would like to reimburse you.' Goodness knows how much a car to Oxford on Christmas Day was going to cost her but perhaps her publisher had some insurance to cover her cancelled flight. Otherwise she might have waved goodbye to the remainder of her royalties.

'Absolutely not,' he said. 'I'm glad to help you get home to your kids.'

'And you two will make it to Anna's family after all.'

'We're going to spend the night in London so Ned can prepare himself,' said Anna. 'He's scared.'

'I'm not. I don't want to make a grand entrance on Christmas Day, that's all.' Ned said, defensively.

The look that passed between Ned and Anna momentarily made Fliss feel like a third-wheel. She peered out of the window into the darkness of the early morning in an attempt to give them some privacy.

'Have you told your kids you're on the way home?' Anna asked Fliss.

'No, I haven't had chance. And they're too old to be getting up this early nowadays. I think I'll surprise them.'

'You said you'd bring extra presents for missing Christmas.'

Fliss hadn't even managed to close Lily's front door behind her. 'Technically, I haven't missed Christmas after all, have I?'

'Give her a chance, Em, she's only just walked in. Merry Christmas, Mum.' Josh gave her a hug and she squeezed him tight.

'Merry Christmas.'

She took her coat and boots off and padded into the lounge to find Lily and Frank sat in front of the fire.

'You made it!' Lily said, standing up to give her a hug. 'Merry Christmas.'

'How did you manage that on Christmas Day?' Frank asked.

Fliss collapsed onto the sofa. 'I got a lift from Ned Nokes.'

'Shut up!' Emma said, wide-eyed. 'The actual Ned Nokes from The Rush?'

'Yes. Although he's not in the band anymore, is he?'

'Can I get you a drink, Fliss? We're on snowballs,' said Frank.

'That would be great, thanks.'

'Oh my god, Mum. I can't believe you went on a plane with Ned Nokes. How did that even happen?'

'The guide that I had, Brun, who drove me around for the book tour, is friends with him. We went out a few times.'

'You went out with Ned Nokes?' Emma almost screamed

it, she was so excited.

'No, Em. He has a girlfriend who is lovely. We went out in a group a few times. You're so excited about this, I think you could let me off the hook about the presents.'

Fliss took the snowball from Frank and sipped it, finding herself immediately transported back to the Christmases of her youth when she and Lily were allowed one snowball on Christmas Day from an age that, looking back, seemed far too young.

'Why don't you stay here tonight?' Lily said. 'It saves everyone packing up today and you can all enjoy yourselves.'

'Are you sure?'

'Of course. We've had such a great time together, it'd be a shame not to see it through. I wouldn't mind a hand with the lunch though. I haven't got the hang of catering for twice the amount of people, let alone for five.'

Fliss went and sat next to her sister and hugged her. 'Thanks, Lil. You've been amazing.'

'Come on then, let's make a start. Frank, you're off the hook.'

'Excellent. Game of Dobble, guys?'

Fliss laughed. It was ages since they'd played Dobble but it used to be Josh's favourite game. She'd definitely join in with that later.

'So how did the book tour go?' Lily asked once they were underway with peeling the potatoes.

'It was amazing. Even on the plane on the way out there, the woman next to me was reading my book! People knew who I was and everyone loves Margot.'

'Wow, that's incredible. Did you manage to see anywhere other than bookshops and libraries?'

'A few places. We went to some hot pools and I went to an open mic night.'

'With Ned and that guy?'

'Brun. Yes, mainly with Brun.' She couldn't hold it in. She needed to share it all with someone. 'Me and Brun...you know.'

'Do I?' Her sister laughed. 'You had a fling with the guy who was escorting you around?'

'Yes but it wasn't a fling.'

Lily stopped peeling and looked at Fliss. 'What was it then?'

She couldn't tell Lily that she was falling in love with Brun. If someone told her that they'd fallen for someone they'd known for barely a week, she'd think they were mad. 'We're more than friends. I don't know how else to explain it. We really like each other but obviously it's not practical to expect anything more when we live so far apart.'

'More than friends? So you slept with him?'

Fliss flicked her eyes towards her sister, telling her all she needed to know.

'Oh, my god. I don't know whether to be pleased that you've finally moved on from Duncan or shocked that you slept with someone you only just met.'

'In my defence, the whole thing was a very intense experience. I feel like I've known him forever.'

'You're in love with him.' Lily had put the peeler down. 'Fliss, this is huge. How did you leave things?' She abandoned her peeling altogether and grabbed a bottle of red wine from the rack and a couple of glasses from the cupboard overhead.

'We might meet up in February.'

'What about before that? Are you going to start sexting?'

'No! I haven't completely lost my mind. I wanted to see how it all feels now that I'm back at home. Being there with him and no responsibilities other than signing books and talking about Margot, it was like a different world. I'm not naive enough to think that it's a basis for a long-term relationship. It's terrible timing for me.'

'It's great timing. Josh will be at university by this time next year.'

'Hopefully,' said Fliss.

'Of course he will. And by then Emma will be almost seventeen and they're not going to need you like they did before. It's important that you start thinking about yourself, and the children are old enough to accept the idea of you having a boyfriend. I'm not saying you need a man but since one's come along when you weren't looking, don't push him away for reasons that don't exist.'

'But we can't put aside our lives to be with each other right now. Maybe in a couple of years it'll be an option but that's not happening now. It's not fair to string him along on the promise of a future when I don't know what that looks like yet. He's already had his heart broken by someone else.'

'If he feels the same way as you, it's probably too late for you to save him from that. I haven't seen you like this, trying to be all coy about what happened. There's no shame in sleeping with someone, but I know you Fliss and there's more to it than that, even if you don't want to admit that to yourself.'

Fliss went over to the kitchen door and listened to make sure the children and Frank were still occupied with Dobble, then she pushed the door to.

'Okay, I do think I'm in love with him but then how can you be in love with someone after a week? We don't know that much about each other and yet I feel like he understands me, which is so odd. The way that he looks at me, Lily, it's incredible. I didn't imagine ever finding someone who feels like that about me. I thought when I eventually wanted to look for a man, I'd have to spend months going through a steady stream of bad dates before I might find someone who wasn't that bad. And now look what's happened when I wasn't ready.'

'You might not feel ready, but things like this never come along at the perfect time.' Lily topped up their wine and then picked up her peeler and started back on the potatoes. 'But you don't need to feel the pressure to make it work. You're the one with more at stake than him. I'm assuming he doesn't have children or a needy ex-husband?'

'No.'

'I would just see how it goes, then. Whatever will be will be.'

'The thing is, I wonder whether whatever happens, this week will always be the best time we ever had together. And on some level, perhaps we should have decided to leave it at that. That's what I had been planning on before the storm, and then once we had that extra time, it made me think it was crazy to let it end.'

'You're all over the place, Fliss. Just try and relax today, after you've helped cooked the lunch, obviously. But for what it's worth, I think it's brilliant.'

Fliss stood up behind her sister and hugged her. 'Thanks, Lil.'

'Now, no more wine until we've got something in the oven.'

The dinner was edible, if not the best example of a Christmas lunch but everyone enjoyed it and Fliss was thankful that she hadn't had to miss it after all.

'I forgot to buy a Christmas pudding,' Fliss said when they'd finished the main course.

'I bought one when I went to pick up the turkey,' said Lily. 'Although all they had left was the posh Heston Blumenthal one so I don't know what that'll be like.'

'I don't want any pudding,' said Emma.

'Is that because you've already eaten a whole selection box?' Josh asked her.

'I have not. I don't like sultanas, that's all.'

'Luckily I bought a non-sultana option as well. Do you like profiteroles?'

'Ooh, yes, please.'

'Can we have both?' Frank and Josh asked at the same time, making everyone laugh.

'You can have whatever you want,' Lily said, dishing up wedges of Christmas pudding for them after she'd plonked a tub of brandy butter in the middle of the table.

'Before we dig in, we need to have a toast,' Frank said.

'Can we have some wine, Mum?' Emma asked.

Fliss gave Frank the nod and he poured a thimble-full of wine each for Josh and Emma, and topped up the other glasses.

'Fliss, we're thrilled you made it back here for today but we're equally thrilled to be celebrating with you all which wouldn't have happened if you hadn't got stranded in Iceland. Which wouldn't have happened if you hadn't gone on the book tour. I don't think we've celebrated this enough. To Fliss, the author.'

'The author!' They all chanted and raised their glasses to her.

With her eyes full of tears, Fliss said, 'Thank you. Merry Christmas.'

'Merry Christmas!'

The rest of the afternoon went by in a blur of the King's speech, numerous rounds of Dobble and snacking on Cheeselets, even though they couldn't possibly be hungry after the huge lunch they'd all eaten.

Eventually, Fliss took her bags upstairs to the room she was going to share with Emma for the night. She opened her case, planning to change into some comfier clothes and found the blanket she'd brought from Snug on the top of her clothes. She pulled it out and buried her face in it to see if there was any trace of Iceland on it. It smelt sheepy, which was comforting and reminded her of her trip to the wool shop with Brun. After she'd changed, she unpacked her knitting so she could take it down and show it to Lily, then her phone pinged.

It was from Brun.

He'd sent a selfie of him sat in one of the chairs in his lounge with the blanket she'd bought for him. It was pulled right up to his nose but she could tell by his eyes that he was smiling underneath. The caption read, 'Merry Christmas, I love the blanket.'

She'd left her gift to him draped over the back of the chair just before she'd left that morning. It was similar to her own blanket but with deeper colours that she thought he would like. Ridiculously, it felt like fate that he had sent this photo now, at the very moment she had just touched her own blanket. Seeing him in the photo with it made her feel connected to him and for the first time since she'd been back in Oxford, she had a glimpse into how things might be for them now. His message made her smile and warmed her heart as she looked at him in the photo. He was there, now, thinking of her. Why wouldn't she want that in her life? Because far from feeling like Brun was someone she could choose to fit into her life or not, she realised that choice was nothing to do with it.

'Merry Christmas, I love you,' she replied.

24

Boxing Day morning was a very relaxed affair and once everyone had enjoyed a lazy breakfast, they packed up all of their stuff and went home to give Lily and Frank a bit of peace and quiet before their London trip.

Although Christmas Day had been great, and it had been lovely to share the day with Lily and Frank for a change, there was nothing like being in your own home to really be able to relax. Josh and Emma disappeared into their rooms and Fliss got changed into her comfiest loungewear, lit the wood-burner and put her new blanket on the sofa ready to curl up with one of the books she'd brought home from Iceland. She made herself a hot chocolate topped with a couple of huge marshmallows because it was still Christmas, and heaved a sigh of relief that she was finally at home with her babies and nothing else to do until January.

Brun had bought her a book about the Icelandic sagas and that was what she chose to read, for no other reason than that he had brought it for her. With her blanket over her, the fire roaring and her hot chocolate finished, she ended up dozing off.

The next thing she knew, the doorbell was ringing. Jumping off the sofa, she went into the hall to find that Josh had already answered the door.

'Josh! How's your Christmas been, mate?'

It was Duncan.

'Yeah, good, thanks.' Josh wasn't pleased to see him, and Fliss didn't blame him after having been unceremoniously dumped at Lily and Frank's.

'Duncan, I thought you were away,' Fliss said, trying to smooth her hair down but knowing that she looked like she'd been dragged through a hedge backwards.

'I've come to pick the kids up,' he said, grinning.

'Oh. Sorry, I didn't think you were having the children after all.' Why had she said sorry to him?

'My plans changed so I thought it'd be nice to spend some time with them.'

'I'm not going,' Josh said.

'Why don't you pop upstairs and tell Emma that Dad's here while we have a word in the kitchen.'

Josh gave his dad a pretty dirty look which filled Fliss's heart with joy, even though a second later she felt bad about it.

Duncan followed her into the kitchen.

'What's going on? You dumped them at Lily's because it didn't suit you to have them and now you're here to pick them up as if nothing's happened.'

A flash of guilt crossed his face but he recovered quickly. 'I was always going to have them from today.'

'No, I distinctly remember a phone call a couple of days ago when you said you wouldn't be having them. Never mind that if I hadn't been able to get home, Lily would have had to unravel all of her plans because of you.'

'My plans changed, I thought you'd be pleased.' He looked stunned that she wasn't. But the fact that he hadn't apologised about any of it meant she couldn't let it go.

'You dumped our children on my sister without even

asking me first, Duncan. It's not fair on them. I'm not going to force them to go with you if they don't want to, it's up to them.' Having seen Josh's reaction, she felt fairly confident that they would want to stay at home with her, especially since they'd only just got back after staying at Lily and Frank's.

'Dad!' Emma came running into the kitchen and flung herself into her dad's arms as if he wasn't the flaky excuse for a father who had left her without warning only a few days ago.

'Do you still want to come and stay?' he asked her.

'With Shona and Dylan?' she asked uncertainly.

He shook his head. 'No, they're still with Dylan's grandparents.' His eyes flicked briefly to Fliss and she knew then that there was trouble in paradise. 'Just the three of us.'

'Yes!' Emma said. 'Can we Mum?'

'You don't need to ask, Em,' he said, 'it's all arranged.'

Whatever she thought of Duncan, she wasn't about to let her daughter see how she really felt about him. 'I'll go and see what Josh wants to do,' she said.

Josh was lying on his bed with his headphones on. He pulled them off when Fliss sat down next to him on the bed.

'I know you don't want to go, Josh. But Emma does and she doesn't see your dad in the same way as you do. She only sees the best in him and she needs you to look out for her.'

Since the divorce, he had been very protective towards Emma which Fliss was grateful for, especially now that Duncan's loyalties were so obviously divided between his old family and his new one. The last thing she wanted was to send her boy off with Duncan when he didn't want to go, but she did have a responsibility to make sure her own feelings didn't factor in the kids' relationship with their dad. She hoped she was gently suggesting something he would feel he wanted to do anyway — look after his sister — rather than guilt-tripping him into it.

'It's shit, Mum. He didn't want us there because Shona thought we were taking his attention away from Dylan. I bet he's come back on his own and that's why it's suddenly okay for us to go back.'

What could she say? He had seen the situation for exactly what it was. But she couldn't let Emma go on her own. Even for Duncan, this behaviour was erratic and she wanted the kids to look out for each other.

'I know. And I completely understand if you'd rather not go. It's your decision.'

'I don't want to go but Em will want to.'

'Even so, I'll back you up, whatever you decide.' Although she was saying it was his decision, she knew he'd decide to go, because his sister wanted to.

'I'll go.'

Fliss leant down and hugged him. 'Thank you, Joshy. I love you and I'm sorry.'

'You don't need to be sorry, Mum.'

'You'd better get your things together,' she said gently, stroking his forehead like she used to when he was little.

He nodded but made no move to get up. Fliss headed back downstairs.

'Okay, Emma, Josh is packing, you'd better get your things together too.'

Emma skipped off, delighted at the prospect of spending time with her dad without the irritation of her half-brother.

'Josh doesn't want to come but he is because Emma wants to.'

'Great. Any chance of a coffee?'

'You've got a nerve, Duncan. If Emma wasn't so blind to the terrible way you treat them both, I would have backed Josh and not let them come with you.'

'They're my kids too.'

'When it suits you.'

'You're the one who flitted off to Iceland and dumped them on me. Shona's still pissed off about that which is why she's stayed on at her parents'.'

'You just said they're your kids too but you only fit them into your life when you can. You're not there for them. What would have happened if Lily hadn't just accepted you turning up on her doorstep? What would have happened if I couldn't have got home from Iceland? We can't rely on you because nothing happens unless it suits you. Children need you to stick to the plan.'

'This was the plan. Today was the plan, Fliss. I don't know what you're so het up about.'

Looking at his face, genuinely believing that he had done nothing wrong, Fliss felt the fight go out of her. What was the point? It wouldn't change anything to keep on with this conversation.

'Fine. Take them but they need to back here by lunchtime the day after tomorrow because we've got tickets to the cinema. And if they want to come home sooner, for any reason, you bring them.'

'Alright, fine,' he said, holding his hands up in surrender.

Having to wave the children off with Duncan, especially knowing that Josh didn't want to go, was difficult. All the excitement at making it home for Christmas had been swept away in a ring of the doorbell. It wasn't as if Duncan wasn't meant to have been spending time with them on Boxing Day, but since he'd changed his plans on a whim to suit himself, she didn't think he'd have had the nerve to turn up as if nothing had happened.

She had learned over the past few years that when she felt like this, the best distraction was writing. Once she got going, it was easy to lose herself in Margot's world and forget anything else that was going on. The times when the children were with Duncan were when many of those words had been written. When it was easy to connect with the kind of solitude her character lived with because she was alone too. But this time it was different. This time, the Iceland of her previous novels abandoned her and she found herself thinking about her Iceland. The one with Brun. Now that she had too much time to think, it was another blow to her mood to find that her writing couldn't provide the same distraction from thinking about him. Was this what the next two weeks were going to be like? Why had she ever suggested that they give each other time to get used to being apart, to see whether they were still going to feel the same about each other now that they were away from the intensity of how their relationship had started. All she wanted to do was fill the void with Brun.

Realising that she wasn't going to achieve anything while she was in this mood and resolving not to contact Brun because she had to prove to herself that she could live without him for more than a single day, Fliss did what any lonely person might do on Boxing Day. She stoked the fire back into life, snuggled up on the sofa and binged Christmas movies with chocolate and tea to hand, replaced by wine once lunchtime arrived.

The following morning, she was thinking more clearly. This time alone was precious; she would've killed for it when the children were younger and she and Duncan were still together, and she wasn't going to be blown off course by him or anything else.

She sat down in front of her laptop. If she was going to make any headway with her writing, she had to lean into the way she felt about Iceland now. It was so intrinsic to her stories, she couldn't abandon it just because it was intricately linked to Brun and how she felt about him. Perhaps now that she was in the middle of writing the fifth book in the series, it was time for Margot to find a soulmate.

Inevitably, Fliss's vision of what Margot's soulmate might look like wasn't a million miles away from being Brun. But rather than an Icelandic tour guide, she made him a police detective who had newly arrived in Reykjavik and who wasn't at all into the idea of using an English freelance psychologist on his cases. Given that Margot had led a solitary life, Fliss didn't think she'd fall into the arms of anyone quite as easily as she had herself, and decided to embark on writing an enemies to lovers storyline for them.

It took her the rest of the day to weave her new character into the beginning of the book that she'd already written and by the time she stopped writing, it was dark and she was hungry. There was hardly any food in the house, at least nothing that she fancied, so she got changed and planned to head to her local pub. They did takeaway meals of a giant Yorkshire pudding, filled with roast potatoes, roast lamb and whatever vegetables were around on that particular day. It was always on the menu in the winter months and Fliss quite often popped round there to collect one if the kids were away. She always made a portion of gravy before she went and warmed it in the microwave when she got back, before slathering plenty of mint sauce over all of it. Her mouth started watering at the thought of it.

After she'd made the gravy, she picked up her phone, put her shoes and coat on and pulled the front door shut behind her. Then her phone rang.

'Mum, I want to come home,' said a tearful Emma.

'Ask Dad to bring you, Em.'

'He said no. But Shona and Dylan are back and her and Dad have been shouting at each other all day.'

Fliss bit back the anger that had immediately risen from within. 'Can you let me talk to Dad?'

She heard muffled voices while Emma handed the phone to Duncan.

'I'm sorry, Fliss,' he began. 'I don't know why Emma's phoned you. Everything's fine here.'

'You said you'd bring them home if they didn't want to stay,' she said firmly.

'We can't be dictated to by Emma every time her nose gets pushed out of joint.'

Enough was enough. She thanked her lucky stars that Emma hadn't rung half an hour later when she might already have had a glass of wine with her dinner.

'I'll come and pick them up. You and Shona obviously have something going on and it gives you some space to deal with that if Josh and Emma come home.'

He didn't argue with her. She knew he didn't want her to know that he was having problems. He'd rather juggle everyone, making nobody happy rather than admit to her that everything wasn't perfect. She should have stood her ground the day before. Her instinct that he was home without Shona and Dylan because something was wrong had been spot on, why didn't she trust herself to say so?

On the way back home, Fliss stopped at the pub and picked up three takeaways instead. It was a huge treat for the children because it wasn't cheap but it was Christmas, and they all deserved a treat.

'I'm sorry, Mum,' said Emma from the darkness of the back of the car just before they got home.

'Em, it's not your fault. It's not up to you two to know what's best all the time. That's my job, and your dad's. He wanted to spend time with you but he has to think about Shona and Dylan now too. He has to be the one to make sure he's giving everyone the best of him and it went a bit wrong this time.'

It wasn't the first time that Fliss had found herself

defending Duncan but she had long realised that she was doing it for her children, not for him, and it didn't stick in her throat the way it had in the beginning.

'Thanks for the tea, it's really nice,' Josh said, devouring his much more quickly than Emma, who was picking at hers, and Fliss who was savouring it.

'That's okay. Give Josh whatever you're not going to manage, Emma, before it gets cold.'

After tea, they sat by the fire and watched *Elf*. It was a tradition they had stumbled into a few years ago and hadn't managed this year because of Fliss being away. Emma curled up on the sofa, her feet resting in Fliss's lap and Josh was slouched in the armchair with his legs draped over one of the arms. It had taken a few more days than she'd hoped, but finally they were having exactly the kind of Christmas that she wanted.

25

The new year started, as always, with a shock to the system as the family went from lazy days at home straight back into school. Both Josh and Emma had mock-exams so the stress levels in the house were sky-high and Fliss was glad to escape to work, which was relatively enjoyable.

She had settled into a pattern of writing in her lunch hour and for a couple of hours after dinner each night while the kids were in their rooms revising and she was happy with the progress she'd been making. She'd contacted her publisher to see whether they would be interested in the next two books in the series. It seemed like the right time to ask while there was some momentum from the book tour to fuel any enthusiasm. As yet, she hadn't heard anything but she'd come to learn that these things always did take time.

The two week break from contact that she and Brun had agreed on was almost up. If anything, it had confirmed for her that the way she felt about him wasn't going to change. Almost everything that had happened to her since she'd been home, she'd framed in the context of having a relationship with him, and what it might be like. On Boxing Day when Duncan had turned up to collect the children with no warning, it would have been wonderful to have been able to talk to Brun about how she felt, knowing that he would have been on her side. She'd love to talk through the changes she was making to her character's life in her writing. She wanted someone to share her life with, and she wanted it to be him.

Once the two weeks were up, Fliss became paralysed with fear. Desperate to text Brun, she worried that perhaps he had changed his mind. He might have realised how difficult it would be to be with someone with considerably more baggage than he had. Someone older than him who had no interest or realistic possibility of giving him any children of his own. These were things they had never had chance to discuss. Was that because they weren't important, or because they hadn't had time? If she got in touch first and then he wanted to call a halt to things, she'd be devastated.

In the end, it was that evening that Brun made the first move with a FaceTime call. Fliss jumped up from the chair where she'd been sat writing and quickly checked how she looked in the mirror over the mantlepiece. After smoothing her hair down and swiping her fingers under her eyes to remove the mascara that had migrated down there over the course of the day, she composed herself and answered the call.

Brun was grinning at her and any worry she'd had that he might not feel the same anymore, disappeared.

'We did it,' he said.

She laughed, as if she had never doubted it. 'We did. How are you? I've missed you.'

'Not more than I have missed you. It is quiet here without you.'

She could tell he was sat in his own lounge. There was a blanket draped over the back of the chair but she could see that it wasn't the one she'd brought him.

'You've got a new blanket, have you been shopping?'

He nodded. 'This one is for you, so we have one each when

you come back.'

Fliss thought her heart might break out of her chest. Why had she doubted him? 'I love it, thank you.'

They chatted for almost an hour about everything and nothing until Fliss heard movement from upstairs and realised what the time was.

'I'd better go. Josh and Emma will be down any minute.'

'Will you have time to talk tomorrow?'

She nodded. 'Yes.'

'Until tomorrow then.' He blew her a kiss and she did the same, then they ended the call without saying anything else.

'Who were you talking to, Mum?' Emma asked, coming into the lounge and collapsing in the corner of the sofa.

'A friend from Iceland.'

'Not Ned Nokes?' Her eyes were wide with anticipation.

'No, Brun. You remember I told you he was driving me and showing me around when I was in Iceland?'

'Oh, yes.'

If Emma thought it was odd that Fliss was carrying on this friendship with her tour guide, she didn't show it. Perhaps there was the occasional upside to this self-centred phase after all.

Over the next couple of weeks, Brun and Fliss established a routine of FaceTiming each other every two or three days with many, many WhatsApp messages in between. Brun was working some evenings doing Northern Lights excursions so they fitted their calls in around that. They had started making tentative plans for Brun to visit for a long weekend at the beginning of March which would coincide with Fliss's school having a leave-out weekend. That meant that she finished work early on the Friday and could go to Heathrow to meet him. She was looking forward to it so much, the only niggle being that she was still undecided about whether to introduce him to Josh and Emma on this visit. She'd organised an AirBnB for him that was close to her house through someone that Abbie knew, but she didn't relish the thought of trying to keep his visit a secret. Nor did she want to introduce him as her special friend or anything excruciating like that. The children were old enough to know what that meant. Luckily she still had a few weeks to decide on a way forward.

The following night on their call, he told her that Ned was playing a small venue in London the following week. It was one of a series of warm-up events for his first solo tour which was starting in the summer. This show was low-key and hadn't been advertised much so only his most fervent fans would be in the audience, along with industry people.

'Ned asked me to see if you would like to go. You could take the kids if you wanted?'

'That will be a definite yes from Emma, I don't even need to ask her. I'm sure Josh will want to tag along too.'

'And he says he will put your names down so that you can go backstage afterwards. Anna will be there too.'

'Wow, that sounds amazing,' Fliss said, thinking that it would blow Emma's mind when she told her she'd be able to go backstage at a Ned Nokes concert. 'Please tell him thanks from us.'

'Okay. I will see him later, we are playing at the open mic night tonight.'

Fliss felt a pang of sadness at missing out on what she knew would be a great night. 'I wish you wouldn't do all the fun things without me,' she said, teasing him.

He laughed. 'None of it is as much fun as when you were here. Gudrun keeps telling me that my eyes are sad. I have told her it is not my eyes but my heart.'

'Don't be sad. It's less than a month until we see each other. Sing that beautiful song with Ned tonight and think of me.'

'I always think of you.'

Fliss wondered whether she'd ever get tired of being adored. She didn't think so. 'Message me and let me know how it goes. I hope you get the biggest cheers.'

Predictably Emma was ecstatic when Fliss told her they'd be meeting Ned and immediately announced that she'd need a new dress for the occasion.

'Will it be like a party? Do you think there will be other famous people there?'

'I don't know, Em. It sounds quite low-key so I doubt it. I think it's more that we get to see him and say hello.'

'Oh my god, Mum. I'm so glad you went to Iceland. I can't believe you're best friends with Ned Nokes.'

There seemed little point in explaining that she wasn't best friends with Ned Nokes.

'We'll go shopping in town at the weekend, then.' She might even get something new to wear herself. It was a while since she'd been to a concert and it was quite exciting.

That evening she met Abbie for a drink. They hadn't managed to catch up with each other since before Fliss went to Iceland and although they chatted regularly on WhatsApp, there was a lot Abbie didn't know. Fliss hadn't shared anything more about Brun with her since she'd called to tell her they'd kissed, and that seemed like a lifetime ago.

They both ordered a large gin and tonic and found a quiet booth in the corner of the posh pub in Summertown where they liked to meet.

'Shall we start from the kiss? I'm dying to know what happened next and you never told me. Was it a holiday romance or just a kiss?'

'Neither, really. We're kind of seeing each other.'

'How can you kind of be seeing someone who lives in a different country? Are you one of those strange couples who correspond and never meet?'

'I think you're getting us confused with people who strike up relationships when one of them is in prison. Obviously we're planning to see each other it's just early days and we don't know how it's going to work yet.' Fliss stirred her straw around her glass, absentmindedly, finding herself quite enjoying chatting about her and Brun.

'So you're planning to go to Iceland again or is he coming here?'

'He's coming here first, in March and then I don't know after that. We're taking it slowly.'

'That's not slow. For you, that's zero to sixty in five seconds. You haven't even been on a date since Duncan left and now you're in an intercontinental relationship.'

Fliss laughed. 'Okay, you do have a point. And we did take a break once I got home to give ourselves a chance to see how we felt. And we both feel the same.'

'So it's really that serious?'

'It is. He's willing to wait, not that I've asked him to, and he knows I can't just move to Iceland. But also, his job is being a tour guide in Iceland which doesn't really translate to anything here. It's tricky for both of us.'

'But you're doing it anyway,' said Abbie. 'Love triumphs.' Then, looking uncertain, 'Do you think it's love?'

Fliss could do nothing but nod with a big grin on her face. 'It is. I've never had the kind of relationship where the other person is interested enough to be invested in everything that you are. Supportive, loyal, kind, loving. That's what he is. And he doesn't know the half of what he's getting into with me but I know he can take it in his stride.'

'Is he meeting the kids when he comes over?'

'I don't know. I mean, he needs to but what do I say? As soon as I introduce him they're going to know what's going on.'

'And why is that a problem? They're not little kids

anymore.'

'I know. It's not that I worry about them seeing me with someone new, it's more about the fact that Duncan is such an unreliable arse since he's been with Shona, and is worse than ever at the moment. I don't want them to think my focus is going to be on Brun and not them anymore. At least when Duncan's an idiot they know they have me.'

'You'd never behave like Duncan, though. Don't tar yourself with the same brush.'

'But Emma especially doesn't see what he's really like. It's different with Josh, he totally gets it and he already carries a lot of responsibility for them both when they're with Duncan. I wouldn't want him to feel any extra burden from me.'

'You have to think of yourself too. Why does Duncan get to start a new life and leave you behind to pick up the pieces with no expectation of anything like that for yourself? You've given yourself over to everyone else for too long, Fliss. It's just as important to show the kids what a single mother who has her life together and is moving on looks like too.'

It was almost exactly what Lily had said. That it was time she started thinking about herself. And that was all well and good but she had no idea how Josh and Emma would take to Brun. She wished she had a better plan just so that she could lay out for them what was going to happen, but she didn't.

'It might help with Emma at least if I push the fact that he's best friends with Ned Nokes,' Fliss said, forgetting that she hadn't mentioned that she'd met Ned to Abbie yet.

'*The* Ned Nokes? From The Rush? Yes, I think that would do it. Some people are impressed by that kind of thing.'

'Not you, though.'

'God, no. Couldn't care less. But I can always take a spare ticket off your hands if that helps?'

'Actually he's asked me and the kids to go to a gig he's doing next week. If I'd known you were a fan, I could have asked for an extra ticket.'

Abbie, flapped her hand and said, 'Oh, next time is fine. Don't worry.'

26

Emma's excitement was translating into stroppy demands for all of the things Fliss needed herself. Mainly the hair straighteners.

'It's more important for me, Mum. Your hair looks fine. Anyway, didn't you straighten it this morning?.'

Fliss wasn't sure in what world her hair could be considered to look fine, let alone acceptable enough to leave the house. It had been raining all day which meant that straightening it that morning had been a total waste of time because the frizz had embraced the damp air and come out to play.

'Emma,' she said, in her firmest, yet most patient voice. 'We are leaving in five minutes. Your hair is perfect. I will not be leaving the house with my hair looking like this, so if you still want to go to the concert, it's my turn with the straighteners.'

Once everyone's hair was done — even Josh had stuck some sort of product in his — they caught the bus to Oxford station and then the train to London Paddington. The venue was south of the river at a place called Omeara that Fliss had never heard of so she decided the easiest thing to do was to get a cab.

The venue was situated in the arches underneath a railway bridge. It was nothing like Fliss had been expecting given how famous Ned was. She'd thought it would be some kind of concert hall whereas this place looked quite small.

'It's really cool,' said Josh.

'We're literally VIPs,' Emma said with a reverent whisper.

Fliss gave their names to the man on the door and they were ushered inside. Josh was right; it was perhaps the coolest place she'd ever been. The railway arches made the space feel intimate, curving around the people that were already milling around. The floors were wooden, the lighting low, and it all felt very high-end and slick. They started in the bar area where it was a nice surprise to find out that the drinks were free which impressed the children yet again. Fliss felt she was going to owe Ned big time for making her the coolest mum ever, even if only for an evening.

After a while, everyone was ushered through into the main space which had a stage at one end, the brick arch covered in wooden panelling, presumably for acoustic reasons. It was sparse compared to the bar area but it still held the same intimate vibe. There were elaborate balustrades running down either side, making two balconies, just a touch higher than the main floor. Several rows of chairs towards the front of the room were already mostly full, and everyone else was stood behind. They managed to get a good spot towards one side, just behind the last row of chairs so that they had a good view and no-one tall could stand in front of them.

The stage was set with a few guitars on stands down one side, and a single chair and microphone. Fliss could feel the sense of anticipation in the room. Looking at the seated people, especially those in the first few rows, they didn't look like Ned Nokes fans, but more like record company people. Most of the people she would assume were fans were standing, which is what she would always want to do at a gig so that she could dance.

'Is it just a guitar, Mum?' Emma asked.

Based on the evidence, Fliss said, 'it looks like it, Em. I went to an open mic night in Iceland where he played guitar and it was really good, I think you'll enjoy it.'

'It's not going to be like The Rush, though, is it?'

'No, I don't think so. Do you think we should leave?'

Predictably Emma rolled her eyes. 'Obviously not.'

A couple of minutes later, the lights went down and Ned came onto the stage to cheers and clapping. Fliss had been right about the fans being at the back because the welcome Ned was getting went from sedate clapping at the front through to whooping and cheering at the back.

He looked much the same as he had when Fliss had seen him in Iceland. It was refreshing that he didn't feel the need to change anything about himself.

'He's got glasses on,' Emma whispered, looking at Fliss in surprise.

'Thanks so much,' he said with a grin on his face. He looked comfortable as he picked up one of his guitars and sat down, picking at the strings, tuning it as he began to speak. 'A lot of you know that I've been working on some new music over the past year and I'm about ready to bring it out into the world.' He paused for some cheers. 'Thanks so much. Some of you might know that I play regularly at an open mic night in Reykjavik and sometimes in London and that's where I've found myself and the kind of music that I really want to play and share with you all.'

He began to play. The room was so silent, it was hard to believe there were probably three hundred people in there. The guitar and Ned's voice resounded around the room and Fliss felt the back of her neck prickle. It was something special.

After a couple of songs, he stood up and changed guitars,

at the same time, someone brought another chair and microphone onto the stage.

'Thanks guys. Now, I have a special guest joining me. I've known this guy for years. We've been through a lot together and we've written a lot together.'

Fliss found herself holding her breath, even though she knew Ned and Brun hadn't known each other that long, there was a tiny part of her that hoped it might be him.

'Please welcome Freddie Banks to the stage!'

The room erupted as The Rush's frontman appeared and Fliss had to step away from Emma to avoid being pummelled in the face when she started jumping up and down clapping her hands over her head. Josh nudged her and smiled, nodding towards his sister.

Ned and Freddie started off by singing an acoustic version of a song by The Rush which sounded amazing, particularly when they stopped singing the chorus and allowed the audience to take over while they played along, looking thrilled to bits that everyone knew their words.

'We wrote this next song after I left the band. It was a strange time but Fred was on my side.' He smiled at his friend, and Freddie nodded an acknowledgement.

'Writing helped you through, right man?' Freddie said. 'And eventually got him out of my spare room.' There was a murmur of laughter and they both began playing again, then Freddie left the stage to cheers and Ned was on his own again.

'I wrote a lot of bad songs in that time but then something changed. It coincided with one of the other big changes I made when I moved to Reykjavik for a while. I needed a bit of perspective.' He was strumming as he spoke. 'And I found it.'

He played a couple more songs, and Fliss could hear the way they'd changed through the set, now sounding more like the songs he'd sung with Brun at the open mic night.

'Now I have another special guest for you. I met this person a year ago, the first time I ventured out by myself in Reykjavik. Don't tell Fred I said this but we've got something special going on.' Everyone laughed and there was a ripple of applause. 'Welcome to the stage, Brun!'

Fliss thought her heart had stopped when she saw Brun walk out onto the stage. She watched as he picked up a guitar and sat down with Ned just as they had at the open mic night.

'So Brun and I play together regularly at the open mic night in Reykjavik and we've written a couple of brilliant songs, even if we say so ourselves.'

Brun let out his hearty laugh that Fliss loved and had missed so much. He was smiling but she could tell he was nervous, although as soon as they started to play, Brun's foot began tapping and he forgot where he was once he was immersed in the job at hand.

'This is really good, Mum,' Josh said, as they launched into the upbeat song they'd played first at the open mic night. Fliss found herself dancing and bopping around almost as much as Emma. Even Josh was moving from side to side in time with the beat.

The applause was pretty deafening and Ned and Brun looked as pleased as anything.

'Thanks guys,' Ned said. 'My friend Brun is going to introduce the next song.'

Ned played a gentle melody while Brun spoke.

'I wrote the words to this song before I knew the person that I wrote them about,' he said. 'And then I met her and the words meant more than ever.'

She could hardly believe that Brun was saying this and at the same time there was a voice in her head questioning whether she should even assume he was talking about her.

She felt as if everyone had turned to stare at her, as if she'd suddenly been outed as his girlfriend in front of all these people. In front of her children.

'But unless you speak Icelandic you won't understand,' Ned interjected, making everyone laugh. Fliss was grateful for that because it stopped her from holding her breath and helped expel the irrational thoughts she was having. Of course no one knew he meant her. Josh and Emma probably didn't even remember the name of the person who had been her guide in Iceland.

'Do you know him?' Emma asked. 'Is he famous in Iceland?'

'I met him and he's a friend of Ned's.'

Once they started playing, Fliss felt all of the things that she'd felt at the open mic night, although this time, Brun wasn't looking into her eyes as he sang the beautiful words that she didn't understand. Nevertheless, she knew he was singing to her and she wondered how she was going to ever carry on with the rest of her life if she couldn't be with him. Every minute. Every day. Forever.

By the end of the song, even Emma had tears in her eyes when she looked at Fliss with a grin as she clapped hard for Ned and Brun, clearly having loved the song as much as everyone else. The room was a cacophony of cheers and applause for what seemed like minutes while Ned and Brun stood on the stage together, graciously accepting the reaction with nods and smiles and expressions of incredulity that flitted between them.

Brun waved as he left the stage. Fliss hoped with all of her heart that he would be backstage afterwards. Surely he had offered her the tickets to the gig so that they could see each other, so that he could surprise her by being there.

The last couple of songs were probably brilliant but Fliss was replaying Brun's song in her mind, so that by the end of the show, she would have told anyone that asked that it had been the last song, for all she noticed of the rest of the set.

'Come on, Mum,' Emma urged as people started to leave. 'Where do we go to get backstage?'

Short of climbing onto the stage, there was nowhere obvious to go, so they headed back out to the bar, planning to ask someone. In the end, there was no need because they found Anna.

'Fliss!' Anna greeted her with a hug and then looked at Josh and Emma. 'It's great to meet you, your mum told us all about you. Come on.'

She led the way past a bouncer and up some stairs to another bar area. It was high up in the arch and even though none of them were exceptionally tall, they could only walk along the centre of the room towards the open door at the other end. It led onto an outdoor terrace, partly covered by a canvas roof that was doing a good job of keeping out the rain which had died down to more of a drizzle. Despite the winter night, there was warmth radiating from a couple of blazing fire pits and the lights that were strung across the space glowed invitingly.

There were only a handful people up there. Anna led them over to where Ned was chatting to a man in a suit. When he saw her, he broke off the conversation saying that he'd catch up with whoever it was later, and his full beam smile landed on Anna, Fliss and the children.

Once he'd kissed Anna and she'd congratulated him on a great gig, he kissed Fliss on both cheeks.

'I'm so glad you could make it.' He had a glint in his eyes which told Fliss that he had been as much a part of this plot to reunite her with Brun as Brun himself.

'It was fantastic. This is Josh and Emma.'

Josh said hello and shook hands with Ned, seeming to take it in his stride, whereas Emma went bright red when Ned greeted her with a kiss on the cheek as well and couldn't say anything.

'We've got some marshmallows over here for toasting,' Anna said, gesturing for Josh and Emma to follow her. And at the same moment, Brun appeared, taking Fliss's hand and leading her back indoors.

Before either of them had said a word, they were in each other's arms, kissing and falling for each other all over again, until Fliss remembered that she wasn't on her own tonight and pulled away, looking behind Brun to see if anyone had been watching them.

'It's okay, they are with Anna.'

'I know. I'm sorry. This is such a wonderful surprise.' She took his beardy face in her hands and kissed him again. 'God, I've missed you so much.'

'I am pleased to hear that.'

'And you planned this?'

'It was Ned's idea.'

'It's the best idea in the world. How long are you here for?'

'We are leaving tomorrow morning. Ned flew us over on a private jet.' His eyes were wide. Fliss knew how he felt. It was like a different world, the one that Ned operated in.

'I have the kids,' she said, with a hint of desperation in her voice as she realised that aside from this stolen moment they weren't going to have any time alone together.

'I know, I suggested that, if you remember,' he said with a chuckle. 'But better this than nothing until March,' he said.

She nodded. 'Definitely. I'd better get back outside'

'Can I meet your children?' He looked hopeful and like he really wanted to.

'Of course. But I need more time to think about how to tell them about us. Is that okay?'

'Yes, Fliss. Anything you want is okay.'

They shared another kiss and stood in a quiet embrace for

a minute or so before Fliss said, 'You go back. I just need to nip to the loo.'

He held onto her hand as she walked away, only letting go once she'd looked back at him and they'd both acknowledged with a shared look that this was the end of the time they'd share alone that evening.

In the bathroom, she reapplied her lipstick to detract from the slight redness that remained from Brun's beard and smiled into the mirror at herself. She'd never imagined that he would be here tonight. It was the kind of thing than happened at the end of a romcom movie or the grand gesture that came in the last chapter of a romance novel. Not something that happened to Felicity Thorne.

When she got back outside, Ned, Anna, Josh and Emma were sat around the fire pits toasting marshmallows along with a couple of men in suits who didn't look like they'd toasted a marshmallow in their lives, and Freddie Banks and his wife. Emma seemed to have got over being starstruck and was chatting to Freddie as easily as she would her Uncle Frank, apparently explaining the intricacies of TikTok.

Brun was stood watching them. Fliss walked over and picked up two marshmallows and sticks and handed one to him, then they sat down near Josh and Emma and began toasting.

'Josh, this is Brun. He helped me find my way around Iceland.'

'I loved that song you did, it sounded amazing,' Josh said. Fliss loved him more than ever for saying that.

'I did too,' Emma said. 'What did the words mean?'

'Ah, they do not translate into English very well. They lose their magic.'

They seemed to accept that and then listened intently while Brun told a farfetched story about how he'd toasted marshmallows on a lava flow.

'It's true,' he said, with a completely straight face when Fliss questioned him at the end of the story.

'They do stuff like that on YouTube all the time,' Josh said, as if she was the only person there who hadn't done that kind of thing before herself.

'It sounds dangerous.'

'It is very dangerous,' Brun said, and Fliss saw the admiration in her son's eyes, giving her hope that when she eventually did tell them that she and Brun were together, Josh would be accepting of him.

It was getting late and Fliss was mindful that it was a school night for all three of them and also needed to make sure that they didn't miss the last train.

'My car will take you,' Ned said.

'But we're going to Oxford,' said Fliss. 'It's okay, we've got train tickets.'

'It's fine, we don't need the car tonight because we're staying at mine. We can get a cab. Please, Fliss.'

'Thank you, Ned. That's really very kind of you.'

He smiled and shrugged. 'My pleasure. Hey, are you two on BeReal?' he asked Josh and Emma. They pulled their phones out and went about swapping details with Ned, giving Brun and Fliss a valuable minute or so to say goodbye.

'I'll see you in March,' she said. 'I'm hoping maybe the kids will be with Duncan and we'll have the weekend to ourselves.'

'I can't wait,' he whispered into her ear as they shared a last hug, no different to the hugs she gave Anna and Ned.

'That was the best night ever,' Emma announced as they sank into the seats in the back of Ned's car.

'Thanks for taking us, Mum,' said Josh, resting his head on her shoulder.

'My pleasure.' It felt lovely to have had this evening, which had ended up being so special, and sharing it with her children. It was on the tip of her tongue to tell them now that Brun was more than a friend but she resisted, not wanting to spoil the happy but exhausted vibe in the car. It could wait for another day.

27

Now that she'd seen Brun, there was no question in her mind that they needed to find a way forward together. The weekend in March was the first step and Fliss was determined to make it a success. In her mind, that meant the children had to know about Brun. There was no point in keeping it a secret when she was so sure that nothing was going to change her mind about him. Watching him on stage at Ned's gig, she'd felt overcome by the love that coursed through her when she knew he was singing to her. Seeing him there was incredible and she knew she'd feel like that about him every time they were reunited after time apart.

Because that was still the reality of the situation. Fliss's settled life in Oxford was the biggest thing to overcome and while she didn't want to rock the boat with that at the moment, something Brun understood, she was more willing now to think about how she could introduce Brun into her life properly. He didn't need to be a secret that she managed to meet up with a few times a year. The brief time he'd spent with Josh and Emma gave her cause to think that the three of them would get along. They'd bonded over marshmallows; it was a start.

'Are you two happy to go to Dad's for the weekend in a

couple of weeks?' she asked over dinner one night.

'Will Shona and Dylan be there?' Emma had started to see them as a barrier to her seeing her dad after what had happened at Christmas.

'Yes. I think you need to expect that to be the case all the time, Em,' she said, gently. 'I know it's not the same having to share him with Shona and Dylan but that's how things are now.'

'It'll be fine, Mum,' said Josh. 'What are you doing that weekend?'

Now was the time to tell them. Although having just explained to Emma about having to share her dad, it seemed unfortunate to have to follow that with her announcement about Brun.

'Brun is coming for the weekend. I'm going to meet him at the airport and then we're going to spend the weekend together.'

'Oh cool.'

It was such a benign reaction that Fliss wasn't sure if Josh had entirely understood what she'd meant.

'He might stay here.' Now she felt like she was asking permission which was ridiculous. Should she just come out and say, 'He's my boyfriend'?

Emma looked at her. 'Are you seeing each other? Is that why you took us to Ned's concert, so that we could meet him?'

'No, I didn't know he was going to be there but yes, we are seeing each other.'

'Are we going to have to move to Iceland?' Emma's eyes were wide with worry.

'No, of course not. Nothing will change, we're just going to see each other occasionally when we can. That's all.'

'I think it's cool, Mum,' Josh said, looking at his sister.

'Well, don't have sex all over the house, it's disgusting.'

'Emma!' Fliss said, almost choking on her mouthful of pasta bake.

Josh had gone bright red and was staring at his plate.

'Sorry, but it is. Having sex again when you're so old is gross.'

Fliss had to bite her tongue to stop herself from explaining that not only teenagers and people trying to have babies had sex. That the sex with Brun had been the best she'd had in her life. Instead she said, 'We'll try to control ourselves.'

And what she'd envisaged as a long, deep and meaningful conversation, introducing her children to the idea of her dating again, had been over in a couple of minutes. Without wanting to prolong the embarrassment for Josh by clarifying, she thought they were probably left with the impression that Brun was less of a long-term partner and more of a weekend booty-call.

Lily and Frank had come round for Sunday lunch. They hadn't seen much of each other since Christmas and WhatsApp was only so useful when it came to keeping up with all the news. Josh and Emma were still in bed and probably would be until the waft of roast lamb became too strong for their stomachs to ignore.

'How's everything then?' Lily asked, sitting down at the kitchen table with Frank and opening the bottle of red wine that Fliss had placed in the middle of the table when she'd laid it earlier.

'Everything's good, thanks. How about you two?'

'Same old,' Lily said.

'We've booked a cruise,' Frank said, as if to point out to his wife that there was something worth mentioning.

'Oooh, lovely! Where to?' Fliss finished tossing the potatoes in oil, seasoned them and pushed the tray into the oven where the lamb had been slow-roasting for a couple of hours and was starting to smell delicious.

'New York on the Queen Mary and then to the Caribbean.'

'Wow, that sounds amazing. I've always thought it would be so romantic to sail to America.'

'It was Frank's turn to choose this year,' said Lily. 'It's a good choice.' She smiled at Frank and blew him a kiss.

Pouring a small glass of wine for herself, Fliss took a seat for the ten minutes she had before she'd need to start prepping the vegetables.

'Isn't your weekend with Brun coming up?' Lily asked.

'Yes, next weekend. He's coming to stay here and the kids are going to Duncan's.'

'I thought you said Abbie was sorting out an Airbnb?'

'It seemed daft to do that since the kids won't be here. Anyway, I've told them now. They seem fine about it as long as we don't have sex all over the house.'

Frank had trouble swallowing his wine and almost choked before he let out a laugh. 'I wish I'd heard that conversation,' he said, once he'd recovered.

'I know. It wasn't how I imagined it would go at all. But they know now. I did start to wonder whether it's even worth sending them to Duncan's but I think it might be too much for us all to be in the house together on Brun's first visit.'

'Agreed. You two need some time alone. You haven't seen each other for months and you perhaps need to be a little slower with the introductions than 'here's my boyfriend, he's staying for the weekend'.'

Fliss had completely forgotten to tell Lily and Frank about the concert. 'They actually met Brun a couple of weeks ago at a Ned Nokes concert we went to.'

'Emma said you'd all been to see Ned Nokes but she didn't mention that they'd met Brun,' said Frank.

'She didn't know who he was then and she was firmly concentrating on Ned and Freddie for most of the evening.

But they did meet and the kids didn't take an instant dislike to him or anything so I thought I'd let them know who he was before he came to stay.'

'Good for you. I'm glad you're not hiding it away. There's nothing like being in love and sharing it with the world,' Lily said.

'Thanks. Right. I'd better make the Yorkshire pudding batter.'

'And if Duncan lets you down for that weekend, we're around to help out.'

Frank shook his head. 'No, Lil, we've got the director's retreat.' Frank's company had a weekend away in a posh hotel every year for all the staff and their families.

'It's okay, I won't need a back-up plan this time. It's not as if I'm out of the country, is it?'

'I don't trust Duncan not to put a spanner in the works, that's all.'

'Worse case scenario, they can come home. Anyway, I have some other news too, you can be the first to know.'

'Come on then, spit it out, it sounds exciting.'

'When I got back from Iceland, I sent my publisher a pitch for the next two books in the series. There's a lot of interest in them over in Iceland, and since they'd sent me there on the book tour, I thought it was worth building on that to try and get another deal with them. Anyway, on Friday I had an email from Eva saying that they want to offer me a deal for the next three books.'

'Oh, Fliss, that's amazing!' Lily got up and hugged her. 'Congratulations!'

'Thanks.' It was lovely to share the news with her sister. Josh and Emma would be pleased but perhaps wouldn't realise how much it meant to her. But now, she'd tell them over lunch and they'd be buoyed by Lily and Frank's excitement.

'Is it a better deal now that they're doing so well in Iceland?' Frank asked.

'I don't know yet, she's sending the contract over on Monday. But even if it's the same deal, I think it'll be okay. If I can get royalties like the last ones every quarter, I'd be very happy.'

'They might start to market the books a bit more now that they've seen how popular they've been in Iceland. It gives them something to go on, I suppose, once they see why people like them.'

'Definitely. It's the main character, Margot, that people really relate to. I've started writing the fifth book and I'm giving her a love interest. It felt like the right time.'

'I wonder why that's suddenly become a plot point?' Lily teased.

'Oh, shut up and pour some more wine.'

Once the dinner was ready, Fliss called the kids down. They both appeared, bleary-eyed as if they had just got up but they'd at least managed to get dressed.

'We're celebrating,' Frank said, once they were all sat down and ready to eat. 'Your mother has got another publishing deal.'

'Oh, nice one, Mum,' said Josh, smiling and then digging into his roast. It was exactly the reaction that Fliss would have predicted. He was pleased but he was still at the age where it was hard to appreciate that parents were people with their own lives.

'It's great, isn't it?' Lily said to Emma.

'Yes, does that mean we can upgrade the Netflix to more than one screen?'

'It might,' Fliss said. 'We'll wait and see.'

Emma rolled her eyes and Fliss grinned at Lily and Frank. 'Thank you,' she mouthed, and raised her glass to them.

What she did know was that Brun would be thrilled. He'd

been so supportive throughout the book tour, and had been astounded that her publisher hadn't been snapping up the sequels before the ink was dry on 'The End'. He would think that she deserved the new contract and would know how much it meant to her, perhaps more than anyone else, even Lily and Frank.

She was in two minds about whether to tell him before the weekend or whether to wait and surprise him with it. In the end, she decided to wait because she wanted to see his reaction first hand. She could imagine that he would let out one of his big laughs and pull her into a hug, maybe pick her up and twirl her around. That's what she was hoping for.

With just days to go until they saw each other, all she could think about was what it would be like to see him again. To kiss him without thinking that the children could walk in at any moment. To share an embrace without having to pull away too soon because they were with other people. She wanted to see him with no agenda other than to be together.

28

Since getting back from London, Brun had been struggling with the anti-climax. It had been such a last minute idea from Ned that he should go, he'd had no time to build up any anticipation for seeing Fliss again. That, coupled with the fact he'd been nervous about performing in front of hundreds of people for the first time in his life, a good proportion of whom were industry professionals, meant that of the entire experience, seeing Fliss had been a tiny moment that he was left feeling he hadn't made the most of.

There had been lots of good things about the trip, not least the opportunity to fly in a private jet, meet Freddie Banks and play in a stunning venue that he wouldn't have dreamed of before. But the pace of parts of Ned's life, in the time he spent outside of Iceland, was unfathomable to Brun. In Iceland, Ned lived very much like Brun; unhurried with nothing more pressing to do than be on time for the odd open mic night. What they'd had to fit in to the few short hours they'd been in London would have taken Brun a few days to accomplish. They'd arrived at Ned's house in London and before they'd even sat down, Ned was off for meetings with his new record company, his publicist and other people Brun hadn't even been aware existed in Ned's life before. He finally realised why Ned loved living in Reykjavik so much, where none of these things could call on his time, or at least it was easier for him to ignore them.

A couple of days after they'd got back, Ned had called round to tell him that the song with the Icelandic lyrics was the favourite by far of all the songs he'd played that night in London and that his record company wanted to release it.

'You'd have credit as a writer and all you'd need to do is come to London so we can record it.'

'I'm not sure,' Brun said. 'We didn't write it for that reason. It feels wrong to sell it.'

'It just means it can be shared with more people. It doesn't have to be about the money, it's not selling out,' said Ned.

But that's exactly what it felt like to Brun. Especially now that the song was inextricably linked to Fliss. It would feel like he'd taken those special words, which were only for her, and given them to the whole world.

'Take some time to think about it,' Ned said, clapping Brun on the shoulder as he got up to leave.

Brun wrestled with the idea of allowing Ned to go ahead with the song but kept coming back to the fact that it felt too personal to share. It would be Ned's first release as a solo artist which only added to the pressure on Brun to say yes. They'd chosen his song. His words. He couldn't help but be flattered but he felt like Ned's career was riding on him. Whichever song Ned chose to release first would be a surefire hit but the fact that Brun had to give the go ahead, or not, was a horrible position to be in. He decided to leave the decision until he'd had chance to talk to Fliss about it. He knew she felt the same way about the song and wasn't sure what her reaction would be to it becoming a huge hit. Now that they were together it seemed only right to make a monumental decision like this together.

'How was it seeing Fliss again?' Rachel asked him at the

open mic night that week.

'It was great, but over too quickly.'

'But it's not long now until you go and visit, is it?'

'No, it is this weekend. I am looking forward to having her to myself again for a couple of days.'

'Anna and Ned cramped your style, did they?'

Brun laughed. 'Because we kept it a surprise from her, I only saw her after the gig and she couldn't stay too long because of her kids.'

'So she introduced you?'

He nodded. 'Yes, they are great kids. Chatty and easy to be with, like their mother.' It had been strange seeing Fliss being a mother. She was no different really, but he could tell that her focus, even subconsciously was on her kids in a way that it hadn't been when she'd been in Reykjavik. Then, especially once the storm had arrived, she was limited with what she could do about anything that might have been going on at home. He wasn't oblivious to the fact that this wouldn't normally be the case for her.

'It's good that you got along. I guess that bodes well for the future.'

'I hope so. We will see how the weekend goes and take it from there.'

He didn't want to allow himself to put too much importance on the weekend in Oxford. They had put it in their calendars to mark the moment of embarking on a proper relationship. To turn the result of their brief time apart, as they tested out how they felt for each other outside of the bubble of their week together in Reykjavik, into something solid. But for Brun, the moment he saw Fliss after the concert in London, he knew he felt more strongly for her than he'd even realised before and now, the weekend wasn't as significant as it had been before that night. It was one meet-up of numerous to come, that hopefully as time went on, would become more frequent and for longer periods of time than a snatched weekend in Oxford or Reykjavik.

29

Fliss waited in the arrivals hall in terminal two at London Heathrow, standing behind the barrier with butterflies in her stomach as she waited for Brun to appear. The feeling in her stomach was solely to do with the anticipation of seeing him again rather than anything else. She was confident that she had everything covered to ensure she and Brun had the weekend to themselves.

The kids had gone off to school with their weekend bags and she'd texted Duncan before she left Oxford to make sure he was expecting to pick them up after school. The house was super tidy and she'd been to the hairdressers the night before and had a blow-dry so her hair looked half-decent for a change. She was wearing a dress with a cropped jumper over the top and her favourite ankle boots which had a heel, making her feel like she had dressed up. Unfortunately, since it was March, all of this was covered with her trusty Seasalt parka but there wasn't much she could do about that since she wasn't willing to freeze.

Another stream of people began to come through the door and Fliss spotted him before he saw her. He had a rucksack on his back and was carrying his coat over one arm. He was wearing dark jeans and a navy blue jumper with a shirt underneath. He looked smart and it suited him. The only other time she'd seen him look like that was for the party night book-signing at *Hús Máls og Menningar* and that night was ingrained in her memory. She wanted him.

She moved to the end of the barrier and stood there waiting for him to see her. Once he did, she was rewarded with the biggest smile she had ever seen, and he strode towards her, his arms wide, ready for her to fall into them.

It felt more wonderful than she could have imagined. She'd missed his sturdy body against hers; how safe it made her feel. And she'd missed his beardy kisses.

'You look wonderful,' he said, his eyes shining as he pulled away to look at her.

'So do you. And you smell amazing,' she said, unable to help herself.

He laughed loudly and hugged her again.

'So what is the plan?' They began strolling along, Brun had his arm across her shoulders and Fliss realised that it was one of the only times that they'd walked side-by-side without battling through a snowstorm.

'I thought we could get a coffee here while we wait for the train back to Oxford and then have a quiet night in?'

Brun grinned and pulled her closer. 'That sounds perfect.'

There was a Caffè Nero in the arrivals hall which was as good a place as any. They had almost an hour before they needed to catch the Tube to Paddington.

He sat at a table with their coats and his bag while Fliss bought them coffee and a couple of muffins to see them through until dinner time.

'It was so great to see you at Ned's gig but I wished we'd had more time,' Brun said.

'Could you see me when you were on stage?'

He shook his head. 'No, only the people at the front because the lights are too bright. I wanted to see you, to sing to you.'

She took his hand. 'I knew you were, even if you couldn't see me.'

'I need to talk to you about that song.'

'I have something to tell you too.'

'You go first,' he said.

'Okay. I've been offered a three book deal by my publisher.'

'Fliss! That is amazing news! Congratulations. I am so pleased that they have realised the series needs to continue. So that means the book tour must have been a success?'

'I think so.' She was thrilled with Brun's reaction. She had plenty of support from her sister and Frank and Abbie but this felt different. It felt like she'd got someone on her side again.

'So we need to celebrate. Do you have any plans for the weekend?'

'No, my plan begins and ends with meeting you at the airport today.'

'When Ned knew I was coming, he offered me the use of his house. I was not sure how far away Oxford is and whether we would need somewhere to stay tonight so I accepted. Would you like to stay there with me? It is in a nice area where I could take you to dinner tonight.'

It was a lovely offer and there was no reason why they shouldn't stay in London for the night. It would be fun to do something like this on the fly, completely unplanned for a change.

'That sounds great. If you're sure.'

'Sure. I stayed there when we came over for the gig so I know where it is. I guess we could get a Tube?'

'Okay. It's quite exciting.' It felt like such a treat to be able to stay in Central London for the night without having to pay for an expensive hotel.

'Ned says there is a bottle of champagne in the fridge.'

'What did he think we were celebrating?'

Brun shrugged. 'I think it is any excuse for champagne if you are Ned Nokes.'

They finished their coffee and caught the Tube to South Kensington from where it was only a five minute walk to Ned's house. It was one of those white regency style terraces with the columns either side of the front door. Brun took out his phone and held it against a sensor next to the front door. The lock released and he opened the door, gesturing for Fliss to go in first.

The hallway was dark, but that was because the windows at the front of the house were shuttered inside and Brun said that Ned preferred to keep them closed all of the time. They walked through to the kitchen and the lights came on automatically. It was the kind of kitchen Fliss dreamed of having in her house but hers would be the wrong sort of house; too small for a start. The kitchen island by itself was bigger than Fliss's kitchen and there were no handles on the shiny dark blue units which gave it an impossibly sleek finish.

'Wow, this is gorgeous,' said Fliss.

'We need some light.' Brun was doing something on his phone and then a blind which was covering the whole of one wall began to lift revealing floor-to-ceiling doors that led out to a walled garden and letting daylight into the dark house, waking it up. 'That is better.'

'Can I have a look upstairs?' Fliss said, curiosity getting the better of her.

Brun grinned. 'Why don't you go and find the guest room. I'll bring the champagne up in a minute.'

In contrast to the wooden flooring downstairs, the rest of the house was carpeted in thick cream carpet which sank beneath Fliss's feet, feeling luxurious. The house wasn't ostentatious, it was simply furnished but with immaculate attention to detail on the decor that made it feel more like a top-end hotel than someone's house. Fliss poked her head around the door of every room, discovering Ned and Anna's room which had the biggest bed and a few personal items on the top of the chest of drawers, like perfumes and aftershave. It had a walk-in wardrobe which presumably had been a bedroom once, and an ensuite that led off that. Then there was a guest room which had a thoughtful stack of towels at the foot of the bed and some Molton Brown toiletries arranged tastefully on the bedside table, again there was an ensuite with a walk-in shower. The final room was clearly Ned's. There were framed tour posters of The Rush which Fliss peered at with interest now that she knew Ned and had met Freddie, and there were numerous guitars nestled in an open-fronted flight case, the kind that bands use to transport their equipment.

'Impressive, isn't it?' Brun said, making her jump. She hadn't heard him coming because of the carpet and lack of squeaky floorboards.

'I don't think I could live somewhere like this,' Fliss lied. More to convince herself than because it was true.

'Wouldn't it be terrible?' Brun said, smiling at her as he handed her a glass of bubbly.

'I think I've got too much stuff that would look out of place. I'd need a lot more cupboards to keep up this kind of look.'

Brun led the way into the guest room. He put his glass down on the bedside table and jumped onto the bed, landing horizontally. Fliss climbed up next to him, still holding her glass.

'We should toast something,' she said.

'It has to be to us. To this weekend being the first of many times we see each other in the future.'

'Perfect,' said Fliss, and then insisted that they do the cheesy thing of linking their arms through each other's as they took a sip at the same time.

'It really feels like this is the beginning.' Brun was propped up on one elbow, facing her, his eyes shining.

Since Iceland, there were some practical considerations that had been weighing on Fliss's mind. Things that they hadn't discussed before but that were important in the context of starting a relationship.

'Can we talk about some things, first,' she began, realising that she was about to kill the mood but there was never going to be a good time.

'Sure,' he said, some of the spark going out of his expression as he waited to hear what had made Fliss sound quite so serious in the midst of their reunion.

'I'm older than you by... I think six years?'

He nodded, raising his eyebrows in amusement.

'I have teenagers...'

'Very nice teenagers from what I saw,' he said, smiling.

'Thanks. The thing is, I don't think I would want to have any more children. But you might want to, so I think it's something we ought to at least discuss before... well, before we get too serious.' Although it was way too late for that.

He took her hand. 'How long have you been thinking about this?'

'God, probably too long. It's a big thing to ask you not to want kids. I can't ask you that. I mean, if you were desperate we could think about it. But I am forty-one. That's quite old in the maternity world and it's hard work having babies.'

He gave one of his guffaws, taking Fliss by surprise. 'I love you so much!' he said, pulling her into his arms.

It wasn't the reaction she had expected. She thought they'd have a long, serious talk about the whole subject, perhaps struggle to reach any kind of compromise since she'd assumed Brun would want kids.

'Does this mean you don't mind about any of that?'

'I don't mind at all. I want to be with you, Fliss. I am not interested in asking you to become a mother again. You have been through all of that and I am sure, if you are anything like my sister-in-law, that you look forward to having some time to yourself as they grow older. It has allowed you time to build your career as an author and now that is flourishing just as your children are flourishing. It is how things are meant to be.'

'Have you never wanted children?'

'Of course, but I realised some years ago that it would not be something for me and I am okay with that. Before Kristin, I had a relationship for almost ten years and we did try to have a baby and it did not happen for us. We spent a long time grieving a child we had never had. We had to be at peace with that situation or we had to adopt or something else instead. In the end, it was what broke us. So I knew then that I would not be a parent.'

'That's how it's been for my sister, Lily. They tried so hard, it was heartbreaking to watch but she and Frank are stronger because of it. I can understand that at some point you have to know when to let a dream go.'

'Maybe if you did not have a family and wanted one, it would be different but this is not something I need, Fliss. I need you, that is all.'

He leant towards her and kissed her gently.

Lingering.

Teasing.

She took a deep breath. After that conversation, she was full of emotion, and relief. And he hadn't even mentioned that she was forty-one so she was going to assume that he didn't care about that either.

In celebration of the weekend, she'd treated herself to some new underwear. It was navy-blue lace, still sensible rather than skimpy but she felt amazing. She pulled her dress over her head, enjoying Brun's appreciative look when she revealed herself. Because at this minute, she didn't feel like the forty-one year old mother of two teenagers, she felt like a sultry, sex-goddess.

Straddling him, she allowed him to run his hands over her skin, trying not to flinch, although she was melting at his touch and wanted to fall into him. She waited until his breathing became heavier, his touches more urgent, then she undid his belt and reached inside his jeans, taking charge of him and seeing on his face how much he was loving her do that. His eyes were closed and his hands were exploring her thighs and bottom, before his thumb settled somewhere that made her gasp. His eyes shot open and knowing he was in charge now, he flipped her over and pulled his clothes off. He eased her lace briefs down her thighs with two fingers, carefully but too slowly for Fliss who didn't think she could wait a moment longer to have him inside her. The instant he was, they both soared to the finish together, wrapped around each other as if it were the first time, the last time, the only time they might be together.

Later that evening, after they had re-acquainted themselves with each other and then been to an intimate Italian restaurant for dinner, they sat in the lounge at Ned's house drinking tea. The champagne had been polished off before they went out, and after more wine at dinner, they were both a little bleary-eyed.

'What were you going to tell me earlier,' Fliss asked him, realising that they had spent most of the evening talking about her books and reminiscing about her trip to Iceland. 'We were at the airport. Something to do with the song,' she added, to jog his memory. They'd talked about so much since then, she wasn't surprised he'd forgotten.

'Ah, yes. Ned has asked me if he can release the song with the Icelandic words as his first solo single.'

'Wow, that's amazing! You wrote that song and he loves it enough to want it to be his first single.'

Brun smiled. 'Yes, it is amazing, and because we wrote it together I would get royalties. But it feels like our song, yours and mine. We have played it only at the open mic night and then at the gig in London. I did not expect it to be anything more. It feels wrong to make money from it.'

'Wouldn't it always be our song, even if it becomes a hit for Ned?'

He shrugged. 'People will start to google the lyrics and try to translate them and it will lose its magic.'

Fliss shifted from her corner of the vast sofa so that she was closer to him. 'If people can't translate it, then they won't know or understand what you wrote it to say. Maybe that's okay? It will still be special to anyone who speaks Icelandic,' she said, remembering how Gudrun had looked and what she'd said after they'd heard it for the first time at the open mic night in Reykjavik. 'And to me.'

'So you think it would be okay?'

'I do. I think it's an amazing opportunity for you. People dream of writing a hit and that's what you've done. I know that you didn't write it to make money. That's all that matters. No-one can replicate the way either of us feel when you play that song, Brun. It'll always be ours.'

He pulled her into him and hugged her. 'Thank you. I will tell Ned yes, then.'

'You're sure that's what you want? It's your decision, not mine.'

'Yes, I admit I am excited about recording it with Ned. It will be an unbelievable experience.'

'You're going to play and sing on the actual single?' She sat up, grinning at him. 'You're going to be a star, just like Ned!'

Brun let out one of his guffaws of laughter. 'That is not for me. I am helping Ned out because he can't pronounce Icelandic words to save his life. It is for my country.'

'Well, whatever your motivation, it's very sexy.'

Brun pushed her gently onto her back and began tickling her, making her laugh so hard that no sound came out.

'*Mjög fyndið!*'

'I mean it!' she tried to say, although she couldn't get the words out. The only way to defend herself was to kiss him which was difficult when he had her at arms length but she managed to pull him towards her and he soon forgot about the tickling in favour of more kissing.

They moved upstairs to the bedroom but before they settled down to sleep, Fliss checked her phone. It was all good. No messages from anyone, although her battery was about to die and she hadn't brought her charger with her, not expecting to be staying over.

'Night, Brun,' she whispered, curling up with her back against his chest.

'Goodnight, my love.' He wrapped his arm around her waist and pulled her closer to him.

Fliss hadn't felt so content since the last night they'd spent together in Iceland. She had him back and though it might be a while until they could be together again, tonight they had made memories to last her through the times when they were apart. And they still had two whole days together.

The following morning, they left the house early, deciding to stop somewhere for breakfast on the way to the station. They came across a small cafe that had pancakes and waffles as well as coffee that smelled amazing when they walked past, tempting them inside. It was lovely to have a leisurely breakfast together as if it was something they might do all the time.

Afterwards, they strolled through Hyde Park, which was full of runners and families with small children who were early-risers, towards Paddington Station where they caught the train to Oxford.

As they alighted the bus they'd caught from Oxford station back to Summertown at the stop nearest Fliss's house, she began to feel inexplicably nervous. It felt strange for Brun to be in her place for the first time when until now, she'd only known him in places familiar to him.

'The house is a bit of a mess,' she said, beginning to chatter nervously. 'And it's not as warm as yours, even with the wood-burner on and we're so low on logs, I should have ordered another load.'

He squeezed her hand and smiled at her, a hint of laughter in his eyes. 'I do not care about any of that. I am here only to see you, to be with you.'

That didn't make her feel any better and when they turned into her street and she saw Duncan's car parked outside her house, her heart sank even further.

'That's Duncan's car,' said Fliss, not able to think of a reason why he would be at her house.

'Okay. Perhaps Josh or Emma needed to come back for something?'

That was the most rational explanation. 'Probably.'

The front door was ajar. She went inside to find Duncan in the kitchen on his phone, pacing up and down as he spoke to whoever it was. His agitation was clear and Fliss knew that something was wrong.

She waited for what felt like minutes but was only the time it took for him to thank the person and end the call.

'What's happened? Are the children alright?'

'Emma's missing.'

30

'Where's Josh?' She couldn't process what Duncan meant. What did it mean? Emma's missing. Josh would be able to tell her.

'I'm here, Mum.' He came into the kitchen from the lounge, past Brun who was stood in the doorway looking understandably perplexed.

She and Josh hugged. 'What does your dad mean, Emma's missing? What happened? Do you know where she went?'

'She was upset last night before we went to bed. We talked and I thought she was okay but then this morning she was gone.'

'What was she upset about?'

Josh shot Duncan a telling look.

'What happened?' She looked from Josh to Duncan. She could tell that Duncan was daring Josh to tell her whatever it was and she could also see that Josh wasn't sure what would be the right thing to do. She broke the eye contact between the two of them by standing in front of Josh. 'It's okay, just tell me, whatever it is.'

'Dad and Shona were arguing…'

'Hang on a minute,' Duncan began.

'Shut up, Duncan,' Fliss said firmly.

'Emma was really upset and said she wanted to come home. She went down to ask Dad and she heard Shona saying… some stuff about us. She came back upstairs and we talked it through. I thought she was alright after that because we decided to come home by ourselves this morning. Then when she wasn't there this morning, I thought she'd be here. But she isn't.'

Fliss turned on Duncan. 'How could you let this happen? It's once in a blue moon that I ever ask you to have the kids and you can't even make them welcome when they're your children!'

Duncan did look shamefaced but quickly hit back with, 'Your phone's been off. What if she'd tried to call you? Why did you tell them you'd be here when you weren't? Where were you last night?'

'That's none of your business and that's not why she's gone. She's missing because she wasn't welcome at her father's house!'

'And her mother wasn't here for her!'

Fliss took her phone out of her bag and plugged it into the charger that was on the kitchen counter. It took a few moments for it to spring into life and she took those moments to gather herself. It was awful for Josh to hear this. She had to try and calm things down. At the moment, it didn't matter whose fault it was that Emma was gone, they just needed to find her.

'Have you contacted her friends?' she asked and Josh nodded.

'Everyone we could think of. Abbie is getting Ellie to contact all of their school friends,' he said.

Fliss's phone started to ping and everyone gathered around to see if there was anything from Emma.

There were several missed calls which had started in the early hours of the morning, long after Fliss's phone had died.

The last one had been at six am and there was a voicemail message.

'Mum, where are you? I've come home but I forgot my key. I thought you were going to be here? We need to come home. Dad doesn't want us. I don't know what to do.' The last sentence was accompanied by a sob before the message ended.

Fliss gulped for air. It was her fault. Emma had tried to call and she hadn't been there. She'd been off with Brun, not giving her children a second thought for the entire night. And now this had happened.

She felt strong arms around her, and allowed Brun to lead her into the lounge where he sat her down next to him on the sofa.

'It's my fault,' she stuttered.

'It is not your fault,' he said, the certainty in his voice a momentary comfort until her guilt overwhelmed her again.

'If you hadn't swanned off and let your phone die, this wouldn't have happened,' Duncan said, appearing in the doorway.

'That is not fair,' Brun said. 'Fliss left the children in your care. She had planned to be away and should not have needed to worry about them.'

'It's okay, Brun,' said Fliss, having difficulty reconciling the fact that Brun was here with Duncan, providing evidence of exactly what she was being accused of.

'And who are you anyway?' Duncan asked. 'Had a fling with a neanderthal, have you Fliss?'

'Duncan!'

Brun stood up and walked towards Duncan, his broad frame dwarfing the other man and for a moment Duncan looked worried.

'Do not speak to her like that. Everyone is upset but it is not helping anyone to be rude or place the blame.'

'This is nothing to do with you,' Duncan sneered, as soon as he realised Brun wasn't going to start a fight.

'Dad, stop it!'

Duncan turned away. 'I'm going out to look for her. You wait here and keep telling yourself it's not your fault!'

Fliss dissolved into tears the moment he had gone.

'Mum, it's not your fault. It's Dad and Shona. She hates us and he didn't stick up for us. He said he'd sort something out to get rid of us, and Emma was gutted. She didn't want to stay. I should have left with her last night but I thought it'd be better to come home today. I don't know why she didn't wait.'

Fliss and Josh embraced each other, crying into each other's shoulders while Brun watched over them.

'I know it is obvious, but have you tried to call her? Brun asked Josh once they had stopped.

'Yes, there's no answer.'

'And neither of you have a tracker for her on your phones?'

'No, I don't think so,' said Fliss. 'Do we Josh?' He was always her first port of call for anything technical.

'No but I have an idea.' He pulled his phone out and pressed the screen a few times. 'I don't know why I didn't think of this before. Snapmaps.'

'I thought both of you had turned off the location thing on that app,' Fliss said, sniffing and reaching into her pocket for a tissue. 'I did ask you to.'

'It's just an idea, Mum,' said Josh. 'I don't know if she has it on or not but it's worth a try.'

He looked at his phone and frowned. 'It says she's here.'

'But she isn't. Are you sure that's now and not this morning when she rang me?'

'It's now.'

'Perhaps she left her phone outside, has anyone checked

the garden?' Brun said, already heading outside.

They both followed him, searching the garden for any sign that Emma had been there, or that she'd left her phone.

'Do you have a shed?' Brun asked. To be fair, the bottom of the garden was so overgrown that if there was one, it wasn't obvious.

'No, nothing like that' said Fliss, beginning to despair again.

Brun strode down to the bottom of the garden and stood there, carefully scanning around. Then he vaulted the fence that was the boundary between Fliss's garden and her neighbour's.

'What's he doing?' Josh asked, looking surprised and impressed.

'I don't know,' Fliss said, and went to lean over the fence to see.

He was holding the neighbour's shed door open where Emma was asleep, curled up under her coat on some garden furniture.

'Emma!' called Josh, 'Em, wake up!'

Fliss was crying happy tears as she watched Emma wake up, wondering why Brun was standing over her. He led her out of the shed and lifted her over the fence into Fliss's garden.

'Oh my god, Emma. We had no idea where you were!' Fliss said, squeezing her daughter as if she was never going to let go. 'What were you doing in there?'

'I was cold so I thought I'd wait in there until I saw you come home. Then I must have fallen asleep.'

'And you walked all the way here from Dad's house in the middle of the night?'

'Shall we go inside and warm up,' Brun suggested.

Fliss made tea for them all while Brun lit the fire in an attempt to make the place feel cosy for Emma who was feeling the chill and was sat on the sofa with her coat on.

'I've rung Dad to let him know,' Josh said, coming into the kitchen. It was something Fliss hadn't even thought of. 'He said he'd come over later with our stuff.'

'Thank you for thinking about that.'

'What will happen now? Emma won't want to go to Dad's again.'

Fliss could hear the worry in his voice.

'Don't worry, Joshy,' she said, giving him a hug. 'I'll talk to Dad. If it's too difficult for him to have you to stay, that's fine. He just needs to tell me and we can stick to outings for dinner and things like that so that you can see him.'

Fliss and Josh went into the lounge where Emma was curled up in the corner of the sofa with the blanket from Iceland while Brun was telling her about excursions when things had got a bit hairy, presumably in an attempt to put her adventure into context.

It seemed crazy now to have been so frantic when all the time she was asleep in the shed next door, but for Fliss it was about more than that. This was a wake-up call that she should have seen coming. Duncan wasn't reliable. His priorities had changed, if not when he started having an affair with Shona, then certainly now that Dylan was here. It was sad but true that his first-born children were less important to him than his new family. She had given him space when Dylan was born, aware that he needed to be the one setting the agenda for how his new child interacted with Josh and Emma and her trip to Iceland was really the first time since then that she'd pushed for something more than he was willing to give her. And it had back-fired. She'd been so caught up in everything that had happened during and after that trip that she hadn't stopped to think. When she had suggested this weekend to him, she should have questioned whether he really could give the time to it or whether he said yes out of duty. So although she could kill Duncan for breaking his daughter's heart, she should have known better than to put Josh and Emma in that position again.

They'd finished their tea and Josh was quizzing Brun about whether he really had seen a volcano erupt when Emma announced she was going to have a bath and then would watch Netflix in bed.

'If you're going to hog Netflix for the rest of the day I'm going to watch an episode of Cobra Kai while you're in the bath,' said Josh, leaving the room at a sprint and taking the stairs two at a time.

'I'm sorry, Mum. I shouldn't have come home without talking to you,' Emma said, giving Fliss a hug.

'It's okay, lovely. As long as you're okay, nothing else matters.'

When Emma had left the room, Fliss breathed a sigh of relief and leant back on her chair with her eyes closed for a moment.

'This isn't what I had planned,' she said.

'I didn't think so,' he said, smiling. 'The weekend starts here?'

'I don't think it does.' She looked at him, hoping he would know how she was feeling without having to explain herself. Because she wasn't sure what to say. 'Maybe it's better if we call this the end of the weekend.'

He frowned. 'You mean I should leave?'

'I have a lot to sort out. Duncan is bringing the kids stuff back later and we have some serious talking to do.' She could see the hurt in his eyes but her priority was Josh and Emma. She was never going to get her head back into being Brun's girlfriend for the rest of the weekend.

'I would like to stay and support you, Fliss. You don't have to be in this by yourself. I know it is your family but if we are going to be together, these are things I can be part of, to help.'

Fliss moved from her chair to sit next to him on the sofa. What she was about to say, what she needed to say even though it was making her heart break, brought tears to her eyes. She could see Brun register that it wasn't going to be something he wanted to hear and he turned away, swiping his fingers across his own eyes.

He stood up. 'I think I had better leave you to all of this. I can stay at Ned's for the rest of the weekend.'

She tried to catch his fingers in hers but he pulled away. She didn't want to hurt him but at the same time, the thought of him being here, with Duncan accusing her of being a bad mother because she'd been with Brun when Emma went missing, was too hard to bear. She had to be strong when she saw Duncan again. Having Brun here would just be a reminder of the lapse in judgement she'd made by agreeing to stay in London with him, unplanned.

'I'll call you,' she said weakly, knowing her words weren't enough but not knowing what else she could say.

'There is no need,' Brun said, the hurt in his eyes giving way to a steely dispassion as he grabbed the bag he had left next to the front door. 'Good bye, Fliss.'

31

For the next few weeks, Fliss operated in a state of high activity, not allowing herself a single moment to think about how she felt at all. If her mind wandered, it wasn't for long because thinking of Brun filled her with shame at how she had treated him and sorrow at how she had broken his heart, much less her own. She couldn't contemplate the luxury of feeling sorry for herself because it was entirely her own fault.

The writing of the fifth book in the series was a godsend because she could lose herself for hours in thinking about plot points and even how the next book in the series might shape up. She found herself writing more intricately about the case that Margot was helping to solve, purely because she'd given it so much thought. But what she'd gained in plot nuances, she'd lost in Margot's fledgling relationship with the detective. She couldn't bring herself to write that kind of happiness for Margot when she'd lost it for herself. Instead, the enemies-to-lovers storyline that she'd started, became an enemy-to-criminal one when she decided that the detective was a baddie.

After that terrible weekend, she hadn't spoken to Brun properly. She'd attempted to explain herself in a long email, telling him quite honestly that she felt so guilty about leaving her children that weekend, she couldn't forgive herself.

Having spoken to Duncan, she'd established that he was unable to give Josh and Emma the kind of parenting that they and Fliss expected of him and in some ways, she was glad that he'd finally admitted it. It made everything easier now that they knew where they stood. But it meant that Fliss didn't have anyone to call on, apart from Lily and Frank, if she needed some alone time. She felt like more of a single parent than ever before.

Luckily, Abbie was perfectly happy to ignore Fliss fobbing her off every time she tried to organise a trip to the pub or a Saturday morning coffee, and eventually turned up on the doorstep with a bottle of wine.

'I said I couldn't do tonight,' Fliss said when she opened the door.

'You do look very busy,' said Abbie, bustling past her into the kitchen.

Fliss had got into the habit of putting her pyjamas on every evening when she got home from work. Josh had commented on it a couple of times, going so far as to say it was weird, but she'd assured him it was just while she was writing as it helped to be comfortable. The kids were upstairs as had become their habit every evening after dinner.

'I'm right in the middle of an important chapter,' she said, still thinking that she might be able to stop Abbie from making herself at home, even though she was already pouring two glasses of wine.

'Okay, take five minutes to make some notes so you don't lose your thread.'

Annoyingly, Fliss hadn't actually been writing but had been researching some forensic psychology techniques. 'Well, I've stopped now. It's fine.'

Abbie smiled brightly, ignoring Fliss's tone of irritation, and settled herself at the kitchen table. 'So, how're things with you?'

Fliss hadn't actually told Abbie that she and Brun were over, she'd simply stopped telling her anything. It had been much the same when Duncan had left. In fact, there were quite a few parallels now she thought about it.

'Things are great, thanks. My publisher bought the next three books so I've delivered the two I'd already written and I'm writing the third.'

'That's brilliant news! Congratulations.'

Abbie's enthusiasm thawed Fliss a little bit. 'How are you? How did Finn and Ellie get on with the mocks?'

'Not too bad. I think Finn had a bit of a wake-up call at how much work he's going to need to put in to get the grades he wants but it wasn't awful. Has Josh decided on his first choice university yet?'

'We're supposed to be going to Bristol to look around in a couple of weeks. I think he's quite keen on Cardiff but the grades are high there for psychology.'

Abbie nodded. 'Finn's looking at Manchester. He really fancies St Andrews but it's miles away so we've been trying to talk him out of it.'

'It'd be nice for visiting him at weekends though,' said Fliss, finally feeling like she might be enjoying her friend's company after a few sips of wine and some adult conversation.

'Anyway, how are things with you and Brun?'

Fliss's eyes filled with tears and she stared into her wine, concentrating hard on not allowing herself to cry.

'Is it because of what happened with Emma?' Abbie asked gently, handing her a tissue from the box on the side.

Fliss nodded. 'I can't have a relationship when the kids still need me. If I hadn't been in London with Brun that night...'

'It wasn't your fault.'

'We stayed on a whim and my phone went dead. What

kind of mother lets that happen when her kids might need to contact her? It's unforgivable.'

'Fliss. They were with Duncan. You shouldn't have to even think about their welfare when they're with him. You deserve some downtime from that. Do you think he's worried about them every minute he's not with them? Don't let him drag you back to where you were three years ago.'

'I'm…' She was about to argue. To say that this wasn't what she was like three years ago when Duncan left. But it was. She'd been a reclusive mess then as well.

Now she did start crying. For what she'd lost and for allowing herself to be unwittingly manipulated by Duncan into feeling like all of this was her fault.

For hurting Brun.

She wept while Abbie held her. How could she be hurting like this? It was worse than before. Worse than when Duncan had left. Worse because she'd lost more.

Finally she took another tissue and blew her nose.

'Shit, Abbie. Look at me.'

'You look fine,' she said with a smile. 'More importantly what are you going to do now?'

'I don't know. It's been weeks and we haven't spoken.'

'I assume you're talking about Brun. What do you want to happen? If you forget all of this stuff that's happened with the kids and Duncan, what would you have in your dream scenario?'

She didn't need to think. 'I'd want Brun. But I don't think he'd want me now, not after the way I treated him.' An involuntary sob escaped. 'He wanted to stay and help me. He was trying to stick up for me against Duncan and I sent him away. I thought it would make things worse if he stayed and all it's done is ruin the best thing that had happened to me in years.'

'Are you sure it's ruined?'

Fliss nodded. 'I emailed him and he didn't reply.'

'To tell him it was over?'

She nodded.

'Well, what's he meant to say to that?'

Fliss laughed through her tears. 'I don't know!'

'If he feels the same way, don't you think he'd be willing to give you a second chance?'

'Yes, I think he would but nothing's changed. I can't go to him and offer anything more than before.' She blew her nose and took a gulp of wine.

'As far as I know, apologies aren't conditional on anything,' said Abbie. 'He was willing to stay that weekend. Most men would have seen that whole domestic thing going on, all the complication between you and Duncan, and run a mile. He loves you, that was why he didn't do that.'

'And I made him leave.' The sobs threatened again as she remembered the look in his eyes as he left.

'You were scared, Fliss. It's a huge step to let someone into your life like this again. That day with Emma was a very high-tension situation and you panicked. I'm sure you can explain that to him.'

'But what if it happens again? What if I push him away again?'

'Do you wish you hadn't done that this time? Any regrets, Fliss?' Abbie was getting quite animated now.

'Okay, I know what you mean. But if you'd told me I'd panic like that and do what I did, I'd never have believed you, and that's what happened.'

'Things are different now, though, right? Emma told me that the kids aren't seeing Duncan like before. They're just having dinner with him, nothing too intense,' she said, making Duncan sound like he couldn't take it, and making Fliss smile.

Fliss sighed. 'You're right. I don't think we'd be in that

situation again. And I would never wish Brun away again.' Because she knew it was the worst mistake she'd ever made. She just wasn't sure how to make it right.

32

Since Oxford, Brun had worked on every excursion he could in an effort to keep himself busy. Even though he'd been alone after Fliss left Iceland before, this time it was different because he knew he was never going to see her again. It was hard to think about how the end had come about, not because either of them had fallen out of love with each other but because it was bad timing.

The email she'd sent had said exactly that, amongst the many, many lines of apologies. Bad timing. She had to devote herself to her children now that her ex-husband was unable to commit himself to them in the way he had before. Perhaps pre-empting what he might say after some of their conversations in Iceland, she had specifically told him not to think about offering to wait for her. She'd signed off by thanking him for one of the most amazing weeks of her life, saying that she'd always remember him with love in her heart. It was a definite goodbye.

The hurt and anger he'd come away from Oxford with had waned. Talking it through with his sister-in-law, Olga, had helped. She'd explained to him about the ever-present motherly guilt that Fliss would have been overwhelmed with when Emma went missing and how this most likely clouded her judgment of the situation. So although he still hurt, it helped to understand why Fliss had reacted so strongly.

He'd not played at the open mic night since then, and Ned couldn't play that song without him. Ned had been pretty understanding about the whole situation and hadn't asked again about recording the song. Although what did it matter now? It wasn't their song anymore and Fliss had given him her blessing to do it. It was only his broken heart holding him back, knowing he couldn't sing the song without his voice breaking too.

The day before the next open mic night, Ned came knocking at his door.

'Are you coming tomorrow night?'

Brun shrugged. 'Yes, if everyone is going. The aurora forecast is terrible this week so I am not working.'

'Look, I know you don't want to sing that song and I understand why.'

'Thank you.'

Ned took a deep breath. 'But I have to say this. It's a great song and it's wasting away not being played.' His eyes were pleading with Brun and desperation was written all over his face. 'How about we give it a go tomorrow night?'

'I cannot sing those words, Ned. I'm sorry.'

'Okay.' He paused. 'I don't want to be insensitive so please tell me to sod off if you want to. Could we, and I really mean you, write different words? Words that won't break your heart making you think of Fliss? We keep the melody and the English words and change the Icelandic ones. It doesn't have to be a love song just because it sounds like one.'

Brun raised an eyebrow. Perhaps this was what he needed. To pour his feelings into new lyrics that spoke of the loss he was feeling. 'I could try. It probably will not be for tomorrow though.'

'That's okay. Whenever you're ready.' Ned embraced him

and clapped him on the back. 'I appreciate this, Brun.'

'You have done a lot for me Ned, and you did for Fliss. I will write the words and then we will try it out at the open mic night, tomorrow or next week.'

'You're on. Get Jonas to put someone else on the rota for next week just in case the aurora come out to play.'

By the following morning Brun had written new words that he knew he would be able to sing. It was still a song that he would forever associate with Fliss but the words were no longer telling of his love for her but of the crack in his heart at losing her. Singing the words inexplicably helped, he began to realise as he sang them over and over getting them to sink into his brain. It was cathartic as if everything that had been trapped inside of him, all of the sadness and heartbreak was released a little bit with every word he sang.

On his way out, he knocked on Ned and Anna's front door. It was dark and early because he was leading an excursion to the Golden Circle, and Ned opened the door looking like he was still asleep.

'We are on for tonight. I have WhatsApped you a recording of the new lyrics. See what you think but I can play if you want to do it.'

Ned threw his arms around Brun, suddenly wide awake. 'Thanks, man.'

33

Since her publisher had changed their marketing strategy based on what they'd gleaned from the Icelandic market, they were successfully selling Fliss's books everywhere. As her titles slowly but surely climbed the charts, she found herself having to devote more and more time to attending events like bookshop signings and even the odd radio interview.

All of this helped her achieve her goal of not having any time to wallow over Brun. Time had not been the great healer she'd hoped it would be and she still felt raw. So when Eva shared the publisher's plans for a return trip to Iceland for the launch of the third book, she was torn about what to do.

If she didn't think too hard about it, she would have jumped at the chance because she'd loved it last time. Even taking Brun out of the equation, she still would have loved every minute of that trip, connecting with her readers and renewing her inspiration for writing about Margot. The chance to return to launch her next book, knowing that the Icelandic readers would devour it; it was ridiculous to even think about not going.

But Brun was part of the equation. If she'd handled things differently, if they'd not decided to pursue anything when she left Iceland, she could be going back and casually contacting him for a hook up since she happened to be in his area. Wasn't that what people did? Unfortunately — or fortunately — neither of them were those kinds of people. Fliss had no idea whether Brun would have moved on by now and found someone else to write songs about but her gut told her that he would still be feeling as wretched about it all as she was. Contacting him, even if he was single, would open up old wounds, They might not have healed but Fliss liked to think they were beginning to scab over.

'Obviously you're going to say yes,' Lily said, when Fliss called to sound her out about looking after Josh and Emma.

'I probably am,' she admitted. 'Abbie has said she can have the kids round at hers in the daytime. They'll be happy to hang out with Finn and Ellie, so it'd just be overnight.' Although it was only the beginning of July, they had both finished school and were on exam leave with just the odd exam left to take.

'It's fine. It was a pleasure to have them here at Christmas, you know that.'

'Thanks, Lil. And I think this time it'll only be two or three days.'

'Say yes, Fliss and then let me know what you need.'

Josh and Emma were quite happy with the arrangements, grateful to have the freedom to go between their friends' and their aunt and uncle's house. Duncan wasn't exactly out of the picture but they limited their time with him to dinner every couple of weeks or so and they all seemed happy with that for now.

'Do you think you'll see Brun?' Josh asked when she told him she'd decided to go back to Iceland.

'I don't think so,' she said, unsure what gave Josh the impression that Brun was even on her radar any more.

'Come on Mum, you've been miserable since that weekend.'

She was about to brush off his comments but then, for Josh to have picked up on how she'd been feeling she obviously hadn't been hiding it very well. He deserved an explanation.

'I have. But I'm not sure seeing Brun will help.'

'Because you love him?'

Slightly stunned, Fliss said, 'I did love him, yes. It wasn't the right time, though.'

'But that's why you had to think about going there again?'

Fliss laughed. Was this really her seventeen-year-old son who was suddenly so insightful?

'It was amazing last time, with Brun. I suppose Iceland is inextricably linked to him now so it might be strange to go back. A bit scary, if I'm honest.'

'I think it's great, Mum. I wish we could come with you.'

She paused. 'Well, why don't you? I don't know why I didn't think of it before. Your exams will be over, it's perfect timing. Let's all go to Iceland!'

Summer in Iceland was a very different place. With no snow on the roads, and some idea of what she was doing, Fliss had decided there was no need for her to have a chaperone this time and instead had requested to collect a hire car from the airport so that she could show Josh and Emma around herself.

'Are you sure you can drive on the other side of the road?' Emma asked.

'Of course. Trust me, Em. Right. Let's go.'

She pulled out of the car park and headed towards the main road that led to Reykjavik. It felt great to be back. It was a beautiful sunny day, with blue skies and a refreshing breeze, although not quite as warm as it looked. The snow-covered winter landscape had melted to make way for a surprisingly lush countryside dotted with purple lupins and arctic thyme amongst other things that Fliss couldn't name.

There had been so much snow when she left that it was hard to believe it had time to melt away, let alone made way for all this flora and fauna.

The launch event for her new book was the following day at Penninn Eymundsson, a blessing since it was one of the only places that wasn't full of memories of Brun. Then they were planning to stay in Reykjavik for a week to see the sights and have a break after the stress of the exams. It felt like a real adventure.

Eva had given Fliss a budget for the hotel and allowed her to make her own arrangements. She'd settled on a two-bedroom apartment on the top floor of a building close to the Harpa. It had a small kitchen so they could cook for themselves — essential for keeping the cost down and for catering to Emma's whims. There was a carpark not far away so it all seemed pretty perfect.

They spent the afternoon settling in, which eventually included a stroll to the nearest supermarket. It was strange at first for Fliss to get her bearings now that there was no snow. And she was on edge expecting Brun to be around every corner so it was a relief when the kids were happy to laze around the apartment for the rest of the day. In preparation for such an eventuality, she had packed her knitting which hadn't been touched since things had gone wrong with Brun. Now, she felt that urge to knit again. It wasn't snowy or cold enough to need to wear an Icelandic jumper but she remembered how the rhythm of the stitches had soothed her when she'd been anxious about getting home in the storm and she'd somehow known that she'd need that with her while she was here again. This time without Brun.

The following morning, Fliss woke with her knitting strewn across the bed. She must have fallen asleep with it in her hands, still needing to fill every void with activity. Aside from losing a couple of stitches mid-row where she'd stopped, it was intact and salvageable. She got out of bed and opened the blinds to reveal a day as bright as anything, even at six am. It hadn't been dark when they decided to turn in, and without darkness as a signal to sleep, it had felt very strange going to bed. Thank goodness for blackout blinds.

She quietly made a cup of tea and then pottered around getting her outfit ready. She'd chosen a long dress which had a tiered skirt that floated around her ankles. It was fuschia pink with gathered puff sleeves and tiny pleats down the front of the bodice. She'd brought her denim jacket to wear over the top and Emma had insisted the only thing to do was wear white leather trainers, so Fliss had a brand new pair for the occasion.

'What are we meant to do while you're doing the book launch?' Emma asked with a mouthful of cinnamon bun. They'd stopped at a bakery — not *the* bakery, just in case — for breakfast on the way to the bookshop.

'We'll just watch,' Josh said, as if it were obvious.

'I think there will be a chat first which you might find interesting and then I'll be signing books. It might be for a couple of hours, it depends on how it goes. If you get bored you can always go back to the apartment.' She handed the key to Josh just in case.

'Are you nervous?'

'A bit nervous. I'm not sure I'll ever get used to this kind of thing but I love it once I'm there and I can see the readers and see how much they're enjoying the books.'

'You'll be great, Mum.'

They arrived at the bookshop where Fliss was greeted with huge enthusiasm by the same woman she'd met last time. She couldn't pronounce her name; it had an Icelandic sound in it that was almost impossible for anyone else to say, but she was very friendly and found somewhere for the kids to sit while Fliss got herself ready.

There were several rows of chairs crammed into the main floorspace and they were almost all occupied. It was very different to the last time she'd been there, which had been only a signing. A quick scan reassured Fliss that no-one she knew was there and her anxiety began to abate as she started to anticipate the joy of being able to introduce her new book to people who she knew were desperate to read it.

While she was being introduced, after the clapping had died down, Fliss sneaked a look at Josh and Emma and was touched to see them both smiling, pleased and amazed to see the reaction the crowd had to their mum.

The event began with Fliss reading the first chapter of the new book. It was the first time she'd shared these words that she'd written almost two years ago and she felt it was a privilege to be able to do that in person. There was still a nagging doubt about whether they'd like it but every time she looked up when she paused, she could see that everyone in the audience was hanging on her every word. It was amazing.

It seemed like hours later when she finally signed a book for the last person in the line. Josh and Emma had gone back to the apartment and she was looking forward to joining them and opening the bottle of wine she'd picked up the day before.

Just as she was about to put the top back on her pen, another book was placed on the table in front of her. It was closed, the slip of paper with the person's name on poking out from inside the front cover.

She opened the book and saw the name.

It was Brun.

Even though it had been a distinct possibility that he could have been at the event, sat in the front row, waiting for her, since he hadn't been she'd completely put it out of her mind. So now that he was standing in front of her, sturdy, smart and as beautifully beardy as ever, she wasn't ready. She'd let her guard down.

'Brun.'

'Fliss. It is good to see you.' He was smiling. That look from the last time she'd seen him, which had haunted her for months was gone.

Should she sign the book? Is that why he came?

'You too.'

She sat looking at him for a few moments until he glanced at the book and she realised that he was waiting for her to sign it after all. That was why he'd come, and her heart sank with disappointment.

'Thank you for coming,' she said, while what she meant was, 'Are you still angry? Do you still love me? Did you wait for me?' But she had no right to ask him any of those things. After pushing him out of her life, he had to be the one to make the first move. If there was one to be made.

'I am happy to see this book,' he said, as she closed the cover and handed it to him, placing the paper that he'd written his name on, on top of the pile of others.

'I'm glad you came.'

'Me too.'

He stood there for a moment longer, even though it seemed there was nothing else to say.

'I should go, it has been a long day for you.'

He smiled and took a step back.

That was it, he was leaving and she couldn't say anything to stop him.

Perhaps that was why she'd come here. It was a form of closure. She'd known deep down that she would come across him and after the way they'd parted in March, seeing him again underlined for her that it really was over. He hadn't come in and swept her off her feet. He'd come to say goodbye.

At least now, she could go home and begin to start forgetting about what might have been.

She watched him leave the shop, took a deep breath and began to tidy the table, piling the remaining books, of which there were very few, into a neat pile and shoving everything else into her bag. She found the woman with the unpronounceable name and said her goodbyes, thanking them for making her so welcome and requesting that they share some of the many photographs they'd taken during the course of the event with her.

The walk back to the apartment was a welcome chance to catch her breath and compose herself. Of course he wasn't going to turn up and declare his undying love for her. It wasn't lack of love that had kept them apart. If only it was as easy as that.

By the time she got back, she felt exhausted and was looking forward to the glass of wine she'd promised herself. Josh and Emma were in their bedroom, lying on Josh's bed watching something on Netflix together on her laptop. She poured herself a glass of wine and pulled everything out of her bag ready to pack it in her case. The work part of the trip was over and she wouldn't need her notebook and pens again.

The slips of paper that had everyone's names on fell out onto the table and she shuffled them together into a pile ready to bin. There was one which had more writing on it than just someone's name. She frowned, not remembering seeing it earlier.

Dearest Fliss, When I found out you were coming back, I did not want to open old wounds that may have healed. But I had to see you. Now, I am leaving fate to decide whether you see this or not and I leave you to decide whether you feel any differently than the last time we were together. But know that my heart is yours.

Always, Brun.

Her breath caught in her throat. This was everything she wanted. She had no idea how they were going to make it work, but he still loved her and that was all she needed to know.

'I'm just popping out,' she said to the kids, who had barely registered the fact she'd arrived back in the first place and grunted an acknowledgment.

She headed away from the harbour towards Laugavegur, knowing she'd recognise the way to Brun's house from there. Her heart was beating out of her chest in anticipation, all the things she might say running through her mind too quickly for her to register what they might be.

The small gardens either side of the cobbled path that led to the cluster of houses where Brun lived were green, full of flowers and some troll-like ornaments that must have been covered by the snow before. She climbed the stairs to Brun's front door and knocked.

He was there. She could see his shadow move across the window as he came towards the door and she could hardly believe she was there, about to see him again but knowing now that he had forgiven her.

'Hey,' he said, smiling, holding the door open as an invitation to enter.

'Hi. I got your note.'

She went inside and waited as he closed the door behind her.

'I hoped you would.' He seemed reluctant to come to her.

'I am so sorry for what happened when you came to Oxford. I should never have asked you to leave and it's something I've regretted every day since. I was scared and I know that's not an excuse for hurting you the way I did. I don't deserve your heart, Brun.' Saying it all out loud made her feel lighter and, feeling brave, she reached for his hand.

'I know you have been hurting as much as I have. The way I feel about you hasn't changed.'

'I still don't know how it can work but I do know I would like to try again.' She looked into his eyes, willing him to want the same.

'Things have changed for me,' he said.

Fliss gulped, unsure of whether she could stand to hear any more, yet still holding his fingers in hers. Seemingly for the last time.

'Oh, I completely understand,' she said, hoping that a bright smile would keep the tears at bay until she walked back down the steps and out of his life again, this time for good. 'It's been good to see each other to say goodbye. I'll always hold you in my heart too, Brun. What we had was special and I'll never forget it.'

She turned to leave but he kept hold of her hand, forcing her to turn back.

'No, Fliss. I mean, things have changed because I am working with Ned for a while. I will be on tour with him in England until Christmas.'

Still not entirely understanding, Fliss said, 'Oh. That's great.'

'I would like to see you. A lot, while I am there.'

'I'd love that!' she said and threw her arms around him as he gave one of his huge laughs before he picked her up and twirled her around.

'I was hoping so,' he said, burying his face in her hair and planting kisses on her head.

'I love you so much.'

'*Hjarta mitt er þitt.*'

'Am I going to have to learn Icelandic?'

He shook his head. 'You know what it means in here,' he said, placing his hand on his chest.

Fliss started as she meant to go on and took Brun back to the apartment with her. Josh and Emma had finished watching the film and were lying on their beds with their phones in their hands.

'We're going out,' said Fliss.

'Hey guys,' said Brun, making them both look up in surprise.

Emma leapt up and came towards him.

'I wanted to say thanks for finding me in the shed,' she said, unsurely. 'And I'm sorry for ruining your weekend.'

Brun frowned and shook his head. 'No, it was not your fault at all. And it is old history. Can I take you out for a drink? I know a very cool place.'

Once they were ready, he led the way to the hotel that he and Fliss had visited in the storm. It was finished, open and even higher-end than Fliss had expected. He spoke a few words in Icelandic to the woman on the reception desk and then they took a lift to the top floor. The doors opened revealing the way to the outside, which was dressed with an arch of foliage. It led onto the roof terrace which was bathed in sunshine but had large parasols to give shade. With the addition of the furniture, more foliage and the absence of the storm, it felt very different to the last time she'd been there. In the far corner, opposite the sauna, was a small bar area shaded by a canvas sail that was roped to the walls.

'I think we should have champagne,' said Brun, raising his eyebrows at Fliss, who nodded her agreement.

'Can we have champagne?' Emma asked, predictably.

'A sip,' said Fliss, 'but choose a drink for yourselves as well.'

'What are we celebrating?' Josh asked, once they were sat at table with their array of drinks.

Fliss looked to Brun who gave a small nod.

'Brun and I are back together. He's coming to the UK to tour with Ned so hopefully we can see a lot more of each other.'

'That's brilliant,' Josh said, grinning. 'Cheers,' he said, holding his coke aloft.

'*Skål*!' said Brun, passing Fliss a glass of champagne so that they could all clink glasses.

'*Skål*!' They all said in unison.

'Can we come and watch a show?' asked Emma.

'I hope you will come to more than one. Perhaps we can all go on the road together while it is still the holidays?'

Fliss thought she might explode with joy. It seemed like it might work. At least for now. Having the blessing of her children meant everything and she knew that whatever happened, Brun understood that they were her priority. He always had. It was her who had pushed him away at the first sign of trouble when he had always been ready to stand by her side.

The kids went to the edge of the roof to look across the rooftops to the sea and the mountains beyond and Fliss took the opportunity to talk to Brun.

'If I ever panic and push you away again, don't go.'

'My love, I will do everything I can not to leave your side and I hope now that I am no longer a tour guide it will be possible.'

'Don't go anywhere. When you're in the UK, would you stay with me?'

His face broke into a huge smile, knowing what a big step that was for her. 'I would love that, if you are sure?'

'Things are different for me too now. Josh is going to university, they've both settled into a relationship with their dad that's much easier for everyone. I finally feel like I can reclaim my life and I don't want to hide what we have from the kids. We don't need to.'

'Thank you, Fliss,' he said softly.

'And I don't think I will be going back to my job in September. My last royalty statement is more than I could have imagined and I'm going to write full time.'

'So many more things to celebrate!' he said, topping up their glasses.

'To us,' she said, placing her hand on his beardy jaw, loving the feel of it as he pressed his cheek into her hand.

'To us. Do you think the kids will notice if we go downstairs and find a room?'

He laughed loudly at Fliss's shocked expression, that quickly turned into a smile as soon as she realised he was joking. Josh and Emma turned round and began laughing at Brun's laugh, the first time they'd ever heard it. And Fliss didn't think it was possible to be happier than she was on this rooftop in Reykjavik. Iceland had changed her life in more ways than she could have imagined.

She looked up at the sky, as bright now that it was evening as it had been at midday, and thanked her lucky stars for that storm which had been the start of everything.

The End

Author's Note

I can't believe this is the third Iceland story! I knew that if I wrote a third, Brun was going to be the one to find love this time. I also knew that I wanted a slightly older heroine and someone with the kind of life that lots of us are juggling, who perhaps doesn't think they have the time or the freedom to find someone to love. Fliss turned out to be someone I would love to be friends with, especially because she started knitting!

This book may not have been written, at least not with Brun as the hero, if it were not for my friend Sue. She has fancied him from the Snug in Iceland days and urged me to give him his own story. She also suggested his love interest should be called Sue but I did take up her alternative suggestion of Fliss, so hopefully that makes up for it. She'd have preferred it to be a bloodthirsty slasher book but you can't have everything Sue.

Thank you to Catrin, for editing, proof-reading and appreciating the knitting reference in the title. Thanks to Berni Stevens for another fab cover, it's always one of my favourite parts of the process. Thanks to my family, James, Jake and Claudia for attempting to come up with a title. I think it was my suggestion in the end but your input was (mostly) appreciated.

Thank you for choosing to read this book. This Icelandic Romance series is very close to my heart and would never have even become a series if it weren't for the support of fabulous readers like you who let me know that you loved Snug in Iceland and asked for a sequel. Reviews mean such a lot to writers, so if you have time to leave a review for a book you've enjoyed, it really does make all the difference.

The best way to keep in touch is to sign up to my exclusive mailing list at victoriaauthor.co.uk. I'll send a newsletter every month or so to keep you up to date with what I'm up to, as well as any special offers, new releases and exclusive content. You can also find me in all of these places:

Instagram @victoriawalker_author
Facebook Victoria Walker - Author
Twitter @4victoriawalker

Printed in Great Britain
by Amazon